The Piper's Lament

(Book Two Of The Ridge Walker Series)

Alex Breck

Seilachan Fort

Published by Seilachan Fort

www.alexbreckbooks.com

ISBN: 978-0-9933887-0-5

DEDICATION

To the memory of my father, Robert, whose
fondness for the written word unwittingly
set in motion this painful process.

To my family as always for their love,
support and endless patience.

And lastly, to the people of the West
Highlands of Scotland who make my stories
possible.

'The mind is its own place, and in itself can make a heaven of hell, a hell of heaven...'
John Milton, *Paradise Lost*

Chapter 1

'To me, pal, to me!
Aw come on! What was that? How can-'

'Yer joking right? That was the cross of
the season so it was, it's not ma fault
you're a bampot wi' two left feet!'

As three overgrown schoolboys
continued to kick a scrunched up cigarette
packet back and forth across the treacherous
lagoons of pot-holed tarmac, a fourth man, taller
than the rest, attempted to hold on to some last
vestige of propriety. Not so much for his
wretched self, he'd left his self-respect back at
the airport, but more out of consideration for the
long and winding procession of weary and wet
onlookers who were directing scathing looks
towards the four of them.

'What the *hell* am I doing here?'

He pulled his collar up higher against the
lancing rain, but despite his thick matted wig, the
chilly autumn downpour continued to insinuate
its way down his cold wet neck.

At one time, in the not so distant past, he
knew many had considered him a tough guy,
tougher than most. He tried to relax, *an old has-
been might be more accurate, nowadays*, and
allowed himself an expressionless smile as
uncontrollable shivers traversed his body. It was

true he'd survived the internecine darkness of 'The Terror' by being always one step ahead of his numerous pursuers. Later, he mutated into his own barbarous incarnation of 'The Vengeance,' becoming known to exclusive audiences across the world in various starring roles which he played out with a cruel panache.

But it had always been just a performance.

How hard he had tried to assure himself of that fact, as he awoke to begin each and every tranquil day in the intervening months since his retirement. He would try to convince himself that he had just been a jobbing actor, forced to take part in an absurd theatre of death, conjured up by an elitist minority bred to be wholly devoid of emotion. That was, of course, until *he* put the bejesus up them so that they couldn't sleep nights.

'But this bleedin' *rain*! I'm just not used to it these days.'

He glanced up at the morbid clouds and consoled himself with the thought that within the month he should be back tending to his sun-drenched Chilean vineyard alongside his beautiful wife.

His acting days, gladly dispensed with along with the gut-wrenching night sweats, had made a temporary comeback. Not so much a sell-out tour as a one-off reunion gig. *And a non-*

paying one at that, he scolded himself. He shrugged his shoulders in quiet anger as the 40 pounds of body padding became steadily heavier and the relentless damp seeped through his useless "shower proof" jacket.

Death had brought him to this inhospitable mountain-side, half way round the world. *No change there then*. The demise of an old friend, a warrior much like himself and a man who had enjoyed that rare commodity - his respect. Brigadier Archibald MacLelland. *Worth a dozen of these eedjits* he decided as he surveyed the huddled groups battling the unforgiving elements, their sodden funeral coats flapping like so many bedraggled crows.

It warmed him somewhat, to reflect for a moment that he was probably on the wanted list of most of these men here. There would be some good men, perhaps, in respectful attendance at this sombre graveside. But alongside them would be the usual toffee-nosed arseholes who bookended their self-satisfied opinions that they were doing a grand job of defending the realm between their consummate failure to grasp the nettle and their overwhelmingly mistaken delusions of relevance in the 21st century. Compared to the venerable old lion about to be lowered into the ground, they were like hyenas skulking around after a kill hoping to score a few scraps.

He felt his loss keenly now, as he remembered sitting around cosy fires, malt whisky in hand, listening to old Archie's stories from the war. They would each stare into the endless shimmering heat of the hot coals and try to shock the other with tales of foolhardy bravery or plain insanity. And as the first flecks of salmon sky rose up over the snow-covered mountains they would sing subdued laments about conflict and death.

He looked up over the darkening ridge and thought how the young Archibald must have felt, at Arisaig, not so far from here, as he taught the first Commandos the deadly techniques which he prosaically referred to as the 'ungentlemanly arts,' and which came to be known as Special Operations Executive field training. He remembered Archie telling him that the early model for the organisation had come directly from dealing with the IRA and so the two of them would talk late into the night about their personal experiences with the Provos, albeit a generation apart.

When he initially found out about the death, it didn't come as a huge surprise, the Brigadier having been in his early nineties. After flying over and intercepting the odd snippet of 'chatter' however, he began to have serious worries and a niggling hunch began to develop. His mind, twisted as it was after so many years undercover or on the run, would not let it drop. It gnawed at him for several days before he finally cracked and began the suicidal mission he now found himself enmeshed in.

In honour of a fallen gladiator.

I doubt if anyone would do this for *me*, he thought as he limped back to the hearse and climbed carefully into the driver's seat. Then it came to him and he struggled to suppress a hearty laugh. Ridge! His young brother-in-law would be daft enough to do something like this. Loyal too, like a dopey Labrador. He *had* just seen the pair of them, of course, but it had been too risky to break cover. There would be time for all that later.

The two men in dark raincoats interrupted their quiet conversation and glared around at Ridge as he backed off a little.

'Sorry, guys! Just trying to shelter a wee bit from the rain…'

He smirked over at Orla as she raised her eyes to the blackening sky and stifled an infectious laugh with a well placed glove. 'Told you,' she whispered, edging further away and refusing to allow him to gain any advantage from sidling up to her. She had warned him to wear warmer clothing and that with a funeral as large as this would be, it wouldn't matter if they didn't wear strict black formal clothing. But he had dug his heels in as usual.

'This is my funeral suit. I bought it to go to a funeral, that's what it's for. I always wear it to funerals and so I'm going to wear it today.'

So within two minutes of arriving, his legs were soaked and his feet were sodden and heavy. Orla, of course, had opted for a fleece lined North Face jacket and waterproof trousers which he had openly mocked but now desired above anything else.

'What the fuck's their problem, anyway? Do I *look* like a spy?'

They had both agreed only minutes before that the whole thing reminded them of a scene from a *Johnny English* movie where the incompetent hero, supposedly guarding the funeral of a Bond-style agent, watches in horror as the entire gathering of his contemporaries is blown to smithereens. Despite their limited experience of the shadowy world of espionage, Ridge and Orla had decided that they were perhaps the only two 'civilians' in attendance.

Ridge felt his jaw muscles clench. He hadn't been missing any that sleight of hand crap. During their 'adventure,' the two of them had been lucky beyond belief, he knew that. He remembered being nicknamed 'Mr Serendipity' by an American Marine due to his uncanny knack of getting out of serious trouble almost by accident.

On their return, the quiet life had been a little difficult to adjust to in the first few months.

There were various 'strings that had to be pulled' by the more shadowy elements of government to keep the mainstream clipboard and regulations brigade happy. Emotionally, they struggled through an awkward period of adjustment once the initial euphoria at just being safely home had worn off, but thankfully they had managed to reignite their past enthusiasm for a shared life together, helped by some unforeseen but happy developments.

He glanced across at Orla, concerned she would cope with the sombre occasion. She could never be considered a softie, but Ridge knew she had been far closer to the Brigadier than he'd ever been and just recently she could be a little haywire. They exchanged smiles and he decided she would be just fine.

Living these days in a roomy flat in the Southside of Glasgow where Orla had started writing and he earned enough working from home as a software engineer, the two of them had become inseparable. Given this second chance at life together, they were determined to make the most of every minute together. Other people could be a problem though as both of them, but Ridge in particular, had become impatient and intolerant of the lazy minded, soft-bellied culture they had returned to. If it were not for the work on the cottage acting as a diversionary release valve, Ridge felt that he would have lost it by now. They'd recently acquired an old ruin on the remote island of Sorsay close to where his parents still lived.

He'd played amongst its mossy entrails with his brother Gavin through the endless hot summers of his boyhood and after Gavin's tragic death, a young Ridge had promised himself that he would one day restore it and live there for the rest of his life. He was now gradually fulfilling that promise, weekend by weekend, although he couldn't see either of them living there just yet.

He felt Orla gripping his hand as the piper began his lament. He shot her his bravest smile, holding her close as the six men began to lower the coffin slowly into the unfeeling earth. A sudden squall added to the dramatic effect and the weather gods seemed determined not to let old Archie go without a last fanfare of their own. The haunting melody transported Ridge back to the desert hell where he'd prevailed against the odds in his own dance with death and he grimaced up at the sullen sky.

'Still here ya bastards, still here!'

With the formalities over with, the vast gathering began to disperse off the hill and Ridge felt uncomfortable now in his saturated clothing. He laughed as he thought of that age-old excuse, beloved of the middle-aged, that 'it must have shrunk' in the rain. But he knew fine well that he had 'filled out a little' from the gawky boy who ran away to America; 'more meat on a butcher's pencil,' his dad used to say. Still, he could only be classed as a lightweight next to his beautiful wife, all cosied up in her

8

fancy mountain gear. Stretched even more tightly than Ridge's suit, the sight of it made his heart sing, above even the depressing skirl of the pipes. She had the oldest and best excuse ever for her rapid increase in girth.

Orla was pregnant!

Chapter 2

Despite the sadness of the day and the malevolence of the weather, Ridge felt an effusive glow course through him as he counted down, as he now did every day, the number of days left until he would become a father. He still shook his head, as he always did at this point, in bemused amazement at this simple yet life changing biological fact.

He felt like most dads-to-be, he guessed. On one hand, proud and delighted beyond measure but on the other, that deep-seated panic that he wouldn't measure up to the task or that something would go wrong. At just over six months gone Ridge knew Orla and the baby should be safely past any danger. The pregnancy had been uncomplicated and Orla had never looked more radiant. The impending birth had provided the required impetus to get the cottage finished and this in return, by virtue of them having to visit the island more frequently, had greatly helped smooth their re-introduction into the bruised heart of his family. His parents had grasped on to the pregnancy raft as would two drowning sailors, the revitalising effect being just strong enough to restore their feeling that life could perhaps be worth living after all.

Ridge still hadn't spoken too much nor in any detail about his Latin American experience. His mother had continued to be in a fragile state and prone to floods of tears when the topic reared its head. Both parents were content to leave it that their son had done 'something brave and gallant' and beyond that, it had become yet another thing to be filed under the heading 'we'll no talk about that just the now…,' in the same way they had all done ever since Gavin's death.

As the funeral goers started thinning out, Ridge and Orla squelched slowly, hand in hand, down the treacherous slope. Ridge heard the sober and earnest conversations flutter past him in the breeze, each one conducted in the unmistakable clipped tones of perfect Received Pronunciation. He thought of his own father, a rough spoken islander, wise yet uneducated. A man who had sought to bring up his family in a tranquil natural idyll, his only wish being the very best start for his two sons. Yet he had seen his eldest perish in an unforeseeable tragedy then had been forced to endure an agonising cross-examination of his own life as his last remaining child became an international fugitive. As if that had not been enough of a cross for his parents to bear, they had also to grieve the apparent and appallingly violent death of their vivacious young daughter-in-law, a girl they had taken into their hearts as if she had been their own.

Ridge growled as a man accidentally bumped Orla as they made their way down. 'Sorry old chap! These *damned* new brogues…' the man pipped back brightly. 'Aye…yer arse,' Ridge muttered under his breath. *It's wankers like you that got us into all that shite.* But he felt a hand tighten in his and he relaxed again. He

11

would soon be a dad, so what was he getting so uptight about?

And what kind of world were they bringing a child into? Ha! That old chestnut. Despite everything, Ridge remained optimistic, as he still was about most things. Since their return, Scotland had hosted the Commonwealth Games and the resultant upsurge of national pride and media incitement had almost led to a positive vote for independence in the long awaited referendum. Ridge had been ambivalent about the necessity of Scotland becoming a free nation, but anything that would put some distance between him and the two-faced mandarins of Westminster was worthy of his vote any day of the fucking week.

He couldn't help being extremely sceptical about all politicos these days. He and Orla had experienced a darker side of the state, one that only a very few citizens were cognisant of. In some ways, they had unplugged from the 'Matrix.' Ridge knew that the face of democracy that was presented to the unknowing populace was a mask, a sham and that if this façade was ever to slip, if the public *ever* found out what the governing state was really like, then they would truly get their freak on.

Yet, he wondered if this must have always been the way of things and he doubted whether a change of government or constitution would ever alter this fact. A small part of him, despite their experiences, now also believed that perhaps those secretive ghouls who pull the

12

strings were a necessary evil. Men and women like Colm, who do bad things in the name of the common good. Or was that just because he was going to be a father? 'Fuck me, I'll be voting Tory next!' he chortled to himself, as they reached the large granite gateway of the cemetery.

She pulled her hand gently away from him as they went through the gateway. Orla had been fond of the old lady and she remembered how particularly kind she had been to this wild eyed ruffian of a girl not so long ago. It would be nice to show off the bump, something positive on such a sad day. As she leant forward to kiss the widow's cheek, something strange caught her attention. Just out of the corner of her eye, Orla noticed a peculiar looking man who somehow didn't seem to fit the picture. She realised he must be one of the undertakers yet something in the back of her mind jolted her out of the present and spiralled her back into that vortex of terror she had tried so hard to forget. There was something in his shape, the way that he walked, that reminded her of her someone, but she couldn't think who. For some reason she thought of her brother. '*Jeez! No way girl! Yer mad so y'are.*'

She shook her head free of the thought and turned back to the old lady, absentmindedly thinking that it was a shame that Colm hadn't made it over for the funeral. They had both hoped that he would be, especially as there was now going to be an addition to the family. She wasn't allowed to contact him directly; they had a complicated arrangement for communication to avoid either of them from being found by ghosts from their past. 'Anyway…' she thought, patting her stomach for reassurance, 'He's basking in the sunshine, bleedin' miles away. What would he want to come to this godforsaken place for?'

Thinking that Ridge had been milling around just behind her, Orla was surprised to look round and see him involved in a heated discussion over by the gate. A sharp spike of fear pricked her insides as she watched a livid looking Ridge stride away from a sad looking younger guy in generic funeral garb.

'What was all that about, love?'

'You don't want to know!'

'Hold on a mo! I feckin' *do* want to know! Now slow down and tell me what's goin' on will ye?'

'They *know* who we are!

'Who?'

All these guys! The spooks!
The bastards have probably been watching us all along.
Come on, I'll tell you the rest in the car.

Here, take my hand, it's slippy as fuck
down here.'

Watching all of this from a safe distance
was the small figure of a woman, her face all but
obscured by the hood of her rain jacket. Yet if
anyone had taken a moment to peer at her
through the rain it wouldn't have been difficult
to see the hatred on her face. She didn't think
she could have hidden it no matter how hard she
had tried. To have witnessed such a concentrated
gathering of her sworn foes in one place, it was
surely a tactical error not to have attempted
something. She felt positive that if she had
communicated her plans, they would have
considered it worthy of direct action. Except that
she was here on her own time. This was personal.
She stared with contempt at the men and
women filtering out through the gates and
wondered how many had won commendations
for the death and torture of her people. Even she
herself had been awarded a medal for her great
service to this nation of theirs. A circle of tin
pinned to her tiny chest, she remembered with
shame how it had felt like a sword piercing her
breast. At least today, she had the satisfaction of
seeing one of the bastards put under ground and
it gave her a warm glow deep from within. Her
icy cold face flushed with a grim pride as she
imagined how these pillars of the military and
espionage establishment would react if they
knew that she and she alone had been

responsible for the death of Brigadier MacLelland.

Would they be so complacent if they were told that she, merely a slip of a girl, had simply walked in and back out again in broad daylight and in full view of their pitiful security guards and impotent cameras?

Dressing like a gloomy undertaker had come naturally to Colm and with the artificial weight gain and the dark wig he had looked more like a Free Church Elvis impersonator than anything else but, more importantly, he doubted if his own mother would have recognised him.

He hadn't been there just to pay his last respects however. The piper's sad lament had been painful to bear because he knew that no post mortem had been carried out on the old boy and he had already seen the 'secret' SOCO report. The widow was unaware of any malfeasance and had already stressed that she would not countenance any interference with the body. A heart attack had been exactly how he would have wanted to go, she told everyone at the time and so that was the way it was to be. The local doctor, who appeared to be only marginally younger than the Brig himself, had signed the paperwork and so all was well. After all, the lodge was within the Balmoral Estate which meant it had to be among the most secure buildings in the country. It wasn't too likely that there would have been anyone photographed

topless sunbathing here. *You would hope so.*
Even the Queen herself had visited the couple
for a cup of tea just days before the end of her
annual summer holiday.

There had just been one wee problem.

The security around the Estate had been
totally state-of, so he'd been led to believe and
that there was CCTV everywhere was also a
given. However, during the security shift in
which the old man had been discovered, there
had been one more person checked *into* the
Estate than checked out. That made it odds-on
that this person had helped the Brigadier check
out too, permanently...

The police had picked up an obvious
muddy footprint near the locus of death which
had not been matched with any staff on duty that
day. This had been hushed up as it seemed
irrelevant, what with the old codger dying of a
coronary.

Except that Colm knew he hadn't.

Needing to be sure and with time being a
critical factor, he had decided to impersonate one
of the undertakers, principally the driver of the
hearse. Making up a pretext, he contrived to visit
the mortuary hours earlier than scheduled. It had
seemed like a long shot but it became
immediately obvious upon opening the coffin
prior to the 'final journey' that the old fellow
had not had a heart attack as had been reported.

At first glance, Colm accepted that he
had some of the most common coronary
symptoms but only if you had already made up

your mind or had perhaps been ordered not to care too much. His eyes were still wide open and accusatory and the frightening grimace of extreme pain visible across his face told Colm he'd had severe convulsions and an almost immediate onset of rigor mortis so much so that the authorities could do nothing to give him the appearance of being at peace. He saw now why the family had insisted on a closed coffin. But the most powerful indication that he had been poisoned with Strychnine was the fact that Archie's back had frozen in an extreme position of flexion caused by the terrible violence of his spasms. Colm guessed that one of his regular, and therefore well known, afternoon or evening whiskies had been spiked. His skin had also turned that particular shade of reddish-purple that Colm had often seen before. After all, he had despatched more than a few fools this way himself. It would have been too easy for a member of staff to have slipped him the drink and been well away within the half hour or so it would have taken.

But who would have wanted him dead and why now, when he had been retired for quarter of a century?

Colm shivered again as his unerringly accurate gut instinct kicked in and hard with it. He was long since free of his ridiculous outfit and dressed in his customary 'invisible' black casual shirt, jacket and trousers; clean and bone dry. It wasn't the inclement weather either, that had caused the feeling of icy dread to wrap

18

around him like a misty shroud. It was his certain and unmistakable belief that the Brigadier had died because of *him*.

As it often was with certain vocations; in military intelligence you never retired completely and it was rare to live long enough to draw a pension. When you regularly butted heads with powerful governments, massive industrial complexes and a fair smattering of pathologically evil bastards, you accepted implicitly that you were unlikely to die of old age. Bad people often had good memories and long after the collective memory of the great unwashed had been cleansed by the next international incident, there were always old grudges to be settled. But what convinced Colm above anything else that somehow he himself was complicit in the old man's demise was the time factor.

If Brigadier MacLelland had been on a death list, then there would have been a neat red line scored through his name and he would have been shuffled off a decade ago. Colm was pretty sure Archie had been quiet and out of the game for quite some considerable time, until just under two years ago. Around the time when he, himself, had unwittingly brought the maelstrom back to Archie's door. That would have been just after his wee sister, Orla, had apparently blown herself up with an IRA bomb on the steps of the Scots Parliament. The same time that her young husband, the naïve Richard 'Ridge' Walker, was being hunted by MI5, the CIA, the Mexican police and a festering collection of the most execrable gangsters to have ever crawled out of the primordial slime.

You know what they say.

You can choose your friends but you can't choose…

Chapter 3

Ridge jumped up from his near slumber, relieved to hear just a gentle rapping of their substantial apartment door rather than the booming of their clamorous door bell. They were both exhausted after the drive back from Archie's funeral and Orla had already been asleep for some time. They had dissected his brief conversation with Nervous Man all the way back down the road, but could make no sense of it.

> 'He just said he wanted to speak to me *off the record, so to speak…*
> He said it would only take a minute or two and that there was nothing to be worried about. I just-'

> 'Nothin' to be worried about! How the feckin' hell can he say that?'

Orla was livid. It seemed that their sanctuary had been violated already and here she was about to bring a baby into the world and still they wouldn't leave them in peace. Ridge took the brunt of her ire.

> 'Didn't you *think* to ask him what the bleedin' heck he was on about?
> Or how he was after knowing who you were?

Jeez! Are we going to have to go to feckin' South America an' all just to get away from the bastards?'

After talking it through for ages, they both decided that it must have been a mistake on the part of a young inexperienced security agent who had perhaps seen their file at some point and had recognised Ridge. He probably didn't have any idea what had happened previously and had thought that maybe Ridge had been still active in the field.

'He maybe just wanted some filler detail to help close up the file or something like that...' Ridge had told her, somewhat unconvincingly.

'Probably knew he wasn't supposed to talk to you, that's why he said it would be off the record, the eedjit.'

'Yeah...I guess so.' Ridge had shrugged his shoulders as if in agreement whilst staring straight ahead at the road, nervous that she should see through the doubt in his eyes.

He quietly opened the subtly reinforced door, sliding back the triple deadbolts with a practiced nonchalance, to be met by an anxious looking Asian man around the same age as himself. His eyes were red rimmed and straightaway Ridge panicked that there had been an incident outside the building. He and Orla were the only 'local' people in the entire street but that was just the way they liked it. Pollokshields had developed a reputation as being an unsavoury part of Glasgow for non-Asians, partly due to unrelenting media stereotyping, but despite this, the two of them had felt cosseted here since their return. Until the events of the past day. Nonetheless there had been a vicious abduction and subsequent murder of a local white youth from their very doorstep a few years previously and Ridge was careful to keep the slightly built man at arms length.

'Alright? What can I do for you at this time of night?'

'Yes! I am so sorry.
I realise it is becoming very late and for that I apologize most sincerely.
I am here asking you a favour of the most serious nature…'

The man hesitated for only a brief moment, but long enough. Ridge shook his head mutely and made to shut the door.

'No!
I beg of you!
Please hear me out, Ridge Walker!
You are the only man who can help us now!'

Ridge stopped stock still and stood hanging on to the door-frame as if he had been rabbit-punched. Very few people knew him as Ridge. His Sunday name was Richard but as a small child he had struggled with the pronunciation and so had used 'Ridge' instead. After abandoning this nickname as a teenager, he had resurrected it once again after fleeing to America, at which point in time he had wanted to remove himself as far from his previous life as possible. The subsequent events in the US had changed him for ever. On their return he decided that the name change should be permanent but only amongst those very few who were close to him.

He had never seen *this* guy before in his life.

'Sit!'

Ridge gestured to the top step on the communal landing between his flat and the one opposite.

'I thank you my friend. Thank you!'

'I don't mean to be rude or anything, but you are NOT my friend, so can we just cut the crap and you tell me what you want, eh?'

'Yes, of course! My name is Masood and I hope we *can* be friends. I will be brief, I promise you-'

Ridge cleared his throat impatiently and sat down alongside.

'Get on with it then.
But before you start, I'm no' buying anything and I've got a baby on the way so we're totally skint. Aww, shit! *What did I say?*'

Masood had buried his head in his arms and Ridge could hear sobbing, borne out by the tears splashing onto the cold stone steps. Feeling embarrassed for the lad, Ridge put an arm on his shoulder and gave him a manly shake.

'Come on, pal. It's not that bad surely? What's up? How do you know my name anyway?'

Masood sniffed and lifted his head. His long eyelashes held teardrops that could fill a shot glass and Ridge was admittedly more curious than annoyed. The guy should either be an Oscar candidate or he was genuinely upset about something.

'I know about you from a friend of my cousin. You are our last hope!

I have tried everything; no-one else can help me now!
I have money!
Yes, I have plenty money, I can get you cash tonight if you will just-'

Ridge lifted his hands to silence the man.

'Stop! Just hold on a wee minute will you?
I don't want your money!
I was just sayin' I haven't got any to give *you*…that's all, okay?
Now will you *please* just tell me what all this is about?'

Masood sighed and for an awful moment Ridge thought he was about to start bawling all over again. But he seemed to hold himself in check and then the words started to tumble out.

'It's my sister, Nasreen! She has gone and disappeared!
It has been over eleven weeks now. I know she's been kidnapped!
She'd never run away.
Nasreen was very happy here until the marriage proposal.
We know she's in Pakistan. We all went with Mr Saad but there was no sign of her. And we only stayed two days.
Two days? I am telling you!
No-one else cares anymore, they only say if Nasreen has run away to Pakistan then

she's brought the shame of dishonour down on the family so she doesn't deserve their love or support any longer. We are forbidden to speak her name in the house and so it's like she never existed…She didn't even-'

'Hold up!
Has she run away from an arranged marriage? Does that stuff still go on, even here in Glasgow?'

'Yes! I mean no!
It *was* an arranged marriage and it is still a regular custom here but she did not run away from that.'

The man took a deep breath and his brow creased as he focused his watery eyes intently on Ridge. He let out a long sigh and continued to speak quickly and spasmodically.

'Of this I am convinced, Ridge Walker. Nasreen had always been strong. She had already refused to marry the man.
It was over as far as she was concerned. She had already disgraced herself with our family but they had not given up on the idea, nor had the other family in Pakistan. It is a most terrible dishonour to have a cancelled marriage back home. For them it was to be a stepping up of the

ladder to a more respectable position here in Great Britain.

That is why they will have taken her – to force her to agree to the marriage or have her killed if she refuses-'

'Stop! Are you saying your sister's *life* is in danger over this arranged marriage shite?'

'Oh yes, I am quite sure of it, my friend. You must see that they will not lose face if she is killed.

They can easily put the blame on some local dissidents or terrorist malcontents. That way their family can move on with their reputation intact and he can marry another girl instead.'

Ridge sprung to his feet and dusted himself down. He had an inkling where this might be heading but he wasn't having any of it. *Thank fuck Orla's in bed*, he thought. He knew she'd kill him outright for even having this conversation.

'Listen Masood, is it? I'm really sorry for you and your sister and all that but I don't really see how it's got anything to do with me. Now it's getting late and I've had a weird enough day already so if you don't mind I'll wish you the best of luck but I'm tired and heading to my-'

'I'll give you a thousand pounds
tomorrow morning if you even just think
about it overnight!
I promise you! You don't have to be
committing to anything!
Just think about it!'

Despite himself, Ridge couldn't stop a
sudden thought flashing through his mind about
the cost of the wiring at the cottage, before
mentally slapping the idea from his head. *What
are you like? Have you not had your fill of
trouble?*

'Listen Masood! I could take advantage
of you and pocket your cash easy enough
but I know absolutely zip about Pakistan!
I've not even got a passport right now. I
don't see how-'

'You can! You can!
I know that you are the only one who
could find her, Ridge Walker!
I've heard all about how you rescued that
girl from terrorists and how you fought
your way to freedom!
Think how you would feel if it was your
sister?
Or your wife?
What would YOU do if somebody
kidnapped your baby daughter?'

I'll give you *two* thousand pounds tomorrow and eight thousand more when you find Nasreen.'

Ridge was stunned at his reaction to Masood's speculation that he might soon have a daughter and he couldn't believe how much it had got through to him. If he was honest, he'd only paid lip-service to the notion that they might have a baby girl. Sure, he had looked at names with Orla and said all the right things about not minding what the gender would be as long as it had ten fingers and so on but in his own mind he had always pictured a wee boy.

But now he felt differently. How wonderful would it be to have a daughter as beautiful as her mother? Without realising what he was doing, Ridge found himself nodding to Masood and gently closing the door, with a muttered arrangement to meet in a local café the next afternoon.

Chapter 4

After a tortured night of tossing and turning, he awoke cold and alone in the early morning darkness. Anxious as to her whereabouts, he fell out of bed and stumbled wearily through the flat to find Orla sitting in her favourite high backed chair wrapped in a heavy blanket and scowling in her sleep. Feeling instinctively to blame for this dormant surliness he tiptoed into the next room and tried to fill the kettle as quietly as possible. He knew he had failed spectacularly as her shrill tones echoed off the unsympathetic tiled walls of the large tenement kitchen.

> 'And you can make me some toast an'
> marmite to go with the tea!
> Least you can do after keepin' me up half
> the bleedin' night!'

He soon had her won over with a tasty breakfast and together they snuggled back under her blanket on the sofa as he crooned *Wild Is The Wind* softly in her ear. Orla had only acquired a couple of pregnancy related cuisine cravings but as she drifted back to sleep again he decided that, although he loved her more than life itself, her diabolical marmite breath reminded him of rotten silage at the tail end of a Sorsay winter.

At least you *can* sleep, he thought jealously. His jangling brain still raced with the implications of yesterday's events. Despite his nonchalance with Orla he was still deeply worried about the incident at the graveyard. If it was *that* easy to discover who they were and what their movements were, then it would be a dead cert that this flat was also known about. They had royally pissed off a lot of people over the last couple of years and he had little doubt what their fate would be if any former 'co-workers' of either his darling wife or his mysterious brother-in-law were ever to catch up with them.

He wondered if it had been divine intervention, the approach from Masood and the possibility of making a quick twenty grand. He knew it would be complete madness to get involved and that Orla would not countenance it for a second. But at the same time, a cash windfall like that would allow them to finish the cottage and get away from potential danger that much sooner.

They hadn't considered actually living on Sorsay until they reached their dotage, it being just a tad too remote for Orla's cosmopolitan nature. However their circumstances had dramatically changed in the last 24 hours and he knew neither of them would ever feel truly safe in Glasgow again. When they had discussed their various options with Colm and Thad after their miraculous escape from Central America, both men had been of the view that a remote location like Sorsay would be as good a place as any to hide out. Both men were trained killers and they understood implicitly the mindset of the assassin.

The only way to get to Sorsay was by boat and young Seamus the ferryman had been at school with Ridge, having been the best friend of his brother Gavin. Their father's had grown up together and Ridge remembered sitting with Gavin listening in wonder as the two men would regale them with tales of the old days. One of his favourites was when his dad described the time old Seamus, who had always been partial to a drink, had just got a new pair of sunglasses. It had been in the eighties, when mirror shades had been in vogue.

'So there was Seamus, sitting in the ferry shed, proud as punch with his mirror glasses. He sees old Mamie, grabs a stick and gets her to play along with him. Mamie cottons on immediately and grabs his arm to help him down the slip to the ferry, him waggling the stick in front of his feet.

The dozen or so tourists just stand open-mouthed as she helps him into the wee boat and puts his hand over to the tiller. Then Seamus fires up the outboard and heads out across the sea to the mainland with Mamie shouting *left a wee bit, right a bit, you're doing fine Seamus…* and the horrified tourists staring at the blind ferryman and thinking they'd gone mad!'

When he and Orla returned from Central America, most of the islanders had a vague understanding that the family had once again suffered a 'tragedy' of some kind and they had even come to terms with the resurrection of Orla. Most of them had lived on the island for generations, as had his own family, and they took far more stead in the views of the old women of Sorsay than they did of the 'English Newspapers.' There were no actual 'streets' on the small island and each house had only a name for an address, the whole population sharing the same completely irrelevant postcode.

Ridge had admitted that even if someone hired their own boat, it would be almost impossible to land safely and then find one specific house unless they had either lived there previously themselves or were prepared to risk everyone knowing their business within no time. The standard method of giving directions went something like this:

> *Well, ye 'ken the old Henderson house? No, they dinnae stay there the now, they moved away tae Glasgow when young Jamie went tae the college. Ye mind he got that lassie pregnant, aye? Well, ye turn right there 'an past where Seamus keeps his beasts in the winter and ye keep going 'til where the trees fell in the Big Storm. That was guid firewood, so it was. Then it's just o'er the wee hill, no the big hill, mind, at Spook's cottage and then*

34

*down by the old farm bothy. But whit did
ye say yer name was again? Anyways, ye
cannae miss it!*

But he couldn't shake the haunting
feeling in the back of his mind that perhaps the
conversation at the graveyard and last night's
visit were somehow connected. *But how could
they be*? He had no idea what Nervous Man had
wanted to talk to him about. Perhaps Masood
was a setup and Nervous Man had been about to
warn him?

Orla had been right, of course. He should
have been smart enough to extract something
more useful from the man but his first instinct
had been to push him away, to distance that
perilous dark world from the bright and secure
one they thought they inhabited.

He also had still to find out how this
'friend of my cousin' had obtained the lowdown
on what happened with the rescue of Juanita and
his subsequent battles with the drugs cartel. It
was inconceivable that an ordinary young Asian
Glaswegian should have accidentally come by
such information which must have been, to use a
clichéd expression, *beyond classified*.

It had taken a great deal of money,
mostly Colm's money, to rewrite parts of his and
Orla's history with respect to the UK military
and intelligence establishment. With his natural
flair for theatrics, Colm had persuaded them to
accept his smoke and mirror version of events

and, by weaving a epic tale of valour worthy of
an Oliver Stone script, he had contrived to make
Ridge and Orla into 'innocent bystanders drawn
unwittingly into an international crisis,' whilst
bolstering his own shadowy credentials at the
same time.

At the US end of things Thad's dad had
again used his far from inconsiderable wealth
and military muscle to ensure Thad and the
Diamond Dogs emerged unbesmirched by the
whole debacle. The DEA were cock-a-hoop that
from one 'mission,' however left-field it seemed
to have been, there had been so much damage
inflicted on the Central American drugs business.
At one point it looked as if Ridge, Orla and Thad
were going to have to accept a personal
'invitation' to meet with the President which
they had narrowly managed to avoid, courtesy of
first, a hurricane crisis in the US and then
secondly, the closer to home seismic event of
Orla's pregnancy.

All night Ridge had been replaying the
previous 24 hours in his head. As he waited in
trepidation for Orla to reawaken, he knew he had
already decided on the only course of action that
could help answer some of the questions raging
through him. He also knew that Orla would be
violently opposed to this. He rehearsed what he
would say in response to her furious attack. They
needed information and they needed it like
yesterday. What harm could come from meeting
with Masood and finding out more about what

he knew and how he knew it? He would have a coffee, ask a few questions, take a few notes and then say a polite goodbye, walking away with two thousand pounds as generous payment for a night of anguish.

In the end, once he'd taken over an hour to pluck up the courage to broach the subject, her response had blown him away. She just said;

'Sure! You're on, so you are.
It's the only way we'll find out what the shite he's talkin' about.
Will ye be after wanting me to come with you or what?'

He sat shocked, staring at her beaming smile and wondering if he will *ever* understand her, when the doorbell went off like Hogmanay had come early.

Ridge made for the door prepared for anything to happen this time. But he wasn't prepared for this…

It was Colm.

Chapter 5

'Hi bro!
Just here to make sure yer after takin'
good care of my wee Sis!
Jeez! Is it no half freezin' out there?
Get the kettle on, will ye…'

Ridge stood stupefied as his brother-in-law gripped him fleetingly in a strong embrace, his bright eyes shining with emotion. Just as quickly, he was already past, leaving Ridge in his wake and failing miserably to breathe out any appropriate response.

'Orla! Where are you lass?
Take it easy! Sure I can hear you!'

Screaming at the top of her lungs, Orla all but bowled Colm over as she wrapped herself, blanket included, around her strapping brother.

'Ye fookin' big bastard! Why'd ye not call before comin' round?
The spare room's a bleedin' tip so it is an-'

'I'm *not* after staying over, Orla-'

'What! You come all this way from Chile and you can't even stay one night?'

'I just can't me love. Listen. Sit down will you and tell me how you've been.'

Colm turned for a second to Ridge as he spoke.

'Both of you. How have you been coping...with the baby comin' and all? Where's that hot drink, amigo?'

Ridge took the hint and left the two siblings to it. He was surprised therefore when Colm joined him after a few moments and, using the noise from the kettle, he said that he needed to speak with him as soon as possible.

A few minutes later, Ridge could feel the blood still pounding in his neck as he attempted to carry the coffee tray back through.

Shit, he thought. *It's all starting again.*

Orla hadn't stopped talking the whole time Colm had been through in the kitchen and she showed no signs of slowing down as Ridge sat down beside her and took her hand in his. Colm walked over to the window and pushed the net curtain aside an inch or so. He had just informed Ridge that the flat was being watched and Ridge had blurted out the gist of his conversation at the graveyard the day before.

'So we hoped to see you at the funeral, so we did... and then you never showed... and then you're here this morning and...'

Orla glanced up at her brother as he looked sideways at her, smiling that smile.

'You *were* at the funeral? No!
But… how did we not…? But where?
So IT WAS YOU!
I *saw you*, ye big bastard!
You were all done up to look like one of the bleedin' undertakers weren't you? I was sure it was you! You've got that John Wayne sort of walk, from behind. You can't fool yer wee sister that's for sure!'

She shot a furtive look towards her husband. 'I was *gonna* tell you honey but then with all that other stuff an' all I forgot…!' Orla quietened. Her sad eyes slowly lifted to Colm as she began to whisper.

'Aw an' Col… There's been goings-on, so there has. It started yester-'

Colm and Ridge both interrupted Orla at the same time.

'I WAS one of the undertakers…I had to wear that feckin' stuff the whole day.'

'It's OK angel. He knows. I just told him.'

The next two hours vanished in a fog of anxious whispering as Ridge and Orla listened to the calming words of their shadowy relation. Ridge could see his wife trying not to jump at the slightest bang of every tenement door and he held her close while she wept as Colm carefully explained that the Brigadier had been murdered. He ameliorated the blow by omitting to pass on his hunch that the death may be directly connected to the three of them.

Ridge talked about the man at the graveyard and gave a reasonable description of Mr Nervous. Colm agreed with Orla about it being an opportunity missed through understandable panic but to be fair they both admitted that Ridge was the only one of the trio who'd never been specifically trained for any of this cloak and dagger business.

Orla shot fiery bullets towards Ridge as he told Colm about the late night encounter at the apartment door and as he mumbled his rationale for following up on Masood's impassioned request, he heard his words falter and run dry, silenced by a stony face.

'Ridge…
I'm only after sayin' this the once, okay?
Don't even *think* of meeting with this guy again.
I've no feckin' idea what he's about but it's way too close in time to the other stuff from the funeral and the whole

41

thing smells worse than yer bleedin'
stairs out there!

And anyways, ye've got Big Brother out
there watchin' every move you make so
don't be rockin' the boat any worse than
you've already done.'

Chapter 6

It must have been still early when Ridge slipped out of the flat, his tired eyes wincing at the unforgiving sunshine after so little sleep. Colm had only stayed a short while but had stirred up enough anxiety in the two of them to ensure that neither Orla nor Ridge could have slept too soundly.

Orla was now firmly against any further contact with Masood and she'd made no bones about this before crashing out as the dawn emerged. Ridge could accept this, more or less, but it was all the other stuff that had got his dander up. And once he'd got riled then there was little chance that he would ever listen to reason.

For a start, he remained unconvinced that there was a definite connection between the young Asian and Mr Nervous and his spooky crew although he had to accept that the timing *was* a wee bit strange.

But the fact that they'd got a car stationed outside the flat worried him far more. To be honest, he'd not seen anything untoward this morning and the early recce had been partly to see if he could emulate his brother-in-law and catch the fuckers out.

Not had the training… he muttered as he stumbled across the leaf-strewn street.

But who were these elusive watchers? Colm had said he'd found out about a new Glasgow section of MI5 set up specifically to counter the rise of Islamic fundamentalism in West Scotland although this was under the radar at this stage. But Ridge had thought it sounded plausible, what with the video beheadings and the Westminster paranoia about the legions of British youth streaming over to Syria. It was as if a new airline had sprung up; *'Jihadi Jet – one-way only, no booze but the music is to die for.'*

Colm had been sure the goons he'd spotted outside the flat had the whiff of his former 'colleagues' in British intelligence but Ridge had his own hunches. MI5 he could handle. They would be playing by some vague code of conduct, mostly…

But he could think of a colourful smattering of other candidates that could be in the frame for wanting to know where Orla and Ridge were hanging out.

Most worrying would have to be the drugs cartel that they'd been directly responsible for destabilising across the pond. They definitely did not play by the rules plus they had unlimited funds at their disposal. Ridge had plenty experience with tackling wasp's bikes back on Sorsay and even the youngest islander knew that if you didn't quite manage to get the complete nest into your bucket of sea water then there was no greater menace than a threatened wasp. On the bright side, Colm had reminded him that the *narcos* had been left with a less than successful business relationship with their European cousins thanks to their 'honest and noble strike at the cold dark heart of the narcotics industry' as the US President had coined their charmed adventure. Colm reckoned they would probably have written off the pair of them as being dead by now anyway.

And why would they have done that? Because the *other* band of eedjits who'd not shed any tears at their theatrical funeral were the Real IRA whom his darling wife had shafted big style including a solo staging of her very first fake death. The sarcastic bastard in him couldn't keep from wondering how many pretend deaths someone can get away with for fuck's sake.

Then there was something else. Stories of a shadowy wraith had seeped out of 'confidential' memos since their return. Ridge had been terrified by accounts of this unidentified agent, known only by mysterious nicknames like 'Phantom,' or *El Gaitero* – The Piper. He had constantly floated in and out of their story but like the early morning mists off the sea back home, he would never be there when you looked twice. For some reason he could drift through borders and evade the world's best agencies to wreak havoc wherever he chose and Ridge had detected a suspicious reek of consensus amongst the usually non-collaborative organisations – no one wanted to touch this with a barge pole. There were two things that worried Ridge particularly. Firstly, whose side he was on, if any.

The second thing that bothered him was a whole lot closer to home.

And so it had been almost for light relief that Ridge had broken out this damp morning and gone on a fact-finding mission before his meeting with Masood. The way he figured it, they couldn't get into any further bother, just by him seeing the young man plus he could trouser some easy money into the bargain.

Autumn leaves swirled across the pavement, blown by an unseasonably warm breeze and Ridge had that weird almost hungover feeling which made him doubt the validity of his own bodily sensations. His fatigue, coupled with a black coffee on an empty belly, had left him feeling feverish and not a little high.

He and Orla had lead a quiet, bordering on hermit-like, existence since they arrived in Pollokshields, but he was aware of a popular community centre just around the corner and he thought he might find out a bit more about just how commonplace arranged marriages were in this area. Orla had volunteered to write some articles for the local community newsletter so he hoped he'd have a certain amount of currency if he name dropped a wee bit too.

He stopped for a moment, feeling like he was being watched, and an old Merc with blacked out windows swept slowly past, heavy dance beats throbbing monotonously across the wet pavement. Ha! Just getting paranoid now. The streets were polluted with cars like this every evening and the thumping bass had become the default background playlist for Ridge and Orla even though they lived three floors up. What really freaked them out were the eccentric firework shows that lit up all of Pollokshields practically all year round.

Orla would be wandering along Kenmure Street minding her own business while trying to avoid giving in to her pregnancy related cravings for all things spicy as the tempting aromas wafted from numerous take-away joints. Then some big old European saloon would pull up and the back window would slowly descend. From the dark recess of the car a massive rocket would then come screaming out and explode, high above the heads of the unheeding locals. They were starting to get used to it but the latest trend for military grade fire-crackers threatened to initiate a premature birth any day now and neither of them had got around to forgetting the ballistic hell they'd endured back in Mexico.

The entrance to the community centre was thronged with Asian youths all smoking and laughing with each other. Ridge nodded non-committedly and was met by friendly smiles as he edged his way up the steps.

He had a name to ask for and had been repeating it to himself all the way along the road. Rosina Sarwar.

'Hi there! Is Rosina in this early? I'm the partner of a friend of hers, Orla O'Dowd? She writes with Rosina for the community newsletter.

I'm just looking for a wee bit of help
with something.'

Ridge smiled at the slightly built young
lass at the counter, more at his own thoughts,
than anything around him at that moment. He'd
constantly pilloried his wife about her name
since their return and the fact that she had in
effect been a spy all through the first two years
of their marriage without him knowing about it.

'I suppose I should'a guessed, like…'
Ridge would say.
        'With the 'O-O' in your name!
        What were *you* then? 008?'

Then they'd do some 'Mr & Mrs Smith'
fooling around before making love on the old
leather sofa or under the moonlit stars on the
floor of their bay-windowed bedroom.

        'So you must be Richard, right?
        Orla's told me *all about* you!'

He made a mental note to find out *exactly*
what that meant, but just flashed his most
winning smile and allowed himself to be ushered
in by the weary looking Asian woman.

        'Forced marriages?
        Of course they go on!
         I also work for Women's Aid down on
        Albert Drive and there we've seen twice

as many cases since the law changed back in 2011.

I was in a forced marriage myself, years ago. The girls are being better protected now and so more cases are being brought to us but we're still just scratching the surface you know.'

'How did you get out of it?'

'It was not easy, that I can tell you. I had been groomed all my life for it; cooking, cleaning and sewing. My brother's education was important but I was forbidden to go to university and so I ran away. My family quickly found me and begged me to come home, that everything would be different. Little did I know they had already arranged a marriage for me. The night I came home my father beat me badly and within a month I was in Madras to marry a cousin who I'd never met.

I was one of the lucky ones. I became with child and I convinced both families that it would be better if my son, or *daughter* as it turned out, if my son was born in Scotland, as he would get a British passport. When I came home I met a nice lawyer who helped me fight back and paid for my divorce. We're now happily married and I have three beautiful children.'

49

Ridge looked around the vast room and he could see that the centre fulfilled a definite need as there were several groups of different ages all milling around harassed looking community workers and it wasn't even ten in the morning yet. Above them Ridge noticed the old tiled walls were painted with incongruous topless mermaid portrayals and other semi-erotic works. The staff had made a pretty good job of covering the mermaid's modesty with posters about community services and the like and he couldn't help laughing to himself.

Following his gaze, Rosina shrugged her small shoulders.

'What can we do? It used to be a Masonic Lodge back in the eighties and a Seaman's Mission before that. You should see the sea dragon in the toilets!'

'D'ye know anything about a lassie called Nasreen?'

Rosina's eyes half closed with a tired and well used response to such questions but then she sat up and smiled more encouragingly.

'Well, we're not allowed to talk about individual situations but in that particular case it's in the public domain for all to see, thanks to Mr Saad.'

Seeing the confused look on his face, the girl continued.

'It was most peculiar. Imran Saad, you know him, no? He was the local MP here before he lost his seat in the referendum. He took it upon himself to go out to Pakistan to find young Nasreen. Here… I have a newspaper cutting here somewhere… I know I do.
Here it is!'

Ridge took the article and saw a vivacious young girl smiling up at him next to a standard head shot of a middle-aged man. Mr Saad I presume.

'He allegedly spent thousands trying to find her. The popular media-driven theory is that she ran away to join the jihadi cause.'

Ridge detected the sarcastic edge to the girl's voice just then and so he went with his gut instinct.

'But what do *you* think happened?'

The girl flushed and she lowered her eyes for a moment.

'I think it was a publicity exercise for Mr Saad that backfired. He didn't get re-

elected and he's now got a top political job in Pakistan himself. I don't think he had Nasreen's interests at heart or that of her family here in Glasgow. I know there is considerable bad feeling locally and no-one believes the official story.
It's so fashionable these days to assume every young Muslim is poised to head off to join Islamic State and the like. I personally think there was another agenda here altogether but it's too late now. There is nothing that I or anyone can do now I fear.'

Ridge felt his own face flushing with emotion now and ignoring the warning siren going off in his head, he leaned over and touched the surprised girl on the shoulder.

'If I told you, off the record, that I might be able to do something to get Nasreen back, would you help me Rosina?'

The wide eyed girl gulped and nodded.

Here we go again…, Ridge heard himself mutter under his breath.

Chapter 7

'Fuck's sake Andy!
How many times will I huv tae tell ye?
See next time, right? Just dinnae let the
wee cunts in the fuckin' door.
End of. Sorted. No fuckin' *problemo*.
Now get that fuckin' shit swept up and
let us get back tae the fuckin' speech
before some other tosser starts thinking
aboot comin' the cunt...'

Sometimes, just occasionally mind,
Thomas Taggart could feel himself weakening
and he would wonder why the fuck he was even
doing all of this! He'd a decent job with the
'Post' and loads of good mates and all that. He
didn't need this kind of hassle every other week.
   Tonight was one of those moments.
   There they all were, fine and dandy, just
about to start the meeting and this wee ponce up
the front starts shouting his bastarding head off.
Should've spotted him right away, he thought
bitterly. Fucking suede jacket on him. Student
wanker for defo.
   He looked down from his platform and
across the sparsely attended Scout Hall. Andy
was doing his best he grudgingly admitted.
Blood and sawdust could be awkward to sweep
up quickly and this was a whole new ball game

from some of the rough-houses he'd been doorman at back in the day.

'Ladies and gentlemen!
Can I start by thanking you for your forbearance and welcome you to this our Wednesday evening meeting of the newly forged Southside branch of the Scottish Defence Union.
I would like to apologize for the late start and use this as a reminder of the lack of respect that is so common these days for the honest working men and women of Scotland who just want to live in the beautiful and proud country our parents and grandparents knew so well.
Now, we still have our seat at the table within this grand union of Great Britain! An integral part of history and a modern nation to be proud of.
So they tell us!
But is it a land our grandparents would recognize?
Ladies and gentlemen I ask you to think the unthinkable. That soon this country will be overrun with a swarm of Islamic fundamentalists and their ilk.
We must have short memories...
Remember Glasgow Airport!
Remember also that poor wee laddie, lifted from these very streets...
The nationalists want to usher in a brave new world of mass immigration and multi-cultural co-operation.

Today, in this world of double-think and political correctness, it is up to people like us to stand up and say out loud what most of the population think anyway, honest citizens scared into silence by the liberal do-gooders.

We have been poorly served by the politicians of the past. Even forward thinking men like Enoch Powell have only made it harder for right-minded folks like us to speak their mind!

But hear this, my friends. In that great speech back in 1968, Mr Powell forecast that in the early 21st century around one in ten of the UK would be of immigrant stock.

People scoffed back then.

But this HAS come to pass.

I have just witnessed the terrible sights around these streets here, where along with other honest white Scots, I had to literally sweep the Muslim vermin aside in order to proceed along my path.

I urge you all to take a stand and make this land……'

It was another hour or so before Tommy had finished his well-used speech for such small crowds. He knew he could afford to be more controversial at events like this. *Mair fuckin' polis than punters*, he'd decided earlier. Of course there would be a piece in the Record about the wee bit o' bother at the start. Just the sort of press coverage he didn't want. But then,

what was it they said? No such thing as bad
publicity.

Chapter 8

'So, what do you mean about being able to help get Nasreen back? You don't look like a bounty hunter or a civil servant type to be honest.'

'No, that's true,' Ridge glanced around warily. 'This is totally unofficial. I have certain, well, *friends*, you could say, that might be-'

The girl jumped up, her eyes growing ever larger and her hand darted to the edge of her mouth.
'Hey! Not like that!' Ridge noticed several pairs of eyes regarding him less favourably and as he implored the girl to sit back down he heard chair legs scraping on the wooden floor and bodies moving behind him. Rosina seemed to appreciate the genuine horror he'd felt at the thought that he might have been less than noble about his quest and with a flick of her hand the situation became calm once more.

'What I am *trying* to say is that I've got a certain amount of experience in the 'rescue department' but only as a civilian trying to do the right thing. I once found myself in the wrong place at the wrong time and I somehow managed to become a fugitive who had only wanted to find a girl I thought I loved. I made some useful contacts, people who can often circumvent official channels and I might be able to obtain information that could help. That's all I meant…'

Ridge finished weakly and he felt it too, opening his hands beseechingly in a manner the girl would see many times a day in this ramshackle old building.

'Have you had your breakfast yet?' she suggested. Ridge thought things might be brighter after all.

Less than five minutes later he found himself devouring a generous helping of scrambled egg on toast while trying to ignore the vague guilty feeling that perhaps his darling wife, just a short walk away, would have liked to join them.

'So I thought from your reaction back there that you thought I was somehow a human trafficker or something like that. What did you mean about me not being a bounty hunter?'

'You're white,' came the terse reply. She gestured with her hand. 'Like everyone else in this café. You don't come from around here do you? What makes you think you can help Nasreen?'

'I don't *think* anything right now, okay. I'm just trying to find out a wee bit more about the situation so I can work out if there is anything I *can* do, all right? Now you could be a huge help here and tell me what you're on about!'

Rosina looked around the busy room, her mouth tight with exasperation and then after a long sigh placed her coffee down and smiled over to him.

'Okay, you've got half an hour. What do you need to know…?'

It was two hours later that Ridge emerged into a bright late morning sun, his head spinning and his stomach churning from too much strong coffee. He didn't have that long before his next 'meeting' and he badly needed some fresh air and to use the physicality of walking to power up the tired batteries of his internal CPU and then decide what the fuck to do. At this very moment the temptation to just hit 'restore' to a previous backup of 48 hrs was palpable.

He'd already begun to regret his fact-finding mission as it had only highlighted how little he understood the whole situation. No change there, he muttered but without rancour. He'd walked blindly into a nest of vipers before and survived hadn't he? Ah! But this is different, said a wee voice in the back of his head. Now you have a family to think of.

It turned out that the bounty hunters were always Asian males, a more recent trend that had come up from England, particularly among the higher status families who would pay these men to bring their daughters back. They were greatly feared among Asian women as they had little scruples in fulfilling their objectives and would often assault the girls if they resisted. Rosina asserted that Mr Saad would almost definitely have used these men to assist him in looking for Nasreen. Her obvious implication being that if they couldn't find her then how on earth did Ridge expect to?

It hadn't been an altogether pleasant breakfasting experience, he conceded as he strode into the leafy sanctuary of Queen's Park, past the bowling greens now closed for the winter, the grand old building struggling under an onslaught of garish graffiti. Rosina had scorned him that he didn't know the difference between an Indian, Pakistani or Bangladeshi. But when he finally cracked and told her about his own ethnic background and how he could tell who someone's grandparents were on Sorsay just by looking at the shape of their face, then it was her turn to be astonished.

'You never saw an Asian person until you were *how* old?'

Rosina herself was of Indian parents and she was brought up a Hindu, not a Muslim, a distinction she said she knows is lost on most of her fellow Scots. Her parents were reasonably well off with a successful business in Edinburgh and so they could afford to pay for her to be traced although she admitted that she came back to Scotland under her own volition.

'I fell for the lies of my father and the tears of my mother. They told me it would be different when I returned. They promised I could attend college. I got my education that was true. I learned fast.

Usually, girls like me have no life when they return. Our reputation, if you know what I mean, is the most important thing for Asian girls. We have to maintain our family honour, we call it *izzat*. By me running away I was seen as disgracing my family. I had put my own desires above that of my culture, my community and my family.
But my parents had not sought publicity or help with my retrieval, not like Nasreen, and so they had not been so stigmatised. Our *izzat* was not lost. Not like now anyways.'

Ridge watched her stroke her wedding ring absent-mindedly and he could only guess at the suffering she had undergone over in India.

He wondered if he was just being naïve that he found it incomprehensible that this kind of thing still went on in his own country.

'But you're making headway now, surely? I mean, you're educating this community and you're above the radar now, what with all the publicity around everything Islamic?'

'You think?
We've got girls here in the Southside who have been painted as immoral sluts just for running away to find a better life. Some of them are as chaste as nuns and yet now they get followed wherever they go.
Most of them come to me in a worst state than before they ran away because now the families are desperate to marry them off and that usually means to men far away whose families are unaware of their disgraced position.
It's so much worse around here than over in Edinburgh as we've got more lower class Pakistani and Bangladeshi families and many of the girls are more or less illiterate in English. We can't help them as much as we'd like because our cultural boundaries are far stricter than yours and so the more educated middle class among us are forbidden to mix with the poorer

girls and so the problem of runaways just goes on and on.'

Rosina sighed in obvious frustration, like an over-worked school teacher bored of explaining simple concepts to even less interested teenagers.

'My job is to try and empower women who've been born in Scotland just like you and me to lift their heads beyond the confines of our strict communities and reach out to the broader population. This is what we've got to if we're ever going to dispel the stigma of Islam and forge a better way forward. Many of us had been hoping for a 'Yes' vote in the referendum as we thought an independent Scotland might have been more forward thinking when it came to our multi-cultural populations.
But instead we've got the right wing UK government branding asylum seekers as migrant rats down at the English Channel and every one of us here is a potential jihadi.
But now we just have to get on with it and hope for the best.
That's why I'm helping you today, Richard Walker, because I still have hope for the future and I can see hope in your eyes too.'

So here he now was, full of hope and horror in equal amounts, kicking leaves in the park and still toying with the notion that he'd be far better off going straight back to the warmth and safety of his flat. And his beautiful wife.

But he knew he wouldn't.

He had never been able to stop himself getting into situations that he should have walked away from, much like many other young men, he reasoned. Up until a couple of years ago, the worst extent of these things would have been something innocent like missing the last bus home or going up a one way street the wrong way or perhaps going back for 'coffee' when he should've known better.

Since then however he had upgrading his stupidity levels to encompass such activities as marrying an IRA terrorist, stealing the girlfriend of one of the world's most wanted men and going into battle with a group of cross-dressing mercenaries.

He heard himself laugh out loud at that point and it was only then he noticed a group of Asian men watching him intently from an old converted park building now some kind of café. The men were huddled under blankets giving them the appearance of accelerated old age and as he paid greater attention he saw they were sharing a large water pipe and looking very contented with themselves. He waved without thinking and in turn received a cursory nod or wave from the men. He stuck his chin into his chest and walked on a little faster wondering what kind of a place he'd just seen and perhaps smoking pot had become legal or something and nobody had told him.

They could have for all he knew. Despite living in the south of a vibrant and noisy city, neither Ridge nor Orla had been into a pub or club since their return and he couldn't remember the last time he'd had a drink. Because of the baby Ridge had decided to knock the fags on the head too but he still teetered at times and he often found himself walking a little too closely behind a smoker as he inhaled the smoke trailing in their wake. What was it about the smell of tobacco in the outdoors? He'd smoked a lot worse than mere tobacco during his adventures overseas but the attraction of illicit drugs had long since worn off. He'd seen the kind of people who profited from the drugs trade and these days he wouldn't give them the steam off his own piss. The photo warnings that he would put on cocaine packets would be a whole lot more gruesome that an old carcinogenic lung.

But today would be an entirely different and far milder brand of warning-hazard-ahead-extreme-danger-of-death. Last year meeting a stranger in a café to talk about kidnapping and rescue would have been a quiet day at the paper for Ridge. What was the worst thing that could happen? This was his litmus test for decision making these days. Would this result in a death or not? No. Probably not. So proceed? Affirmative. Engage.

Chapter 9

The busy café was cramped and noisy and as Ridge sat defending the tiny flimsy cane table, fingers nervously playing with the sugar sachets, it hit him. This would be the weirdest fucking job interview of his life. *But the travel expenses were good.* He looked in vain for Masood although the many smoked glass mirrors made it virtually impossible to work out just what you were looking at and all he could see were the contemptuous looks from tired shoppers as their cold eyes flashed down to him. The cheek of it! One person hogging a table for two! And he's not even ordered anything!

Just as he started to think he'd been stood up and a wave of relief was beginning to wash over him, Masood appeared out nowhere and thumped down heavily, unadvisedly even, into the coveted chair. Ridge reached across and pumped his hand then sat back to stare out the miserable bastards who were already turning away looking for fresh pickings elsewhere.

Masood looked brighter than their last meeting and he started to fish a brown envelope out of his parka jacket.

'No!
Just leave it there will you!
Can we not wait until there's less people about eh?'

'Yes, I see! It doesn't look so good, does it? A dodgy deal!
But I thank you so much for coming today and there is so much I want to tell you.'

What with the espresso machine going full blast and the general mayhem and clamouring of plates ricocheting off the hard surfaces, Ridge was finding it impossible to hear Masood and he knew they were never going to be able to have the kind of conversation they needed here. He stood up much to the surprise of one of the old battle-axes that had been drawing him dirty looks and her face transformed into a vision of generous munificence as he theatrically offered her his chair in mock politeness. As the woman wedged herself into the seat he shouted down to Masood, 'Come on pal, this place has gone to the dogs lately! Let's go!'

Outside they buttoned up against a colder wind and headed south.

'Know any decent pubs around here?'

Masood just glared at him. 'I don't go into pubs, my friend. I don't drink.'

'Well neither do I, so where do you suggest we go? What was that place back in the park? It looked like some kind of opium den. You know where I mean?'

67

Masood's eyes brightened. 'You mean the shisha bar? Yes, we can go there if you like. It is quiet and we can have a proper talk about everything. Here, take this before I forget. You can count it if you want to but there is two thousand pounds there, just as we agreed.'

Ridge initially pushed his hand away but at the man's insistence he snatched it and thrust it quickly into his coat, somehow feeling like he'd stolen it. No going back now, he thought. And then just as quickly he told himself that there was never going to be, who did he think he was kidding?

Ridge felt a little surprised at his quickening heart rate as they stepped onto the old style verandha of the shisha bar. The men who'd acknowledged him earlier were still there and on close inspection Ridge saw that they were much younger than he'd thought. There seemed to be one water pipe between three men and wafts of exotic spices tempted Ridge's nostrils and he took in the ornately decorated silver chamber that sat atop each one, presumably where the 'whatever' was being burned. Masood seemed to know everyone and shook a great deal of hands once they entered the dimly lit bar. It felt like walking into a large marquee tent like those Ridge remembered seeing Gadaffi holding court in on news bulletins back in the 90's. Both the walls and the ceiling were draped in large swathes of canvas, some decorated with images of ethnic scenes and once his eyes had grown accustomed to the light he began to feel very comfortable being there.

As they threaded their way carefully through the eclectic mis-match of furniture and huge cushions Ridge was reminded of some of the more bohemian venues he'd known in San Francisco. He felt more relaxed still to see there were a couple of white faces over in a corner, a man and a woman, both gazing intently at their electronic devices. Next to them sat two Asian men playing chess.

'So what's your poison Masood? What would you recommend? A wee blast of the water bong then?'

'It's called a hookah, my friend and yes I am particularly fond of the double apple and mint at this establishment. Most refreshing, but perhaps a little chilly for outside sitting today don't you agree? However, they do have an interesting range of teas and some fine pastries if you like that kind of thing. How about a mocktail?'

Ridge could sense a game of cultural one-upmanship beginning and he sat back, comfortable to let Masood have the upper hand on this occasion. He let him explain the history of the shisha bar and how it had the dubious honour of being the first bar in Scotland to be prosecuted for flouting the smoking ban a few years back. So now the pipes were an outdoor feature but customers could have free blankets and hot water bottles if required. Ridge couldn't help wondering how many traditional pubs would offer that kind of service.

The tattered but comprehensive menu was interesting and there seemed to be no sense of urgency for the staff to serve them. Ridge was impressed with the furniture as there wasn't one single piece that matched another. He remembered a review pasted up on the wall of one of his regular haunts in San Fran which had said something like, 'the interior was like the grubby living room of your eccentric aunt who'd been a bit of a goer in the Sixties.'

'So, are there lots of these shisha bars, Masood? I don't remember ever seeing one before.'

'Yes there are a few but they are usually hard to find unless you already know where they are. The elders are very disapproving of them as we're not normally supposed to mix the sexes, especially unchaperoned. There are no Asian women in here right now but later this place will be just like your conventional Scottish pub apart from the

absence of alcohol. There can be music acts playing here and poetry readings and so forth.
The older generation of our community are not happy at all and they accuse these bars of encouraging men to abandon their family responsibilities by spending two or three hours here at a time.'

'Just like a real bar!' Ridge laughed. 'Except your guys don't end up staggering home mortal drunk and puking all over the bathroom!'

'Well yes, that is true but the shisha pipe is considered by many as a health risk and it depends on what you put in it. Normal pipes have the shisha grass which is not a drug of course, but some people do smoke tobacco and other substances too. But the shisha bar is most unlike your bars in that we just come here to mix freely and where else can we go? The Mosque?
Surely it is better for our young people that they can have a place to go while still loving Mohammed and our faith. The alternative is the gangs and violence of your world.'

'Okay Masood, I'm sold! Now, tell me as much as you can about what exactly you want me to do and who else I need to speak to so I can do the best job for you. If she was kidnapped then who did it? The grooms' family? Would he have been involved? Where are they from? Don't worry, I have an empty reporters pad here so don't be shy!'

Chapter 10

Ridge had settled into the relaxed ambience of the shisha bar like he'd been sitting there all his life and he was sipping another intriguing tea when, imperceptibly at first, things began to change around him. The bar had become busier but he could just hear quiet music percolating through the drapes and it sounded like old Beatles stuff, from after they'd met the Maharishi and gone off the reservation somewhat. He'd sampled three different teas by this time, his latest a dark red fruity blend called 'Faeries Blood' which he presumed was a Halloween speciality. Masood had pressed a cake on him so he chose a good old fashioned apple pie and he swore it was the best he'd had since he left San Francisco, a Turkish speciality, he was informed.

They'd had plenty time for Masood to fill him in on Nasreen and Ridge now had a photo of the girl which he found himself reluctant to put down, her large round eyes imploring him to help her. A lot of what Masood had told him about life in the Southside had echoed the theme of his earlier interview and so he could adopt a certain nonchalant air of knowledge and he could sense Masood was impressed with this. At the same time he worried that the man omitted to tell him something vital because of this and so he had interrogated him relentlessly.

However his most pressing question had been parried several times and he'd given up for the time being on finding out just how exactly he had ever cropped up on Masood's radar in the first place. He felt sure that the guy must be arrow-straight and was solely concerned with finding his sister before she came to harm but at the same time he wasn't stupid either and he could also tell when he was being spun. He'd had plenty experience of that after all. It was time to up the ante.

'What makes you so positive that she's even in Pakistan? Had she been there before and aren't there lots of family there still who might know where she is? Why hasn't she followed the gap year trail to Syria and become a jihadi?'

'Of course we have family over there, in the Punjab, but neither Nasreen nor I had seen them since were very small and we'd not been over to Pakistan since then. In fact my trip to help find her was the first time I'd been there since I was about seven years old and to me it was just as familiar as the dark side of the moon. We are Scottish now, Ridge Walker, and my sister was looking forward to the rest of her life here with an education and a good job ahead of her despite what the family may have wanted.'

'Okay! So why the hell would she have allowed herself to be talked into even considering an arranged marriage?'

'It is very difficult my friend. She loves her family, we both do, but they do not give in and they are themselves bound by a code and an honour system that goes back many ages. There is no way my parents would have chosen this path, but it's now beyond the boundaries of the family and so it's just like she'd never been born.'

'And I presume the cops have interviewed the family of the spurned groom?'

'No not exactly.
Not in this country because neither he nor his family have ever set foot outside the city of Islamabad in their lives, this is why a marriage to Nasreen was going to be the biggest thing in their family history and that's why I am positive they have taken her.
She is a prize they will not let go of.
And no, before you ask. The Scottish police have not been to Pakistan as they either don't believe there has been any crime committed or they don't think they can do anything over there. The Pakistani

police have been less than helpful as this happens every day.
This is why I believe that maybe someone like you could make a difference, Ridge Walker.'

By now Ridge had writer's cramp and as he stretched and looked around it was obvious that they were being watched by a group of young men and their demeanour did not look friendly.

'Masood, don't turn too quickly but do you know these guys over there, watching us?'

'Yes, my friend. I have seen them. They are friends of Nasreen I have seen her with before but I don't know them, they are much younger. I think they go to the centre, you know, where you were this morning.'

Ridge smiled over to the men and this provoked a sudden squawking and posturing amongst them as one stood up, preened himself and strode over.

'What's up Masood? This guy a Fed or what?'

The man was barely out of his teens and although he looked threatening as he towered over them, Ridge gauged him at 5' 6" at best and 140 pounds max.

'No Humza! Are you crazy! Sit and join us please! This is a friend of mine who's interested in hearing about Nasreen. That is all!'

'A reporter then! Masood you're a fucking twat so you-'

Ridge jumped to his feet and stared down into his eyes. He instantly caught the familiar whiff of grass. The guy was completely stoned.

'I'm *not* a cop or a reporter, okay! I'm just a friend that's all!
Now do you want to help me find out what the fuck happened to Nasreen?
If not, get the fuck out my face!'

The lad crumbled for a moment and looked helplessly across to his friends for moral support but they'd all turned away laughing. So he took a deep breath, mock punched Ridge's arm and pulled up a large cushion beside them.

'Eh, no need to be like that, pal! We just get too many cunts like that but, snooping around trying to cook up a story. Is that not right Masood?'

Ridge could see that these two men had precious little in common, apart from maybe one thing, the missing girl. He vowed to extract as much juice from this bounty which had literally landed on his lap. Now perhaps at long last, he would get to the real truth about what happened to Nasreen!

Chapter 11.

Once you peeled away the layers of teenage attitude and racial enmity, Humza was just like any other young man in Glasgow, trying to get his shit together in a harsh and unforgiving world where judgements are instant and forgiveness rare. Despite their spiky introduction, Ridge suspected that Humza had the best of intentions and a genuine feeling of concern for the missing girl. It was also becoming obvious that Nasreen might have, perhaps unwittingly, cast a spell over many of the young men that she had come into contact with, but this was a road he chose not to travel on for the moment.

'So, like I was saying, but. There's no chance Nasreen has just run away like a scared wee lassie.
It's fuckin' obvious to me and the lads why she left! Come on Masood!
You know she's gone to find that twat Shahid!'

Ridge saw Masood lower his head in shame and as he felt a jolt of adrenaline surge through him he knew the youngster had struck the mother lode here.

'Masood, what's he talking about? What haven't you been telling me?'

79

'It is true, my friend! Nasreen *had* an acquaintance with this man, Shahid, but I'm sure it was nothing more than that. Nasreen was a respectable daughter despite all of our problems and she wouldn't have been silly enough to be involved with a man like him.'

'What do you mean, a man like him?'

Humza pointed an accusatory finger at Ridge.

'He was becoming a fuckin' nut-job that's what he means!
Always reading the Koran and talking about *jihad* and all that ISIS bollocks! When we were kids, it was *him* who first gave me a toke of a spliff but now he'd be wanting our fuckin' hands chopped off for doing shit like that!'

'Masood?' Ridge aimed his best quizzical eyebrow towards the increasingly harassed young man only to see him break down in tears. Then Humza jumped over and put an arm around the sobbing Masood and as he did so another of the men came over and squeezed in beside them. He was a huge gangly lad, tall as a basketball player and he'd obviously heard everything. Ridge elected to keep quiet as things were just starting to get interesting.

'It's true, but. What Humza says! We looked up tae Shahid at school an' we were all in the same gang, like, and it was totally boss, man, before all the politics and the *rad* stuff took him over! I mean, some of it, we was cool with like, about all you guys fuckin' hating us, taking the piss out of Mohammed an' making out we was all Bin Laden's an' that. Then he took it too far, but, and we didn't hang about with him after that, he was just a loner.'

'Ashif is right!' Humza let go of a broken looking Masood and rejoined the conversation.

'He just lost the plot and none of us really understood what the fuck he was on about after that. He'd have known Nasreen since we was at school, like, but we would never have thought she'd pal up wi' him these days until we saw her having a pure *rager* wi' him just before he disappeared and-'

'Okay,' said Ridge, tentatively, not wanting to interrupt the flow of information but also sensing that the fox might be closing in on the rabbit. He looked directly at Humza now, having realised Masood was just the loving brother who'd been blind to what was really happening with his little sister.

81

'So where is this Shahid? Right now, today?'

'Fuck knows! Nowhere about here. We've looked. In Pakistan, probably. That's where he'd talked about going, to get some training an' that. Funny thing, he'd not been interested in Syria and all that trendy *jihad* stuff over there. He'd been talking about you guys pulling out of Afghanistan an' that and it being a chance to sort out Pakistan an' that, fuck knows what he was doing! All we knew was he'd become a total twat an' wee Nas seemed to have fallen for all his shite!'

'Okay then. So do you think that Nasreen might have gone with him? To Pakistan?'

Masood sat up. 'No! Never! She would not be so silly to do-'

'Fuck up Masood!' Humza threw up his hands angrily and Ashif grabbed his arms to hold him from launching himself over the low table. The big man spoke quietly but with the utmost conviction.

'We don't know where she is but we *do know* she was seeing Shahid. It's fucking obvious to all of us that she's followed him over to Pakistan. You've really no idea about this place. For us, if we want to, like, it's a bastarding conveyor belt. Pollokshields to Pakistan, people joke about how easy it to go there!'

To Ridge, what these young men were saying seemed to have the ring of truth about it and although grateful to them for coming over, he now felt dejected about his prospects of finding Nasreen or getting anythin else of use from Masood. Plus he definitely did not want to be getting involved with anything that had even the merest whiff of terrorism or violence. Orla would kill him long before any jihadi got the chance.

He put away his notebook, drained his tea and thanked them for being so forthright about Nasreen. He gave Masood a look that said, *I need to talk to you outside, now.* As they all stood, Ashif took his arm and whispered, 'Just find her, man. Bring her back to us.'

The sky had become as gloomy as their mood as the two of them left the warmth of the bar and Ridge found himself kicking the same leaves as he'd walked through earlier although this time in fury rather than nervous anticipation.

He wrenched the brown envelope out of his damp pocket and tried to thrust it into Masood's hands but he leapt backwards almost landing in a black puddle the size of Loch Awe.

'Why didn't you tell me the truth about
Nasreen?
Don't you want me to get her back?
What's really going on here Masood?
You've got one minute to level with me
completely, or I'm fucking out of here
and you can stick your two grand up your
arse for all I care!'

'I'm so sorry, my friend! Please! You
must understand!
Of course I want my sister back! This
money I give you is my own. I have had
to borrow just to give it to you and I'm
not a rich man, you must know that.
I apologise for omitting to tell you about
Shahid but I have to admit that even I did
not realise the extent of his involvement
myself until today.
But there is a very good reason why I do
not want his name mentioned when you
travel to Pakistan to find Nasreen.
If Shahid is, as they say he is, a known
radical or worse, then he will be known
to the authorities too and they will have
him on their lists. You must understand.
They have spies everywhere. If you
connect him with Nasreen in their minds
then she will be as good as dead, my
friend.'

Ridge stopped as he realised that tears
were pouring down the other man's ashen face.

'Come here!' Ridge grabbed his arm and propelled him over to a soaking wet wooden bench and together they sat in the gloom. As huge drops of rain cascaded off the trees and down the back of his neck, Ridge wondered how he was going to break the news to Orla.

Right then love! That's me off now! I'm just nipping over to one of the world's largest and corrupt failed states to hunt down a probable Islamic fundamentalist gang member in the most violent terrorist breeding ground that I could find.

He inhaled a lungful of dank, mouldy air and turned to the bowed head alongside him.

'Okay Masood! If we're going to do this, I need everything from you, right! I want to know anything that might help me and especially concerning this Shahid guy. I want to know as much detail as possible about him as you can find. I want to know him inside and out right down to the last insignificant detail.
I want to know what hand he holds it with! Got it?'

Chapter 12

Ridge felt the damp wad of bank notes weigh heavily in his sodden jacket and only then did he question the sanity in trudging around an unfamiliar part of town, alone in the dark, with a month's wages in his pocket. Having long since left the newly re-invigorated Masood, he now felt utterly spent himself. *Where am I?* With the cold rain unrelenting and a low thunder coming from his stomach, rumbling worse than the Glasgow Underground, he suddenly thought of Orla.

Pressing the keys awkwardly with his numb fingers, Ridge ducked under the doorway of a busy sounding bar to escape the worst of the weather. No answer. His chest tightened and he tried again. In the bath? Again nothing. He left a message anyway. He should go home but he wasn't ready for that yet. He wanted this place to seep into his veins tonight. He needed to absorb every possible trace of Nasreen and this place she had lived in.

He could feel a heat radiating out from the doorway of the pub and it was only then he felt colder and found he had been subconsciously edging closer to the opening as if pulled by a tractor beam. But he was saved as a couple of burly women came barging out, accompanied by a clamouring of laughter and an intoxicating wave of hot perfumed air. They giggled and held each other for support under a shared jacket barely big enough to cover one of them and each lit up a cigarette, huddling closer and sharing a secret at the top of their shrill voices. For a brief moment Ridge watched them fascinated but quickly felt that he was intruding and he turned reluctantly to leave the warmth and light.

Back out in the rain he could hear the two women screeching like seagulls all the way down the street and he longed to be back on Sorsay again. He felt alone and strangely alien this dark evening, as if in his mind, he had already left to that other unknown place. Both he and Orla had both mentioned that they often felt ill at ease now they were back in Glasgow and that they worried they would never feel at home in the once welcoming city.

He was desperate for the warmth and company of some good friends but as he splashed through the black puddled pavements he couldn't name one person in Glasgow that he could visit. Since their return it would be fair to say they'd been living quietly but it still hit him like a train. He hadn't one good friend in this, the largest city in Scotland.

Consoling himself with a chocolate bar and a pack of cigarettes, he tried to shrug off his malaise and work out exactly what to say to Orla and then how to proceed. He still needed to find out more before he could go to Pakistan and he didn't even have a passport! *And that was going to be a trial in itself.* The enormity of his task dropped down from the dark sky like a heavy wet fishing net and his legs felt so tired he might

87

have been wading through quicksand. There was nothing else to do, he needed a drink. *Just the one, mind*, he heard himself mutter.

He genuinely hadn't had any alcohol for months and the first pint tasted so good he felt like he should be in a television advert. The pub was packed and although he'd never put a foot in the place before, he had navigated his way to the bar with the consummate skill of a man who has enjoyed a wee refreshment or two in the past. Having said that he hadn't the confidence to go away from the safety of the long traditional wooden bar top itself and so he gripped on and made the best of it.

The wee whisky chaser seemed to possess restorative powers beyond even the mighty IPA which he had almost finished and so he elected to have a little more. Feeling giddy by this time he had the sense to limit the volume slightly by ordering a half pint but still with the 'wee goldie' to follow, a 'half an' a half,' as it was known.

Despite his recent inexperience with the demon drink, Ridge found himself having another round and another after that. He'd sparked up several inane conversations with his fellow patrons as they queued up for service from the harassed bar staff and he felt happy, warm and protected here for the first time since the old Brigadier's funeral. The bar itself was a nondescript affair, rough around the edges but serviceable and homely. It could have been any bar in any town in Scotland. There was nothing to indicate the existence of a parallel universe where men drank tea and smoked water pipes while playing chess and talking about revolution but this time by the bullet not the ballot.

But all too soon he found himself back out in the cold black night shivering and disorientated as if being ripped from the womb. He could vaguely remember himself sliding along the bar as if on the Sorsay ferry on stormy seas; his clothes were wetter now than when he went into the bar and his ears were still reverberating with the angry rebukes of more sober men about not being able to handle his drink and so he surmised that he had in fact been chucked out.

Looking at his watch he couldn't make out the time but knew it must be later than Orla would have wanted. He stared at his phone but couldn't work out how to make it call her and so he decided just to walk home as quickly as he could. It was only then he knew he was lost and he instinctively threw his hand up wildly at the next dark coloured vehicle that approached out of the gloom which for once stopped on a sixpence for him.

As the taxi deposited him outside his flat he hadn't noticed that the main outside door light was off. These lights were supposed to operate on light sensors so always bathed the entrance in an orange light so residents could see which buzzer to press for their particular apartment.

He was vaguely aware that something wasn't quite right and as he fumbled through his pockets for his key he felt more than saw a dark shape emerging from his right. There were spindly but high hedges that separated the tenement flats from the road affording the ground floor residents some degree of privacy and at the main door entrances they were at their tallest, ten feet or more, giving each entranceway a darker more tunnel-like effect.

He peered up and right to see a black shadow in front just as a hand from behind grabbed his hair and pulled him backwards. He felt a sharp pain in his groin and as he began to curl forward a cold fist crashed behind his right ear and he fell into a pool of his own vomit as a hot flood of acid beer gushed across the mossy tarmac.

He turned his shoulder and grabbed a wet boot, only just preventing it from rearranging his face and as he attempted to twist it using his entire bodyweight he was still surprised at how easily the bulk of his attacker became airborne. Then he heard the unmistakable and sickening crack of breaking bone and as he waited for that electric current of pain to rack his weakened body he felt instead the dead weight of a large man fall across his back and then down beside him.

A huge dark face grimacing in agony stared back at him for a brief second before making a half hearted attempt at head butting him. Ridge pulled himself upright to see a tiny black whirlwind rain blows and kicks on his second assailant as he attempted to protect himself while pulling his accomplice off the ground. The little ninja seemed to float as he spun around and delivered another bone shattering kick and then Ridge found himself floundering amongst the sharp winter spikes of the hedge as the two men pushed their way out of the entranceway and stumbled off.

Chapter 13

Ridge allowed his rescuer to escort him up the stairs and he half expected there to be more thugs waiting in the shadows for him. He leant on the door bell wearily and tried to take in what had just happened. It had been a weird day for sure and he started to rehearse what exactly to say to Orla when she eventually answered the door.

Would she be out at this time of night? He shook his head and realised he was now completely sober but when he turned to ask the guy in for a coffee and to say thanks he decided he still had to be off his face. The wee guy, now standing under the bright yellow light of the landing, had pulled off his black woollen beanie hat and somehow transformed into a beautifully coiffured young Asian woman.

'Wow! Didn't see that coming!'

'You didn't see a lot coming now did you, really?
You going to invite me in or just stand gawping like a mutated goldfish?'

'Yeah, yeah, of course! I was just trying to wake my wife up. I don't know where she's got to at this hour.'

Despite his predicament Ridge had to laugh inwardly at his pathetic declaration that he 'had a wife,' as if for one moment this gorgeous wee chick would ever want to shack up for the night with a pissed up numpty covered in blood and sick.

The girl made for the kitchen and as he wandered from room to room he could heat the kettle firing up but as for Orla there was no sign. He sat forlornly at the foot of their bed staring at the space where he expected her to be lying, as if somehow he could conjure her presence just by force of imagination. He listened to comforting sounds from the kitchen and then started up out his half dream in a blind panic. He knew that if she did come back at this precise moment then he would have to start explaining things mighty fast before the street witnessed yet another mighty stramash. It was only then he saw the note sitting on his bedside table. Orla. It simply read –

> *Gone to your folks for a day or two.*
> *Let me know when you're planning to*
> *go away, will you?*
> *O x.*

He staggered back to the kitchen still carrying the letter and ruffled a filthy hand through his hair.

'My wife has left. Gone to my folks.'

'I don't blame her!' came the caustic reply. 'Call me old-fashioned but isn't she supposed to go back to *her* folks?'

> 'Naw! She's not left me, at least I don't think so anyway!
> Talking about being old-fashioned, I still haven't thanked you properly for that down the stairs, by the way.
> My name's Richard Walker or Ridge to my pals and you definitely count as a pal after that tonight!'

The girl flashed him a wide smile and handed him a steaming mug of coffee. Her eyes were a beautiful deep hazel set in a face of flawless honey brown skin and he just noticed that her athletic figure was clad in black 'fatigues' which probably cost more than his entire wardrobe.

> 'My name is Jakia Mehjibin Wadhwa or just Jake to *my* friends and Boo to my very best friends, but I wouldn't worry. You'll not need to remember that one, I promise you. Jake will do for you!'

> He shook her hand. 'Well 'Just Jake' whatever your name is, I'm very glad you happened to be around, I'm not sure what these guys were after.'

The girl looked away and made for the door.

'You got any comfy seats? My feet are killing me, so they are!'

After witnessing her kung-fu skills, this didn't surprise Ridge too much and he led the way through to the lounge.

'Did they rob you?'

He put his hand up inside his jacket fearing the worst but no, the wad of notes was still there. He gagged at the smell from his hands and jumped up in horror at the state he must look in front of this stylish young woman. Making his excuses, he jumped up and went to remove his dirty coat and give himself a quick wash.

'You needn't worry on my account! I've seen a lot worse!'

'Oh yeah?' Ridge shouted from the bathroom. 'Make a habit of this kinda thing do you?'

She was perusing his CD collection when he got back and so he went to stick on whatever was in the player.

'Looks like you're a bit of a Bowie fan?'

'Too right, I am. Guys a legend isn't he?'

'He's a wee bit before my time, to be honest,' she smiled round at him. 'But he's done a few cool songs I suppose!'

'And so you must be a Boo Radleys fan then?'

Her face responded with a question mark.

'The band! That's where the Boo comes from right?'

'Wrong. It comes from *Boudicca*. She was a legendary warrior queen, but I told you not to worry about that!

'So where d'ye learn to fight like that? Kung-fu is it?'

'No, it's just karate. Kyoshinkai karate, or knock-down to give it its better known name. I got free lessons from the work and it just seemed to suit me.'

'You don't look like a bouncer if you don't mind me saying. So what *do* you do then?

'I'm a cop.'

Ridge recoiled and immediately saw that she'd clocked it, big time.

'No, it's okay. I know most people hate us. I've not really done a lot of 'coppering' for a while now. I'm officially a detective, in fact I'm the highest ranking female detective of Pakistani origin in the whole of Police Scotland, I'll have you know!'

'I'm impressed,' Ridge replied, his mind now racing. So was it a coincidence her being here and is *all* of this stuff connected?

'It's a bit of a nuisance really. They pay me an obscene amount of money for doing very little. PR-wise, I'm so precious to them now that I just get shunted around from course to course and presentation to presentation. They love showing me off and are paranoid that I get hurt. That or pregnant!'

Zakia laughed and her eyes gleamed again but then dulled over for a moment which Ridge couldn't help noticing despite his weary state of mind. He tried and failed to see why Jake would have been there for him like that. It didn't make sense. But precious little of the day's events were making too much sense at the moment. He needed a shower, some sleep and to speak to Orla.

'So! Putting on my detective hat for now, who do you think would want to give you a doing, assuming that this wasn't a robbery?
You were pretty drunk when you got out of that taxi weren't you?
Have you wound anyone up lately?
Does this sort of thing happen to you on a regular basis or was this just a one-off?'

'No, I hardly drink at all these days. Honestly!
We live the quiet life here and that's just the way we like it. My wife is writing a book and I do a bit of freelance computer work, you know, programming and stuff.'

Zakia nodded, her eyes drilling into him. Ridge could have just done with crashing out but he figured it was the least he could do to humour her for a bit and there might always be the chance she could actually help him put some of the pieces together. But he knew not to let his guard down. His old instincts were becoming sharper again and she may be a pretty good fighter and all that but he could still give her a few surprises. He trotted out a redacted version of the day's events.

'It gets boring sitting in front of a screen all day so I was just doing a bit of research for my wife and I went over to a shisha bar where maybe I ruffled a few feathers, I'm not sure. But that was this afternoon. In the morning I visited the centre down on Albert Street, you know it? But there weren't any problems or anything that I'm aware of.'

'That you're aware of.
And what about tonight? You could barely walk.
Did you fall off a wagon or what?'

Ridges bristled and looked all around the room rather than at the beautiful woman who was giving him a hard time but then his eyes were drawn back to hers. In the back of his mind he could hear a voice with a distinct Irish brogue telling him that this was kids' stuff compared to what the other beautiful woman in his life would have said! He knew it. And if you were talking about warrior women they didn't come much tougher than Orla.

'I don't know what happened tonight to be honest.
I had a lot on my mind and I was cold and wet and it just seemed like a good idea at the time.
I know how it sounds!
You've probably heard it a hundred times, you think I'm a bevvy-merchant and that's what I sound like, I know, but the truth is I don't go out at all these days

and I haven't touched a drop hardly since my wife fell pregnant, we maybe share the odd can of Guinness but that's-.'

'So that's why you were so drunk? Because you're 'not used to it' not because you had drunk yourself into a stupor?'

Ridge sighed and nodded. 'A bit of both, I suppose.' He needed to change the angle of attack here as he was being slaughtered by this diminutive interrogator.

'So how come you were on the scene so fast anyway?
Do you make a habit of marauding around town in the dark dressed up like a ninja assassin?
Not that I'm complaining mind!'

The girl smiled and sat up in mock schoolgirl attentiveness.

'Well that's the policewoman in me. I too get bored with my job these days and so in the evening I often do this thing where I put on all the black gear and just walk about observing what's going on, trying to figure out why people do what they do. I think I should have been a psychiatrist! So anyway, I was just walking past, probably about twenty minutes before

you got there and I saw these two guys
acting suspiciously outside your door.
Someone had come out the main door
and yet they didn't seem to be in any
hurry to go in and my police instinct told
me to hang around and watch for a few
minutes.
To be honest, I was just on the point of
walking away when you got out the taxi
and as you zigzagged your way towards
them, the two men suddenly developed a
strange fascination with the hedge. That's
when I knew they were going to try and
roll you! Such an easy target, you were
like those poor homeless guys who get a
kicking from fourteen year old boys
testing their bravery buttons.'

Ridge shifted uncomfortably in his seat.
How did he get himself into these situations?
Getting lectured in his own home by a complete
stranger. One to whom he possibly owed his life.

'Well they got more than they bargained
for, thanks to you. I heard you break at
least one bone...'

The words were out before he could stop
himself.

'So! You have some experience of
hearing the violent breaking of bones, Mr
Computer Programmer?

That's very odd I have to say.
But yes! I am fairly sure there will be a
broken tibia, a fractured elbow and most
likely a severely dislocated patella
presenting themselves to the A& E
department of a Glasgow hospital right
about now. And that reminds me I have
to make a quick call or two!'

'Well, I won't keep you another minute. I
need a shower badly.
Thanks again for tonight! I'd hate to
think what would've happened if you
hadn't been on ninja patrol. It's a
comforting thought that our streets are
that much safer!'

Zakia stood and mimed the traditional
police officer putting away their notebook act
before standing to attention and adopting a
hands-behind-the back stance.

'It's all in a day's work, sir. That's what
we're here for.
Just be careful out there.'

They shook hands again and Ridge
escorted his rescuer to the door. As the door
closed he leant heavily against it, suddenly
exhausted. He also had this weird feeling that
when he woke up the next morning he would
find that he'd dreamt all of this and Orla would
be snoring happily right beside him.

With that thought in mind, he fell onto the bed, fully clothed and straight into a series of vividly coloured kung-fu themed dreams of the sort Tarantino would be rightly proud of.

Chapter 14

It was late the next morning as a freshly scrubbed young Andrew Walker stood patiently at the 'fast track' Passport Office in rain lashed Cowcaddens. Only he could know how painfully his head throbbed and why he walked in that peculiar fashion. In his shaking hands he clutched the myriad assortment of identification documents required for renewing his passport quickly. Renewing a passport he'd never possessed, with a birth certificate printed on paper younger than the shiny new shoes he was wearing and in the name of an unfortunate younger brother of his grandfather who'd never made it back from his one and only foreign adventure in 1914.

Aye, it's not what you know but who you know, he was thinking as he focussed on not passing out onto the brutally practical red linoleum floor.

Both he and Orla had been given new identities for everything that required documentation including driving licences, social security and anything else connected to the machinery of the State. According to official records, Richard Walker and Orla O'Dowd had died in a tragic road accident whilst on holiday close to the Mexican resort of Cancun. Their bodies had never been recovered. This had been particularly complicated for Orla as just a few months before this it had been accepted by the authorities that she had already been killed in a suspected botched bombing attempt on the Scots Parliament in Edinburgh.

However, with the personal involvement of their new bestie, the *Pres* himself, their status as the 'brave unsung heroes of democracy' was assured and no amount of governmental and bureaucratic untangling was considered beyond smoothing out for the pair of them. Hidden away back in the flat they even had a White House medal each which they had vowed they would show the kids when they were old enough to understand how crazy the world had been at one time.

Back out on the cold wet streets, he braced himself against the wind and headed back to the train station and a meeting with Masood. Looking for definitive answers before he made the final decision to go, he felt stronger and more purposeful than he had in a long time. He called Orla for the third time that morning. He'd confessed everything to her earlier and she'd practically forced him to check in with her at hourly intervals ever since. He'd been bang on the money about her reaction and that the thing she'd be most aggrieved about would have been a strange female in her flat at midnight.

'Hi love! Yep! It was a breeze! Totally. I'll get the passport in a day or to at the most. You got to hand to these guys, they

105

know how to work the system when it suits them! Catch you after I see Masood.'

Chapter 15

It had been his idea to meet in a more public place this time. He had still been feeling sore and jittery when he'd spoken to Masood but so far he'd left out the excitement of the night before and now he thought he'd probably keep it that way. The guy was having a hard enough time dealing with all this and he doubted Masood would be able to shed much light on the matter anyway.

The kick in the nuts had served one purpose however. It had given him a metaphorical kick up another part of his anatomy and it had been a wholly different Ridge Walker who'd carefully parted the heavy blackout curtains that morning to see if he could spot the 'surveillance team' that Colm had warned him about. Nothing.

He'd tossed and turned all night trying to fit pieces of this jigsaw together. If there had been government people watching then what the fuck were they doing whilst two men were jumping on his genitals? Did they not notice Ms Ninja? Were the two thugs actually the same people Colm had seen? Or was Zakia part of *their* team? It was a very convenient situation that she just happened to be there at the right time. So did that mean they were only trying to warn him off? And if so then it absolutely had to be connected with the Nasreen case. But why? Did they think that roughing him up would scare him off. And surely a serving policewoman wouldn't be stupid enough to get involved with something like this.

Christ, I wish Colm were here right now, he had thought, glancing up in to the trees overlooking the park on the other side of the road. You never know, he laughed, remembering his brother-in-law's penchant for arboreal sleeping arrangements. Colm would know what to do.

So as he dodged past the armed policemen at the entrance of Central Station, he made a mental note to try and find out whether Zakia was actually a serving police officer. Looking at their uniforms, he tried and failed to remember what her full name had been and immediately regretted not taking a note after she'd left. Still, there couldn't be that many Asian female detectives, could there?

Central was still a grand station in the classic sense, with a large white marbled concourse enclosed by attractive Victorian buildings made into shops, ticket offices and station facilities. Over arching all of this was a classic glass and metal structure providing sanctuary for the multitude of pigeons roosting between bombing raids on the ubiquitous multi-national horse burger outlet. He had arranged to meet Masood in a classy café overlooking the main concourse and he figured that the more people bustling about the safer he would be.

But Central Station at lunchtime was a tad busier than he'd anticipated. Trying to shrug off a slight case of agoraphobia brought about by spending too much time in the peace and quiet of his flat he pushed through the throngs of commuters towards the entrance to the café stairs. He thought he'd be able to see who might be watching him better in such a wide open space but it was too hectic and he couldn't stop his brain streaming images from one of those Matt Damon spy movies as he nervously looked to see if he was being tracked by any security cameras.

He caught Masood waving over to him and his first impressions were that he looked brighter and more confident that the wreck of a man he'd left the day before.

> 'Welcome, my friend! It is good of you to come. Please have a seat and we will have a cup of tea while we wait.'

> 'Wait? Wait for what?'

> 'Did I not tell you? I am sorry Ridge! I thought I had already spoken to you about this. Here! Quickly! Take this!'

Masood reached over the table and handed Ridge a familiar looking brown envelope but this time it felt bone dry and considerably more stuffed.

'I have spoken at great length with some of my family and I am very happy to tell you that it now seems that there are more who would welcome the safe return of my sister and consequently they have agreed to assist in the financial arrangements. The envelope contains eight thousand pounds, Ridge Walker, and this is yours to keep providing you take the flight to Pakistan. I have the tickets here also.'

'That's very trusting of you Masood but you don't have to give me it until I bring Nasreen back, I don't need it up front, honestly.'

'Yes of course I trust you, my friend, but let me tell you, there is more good news. When you return with Nasreen I will give you a further ten thousand pounds and on this matter I ask you to trust me also.'

'Wow!'

Ridge pushed back into his chair and almost over-balanced, the tall legs being unprepared for his unusual seated gymnastics and he grabbed onto the faux marble table top.

'Twenty grand, Masood! But I can't take that from you, it's too much!'

110

'For the safe return of my sister it is mere pocket change my friend. However, there is just one stipulation that I must insist on due to the involvement of my family and the considerable sums of money they have advanced me.'

'Go on…'

Ridge was still reeling at the thought of so much cash and whether they could now actually get the cottage re-wired *before* the wee one was born. He knew that Orla would be dubious about the morality of accepting the money but there was also that nesting instinct that he'd noticed and he hoped she would just think of it as an investment in their new and safer life on the island.

'You must take one of our family members with you.
My second cousin to be exact. This will greatly assist you in all matters pertaining to the culture of Pakistan which you freely admit to knowing very little about and it will give my family a certain assurance that you will not attempt to subvert the mission by reckless or inappropriate behaviour!'

'So you don't really trust me then?
Is that what you're saying?'

111

'I trust you with my life, Ridge Walker. But much more than that, I trust you with the life of my sister, whose safe return lies within your hands. Please accept this new arrangement as being a sensible and practical for all concerned!'

Ridge couldn't help feeling annoyed but underneath he also felt considerable relief that he'd have a back up guy and he knew it was obvious that he would have been at a considerable disadvantage being there on his own. But then he'd thought was that not the whole point of him being recruited for this in the first place? The very fact that he had done this on his own before and survived. But only just. And to be fair, he did have more than a little help. But all in all, his ego was prepared to be bruised slightly for twenty thousand pounds.

'Okay! Fair enough then. I suppose he'll come in handy from time to time over there. When is he turning up then?'

Masood was looking behind him and Ridge saw his eyes light up and the biggest smile break out across his face.

'Now, my friend! Right now! She is here!'

'She!' Ridge spluttered and stood up, turning awkwardly, his chair becoming airborne at last and launching itself under the legs of a passing waiter who should have fallen over the balcony had he not had the reactions and suppleness of an acrobat.

'Causing mayhem again are we!' the girl whispered softly in his ear as he struggled to maintain both his dignity and his sanity.

'Ridge Walker, can I introduce you to my wonderful second cousin Zakia?

The girl smiled demurely at him stretching out a petite olive coloured hand while all the time holding his gaze with those piercing black eyes which couldn't hide more than a little hint of amusement.

'Pleased to meet you, Ridge Walker! Have you ordered yet Masood? That coffee smells very good indeed!'

Ridge stood rooted to the spot for what seemed like an eternity until he felt the waiter thrust the errant chair into the back of his legs and then strut off with a dramatic flounce. He couldn't work out what was going on and now he felt trapped in some weird nightmare. First the ridiculous amount of cash he'd been given and now this apparition from last night back to haunt him. As he sat carefully down, half-listening to their polite talk about various aunts and uncles he felt his face hot and fiery and there was sweat gathering behind his knees. His earlier calm and professional demeanour was melting and he knew he had to get away before he tossed all his toys out of the pram.

> 'Back in a minute, Masood. Coffee, black, large mug if they have them.'

He crashed into the toilets, the cheap door ricocheting off the tiled walls as he headed straight for a sink and turned the cold tap on full blast. Ripping off his coat and shirt he bent over and filled his hands with the icy water. Ignoring the quizzical looks from the man next to him who was trying not to stare at the myriad wine coloured scars across Ridge's torso, he splashed his face again and again.

He stared into the mirror, trying to see the man in there behind the eyes. Did he know what the fuck he was getting himself into? After everything that he'd been through before, can that man in there handle whatever was going to be thrown at him? He looked intently to see any sign of weakness or uncertainty. He saw mostly anger. Anger at being duped for sure. And he also saw in those eyes a steely determination that he would never let any person on this planet get the better of him ever again. So, this is how it would be played. Game on!

Chapter 16

After Ridge rejoined the table it was only a few minutes before Masood left the two of them, *to get to know one another.* 'That should be interesting,' Ridge had said with such an edge in his voice that Masood sensed that perhaps he should find himself something urgent to take care of somewhere else. He left the flight tickets on the table and asked Ridge to call him that evening.

Masood had moved barely out of earshot when Ridge slammed his hand down and turned to the bemused woman on the other side of the table. Zakia in turn looked up to the skies and tutted like an ever so slightly harassed primary school teacher.

'So! Are you going to tell me what the fuck is going on, Zakia or *Jake* or whatever the fuck your real name is? And this time I want the truth, because if I don't feel like I'm getting the real deal from you in the next two minutes then I'm walking and you muppets have just wasted ten thousand pounds!'

'Temper temper!
Remember who you're talking to Ridge Walker!
Or is that Richard?

Or should it be Andrew now?
Or whatever 'the fuck' your real name is!'

'Okay! Fair point. I'm listening…'

'What do you need to know?
That I am a policewoman? True.
That I am Masood's second cousin? True.
That I and some of my family want
Nasreen found quickly? True.
That you will never find her without my
assistance? True.
And that together we will make a most
formidable team don't you think?'

The sudden and unexpected compliment
wrong-footed him.

'But, about last night? How did you, I
mean what were you-'

'What was I doing outside your flat last
night? Well don't flatter yourself! You're
not my type, I assure you!
I was following you that's all. I already
told you that's what I like to do, did I not?
I watched you wander the wet streets of
Glasgow like some latter day Holden
Caulfield! I waited patiently while you
drank yourself into oblivion and then I
also got a taxi, but mine turned out to be
a more direct and therefore faster taxi, a
tangible benefit of being sober and aware

116

of what's going on! Maybe you should bear that in mind if we are going to work together!

I then arrived at your flat where I found our two friends.'

The waitress came over and Zakia ordered two lattes whilst Ridge stared out over the concourse below and all the busy people oblivious to the drama being played out at his table. But was *he* being played? That was the kicker.

'So, the rest of my story you already know. I do not know what these people were doing and unfortunately they did not appear at any local hospitals so it may take some time to ascertain their identities. I fear they must be in some quite considerable distress by now. Now, let's see these flight arrangements! Economy class. Oh dear! We are going to have to become very close friends over the next few weeks!'

Chapter 17

The following week was mostly taken up with Ridge trying to keep the peace with Orla and his family. He joined her over on Sorsay and both of them made a reasonable pretence of working on practical aspects of the cottage and getting various increasingly expensive estimates from the only qualified electrician on the island. They also spent an inordinate amount of time just holding hands, talking about babies and savouring the peace and quiet together and Ridge would gently caress her growing bump and wonder why he had agreed to leave them even for only ten days or so. He'd picked up his new passport and visa before leaving and had had a further meeting with Zakia where she'd given him her 'idiots guide to Pakistan' lecture plus the usual guide books and internet links.

On Sorsay, they'd decided to keep his folks out of the loop and so to the rest of the family he had been lucky enough to win a contract to carry out a lucrative system re-fit for an Indian call centre network. To begin with, Orla had not been overly happy about the situation and in order to mollify her, he had asked Zakia to phone her and the two of them seemed to hit it off immediately, their mutual disdain for his comical shortcomings cementing an instant bond between them. With Zakia duly inducted into the 'sisterhood of kick-ass bitches,' as Orla aptly christened their friendship, the only other potential blot on the horizon remained the myriad assortment of international terrorism he could shortly be facing.

Zakia had played down the likelihood of any darker forces at work outside that of the usual deadly sins of pride, envy and greed which in her professional capacity she and her colleagues encountered every single day of the week. As regards her employment situation, she had elected to keep quiet about their trip to Pakistan and so their rescue mission had been neatly wrapped up in overdue holiday and overtime.

All of this Zakia had communicated to Orla and it served to downgrade the potential threat levels enormously and, over the course of the week, the overall picture of the trip had been gradually being painted as a simple family get together coupled with a modicum of strongly worded persuasion and an escorted return to safety.

Ridge was happy that the hormones responsible for the healthy development of their unborn child had somehow softened the reasoning abilities of his beautiful wife as the last thing he wanted to happen while he was away was any difficulties with the so far perfect pregnancy.

But in no way did he buy the story that this would be easy or straightforward. There were too many unanswered questions right here in Scotland and that was before they'd even got to Pakistan.

The relentless in-flight movies continued unabated as Ridge tried to adjust his seating position for the hundredth time but it was no use. Cramp stabbed at his legs and he had long since lost any sensation of feeling in his backside. He glanced enviously at the sleeping Zakia, small and supple enough to be able to curl up like a cat. They were on their second aircraft and only seven hours into their 22 hour journey but he was already counting down the hours until they arrived at Qatar and he could stretch his legs for an hour before the last leg to the airport at Rawalpindi in Pakistan.

Zakia had given him plenty to read and he could sense a mocking attitude in her voice as she told him she'd be testing him on it all later. She would never be lost in any crowd, resplendent in a pair of skin tight luminous orange leggings and of course he'd begun their flight to London by offending her, making a joke about her looking like an escapee from Guantanamo Bay. Their four hour changeover had been spent mostly apart but he was determined not to be shown up in any later exam and so he'd devoured most of the data already. It all made sobering reading.

He'd read with amazement all the 'official' Government paraphernalia like the Foreign and Commonwealth advice on 'missing persons abroad' and it was like a step back into Colonial times. The official line seemed to be that the British Embassies or Consulates would do very little in the way of practical help. If you were trying to find someone in Pakistan for example, they would not provide any financial assistance nor attempt to involve the local police authorities on your behalf. He saw why the previous attempts to find Nasreen had foundered and also why Zakia had opted to come with him in an unofficial capacity.

The UK cops were not allowed to get involved unless specifically asked by the local plods and to make matters worse an individual could not make contact with the international policing bodies like Interpol. That had to come from the British police. He was staggered to see that the FCO brochures were unsubtly suggesting that you'd be better off using a paid service like private detectives and that was when it hit him. *Fuck me! Is that what I am now, a private eye?*

As far as he could make out the British would not help him search for Nasreen and even if he found her they wouldn't help with any rescue operation. But they would help him find a local printer if he wanted to make up some posters! He couldn't help thinking that the Yanks would have been a better bet with this kind of thing and he remembered the way they'd sent the tooled up choppers into that apocalyptic hell-hole where he was close to death and won the day with a minimal amount of paperwork. 'As for our lot,' he muttered quietly to himself, 'unless we're going to look for a fucking lost cat it looks a lot like, *you're on your own, old chap, best of British*!'

His pessimism took a dent by his ability to arrange an 8am appointment with the British Consulate in Islamabad the day after tomorrow whilst browsing the delights of duty free. He did this partly as a fingers up to Zakia but also because that hadn't been done last time and he didn't have a clue what else to start with anyway.

They'd ended up having a brief, intense and fairly one-sided conversation with Zakia finally opening up like a rare orchid under a fleeting sun. Ridge had shown enough commonsense to ameliorate his behaviour so as to encourage her to talk as he knew the small but tough woman would be as least as valuable as she had promised to him just days before. But he was still taken aback by the force of her argument and found he had little ammunition to counter her tirade.

> 'Do you have any idea how it feels to be a Muslim woman in Scotland right now? To be viewed as a foreigner in our own country? A threat to national security? And even worse if we choose to wear the niqab or the hijab! I don't feel the need to wear a headscarf to express my faith but at the same time I totally understand why some other women might want to and

let's remember it's still their right, at
least in Scotland.
Even forgetting the whole religion thing,
it's not up to a bunch of white men to
dictate what *any* woman is allowed to
wear!'

'But it is a bit threatening for the locals
isn't it?
When you've got all these women cutting
about in full veils and all that. Wasn't
there a story about a suspected terrorist
escaping custody dressed as a woman?'

'Ridge!
Do you know how many Muslims there
are in Scotland right now?'

He shook his head, lamely.

'About 100,000 or so. And do you know
how many women actually wear the
niqab? Around 200. A tiny minority! So
why does it always get front-page
headlines and endless gassing on the TV?'

Zakia had given him reams of
information about recent events in Pakistan and
all the political shenanigans over the last few
years and he seriously doubted if he'd have got
on the plane if he'd realised just what a viper's
nest they were flying into.

The way he saw it, the first priority was to get safely landed and then get the fuck out of Dodge as quickly as possible. He had only been dimly aware of a suicide bombing at Karachi airport back in the summer. Why would it have registered more than a tremor on his emotional seismograph back then? Now that his darling wife's family bombing business had folded, he had completely lost interest in such matters. But over in that part of the world, bomb disasters were a regular event after all, like floods and train crashes. And now, squirming in this cramped aircraft, speeding through the darkness ever closer to another Pakistani airport, they had become acutely relevant.

He had already acknowledged to himself that the Karachi airport disaster had unnerved him considerably over the last few hours mainly because there was precious little he himself could do. He'd tried to console himself with the fact that it had all been several months ago until Zakia dropkicked the breaking news that around sixty people had been wiped out in a Lahore suicide attack just at the very moment their plane had taken off from Heathrow. He had never been a very relaxed passenger, even in a car. Now he felt utterly helpless.

It's too late to start being scared now, he told himself as he called up the venerable BBC news app on his phone and determined to squeeze every bit of information he could out of Zakia and any other source he could find online before the plane hit the tarmac, hopefully wheels first.

The footage was grim, particularly on some of the international stations. They both watched in stunned silence as a ghastly parade of badly wounded were stretchered past the melee of onlookers, many bathed in the crimson blood of others, their cell phone video pictures shaking in an all too vivid reality horror show. The bomber had struck a popular tourist ceremony at a border crossing with India where both sides performed a carefully orchestrated ceremony, a rich feast of colour and culture repeated at the exact same time each day for the eager consumption of thousands of local and international visitors.

Now hundreds of injured were strewn across a once immaculate parade ground as gaudy ceremonial ribbons and banners fought and lost the battle for grabbing the attention of horrified eyes. It had only taken a second to transform the once perfect landscape of clockwork precision into a chaos which no amount of rehearsal could have ever have anticipated. Against this vision of hell so quickly conjured up, the army and medical corps were striving to restore the time worn appearance of order while heartless cameras continued to zoom into the anguished and bloodied faces of the wounded until Zakia snatched the phone from his lap and switched it off.

'What are you doing?' Ridge exclaimed. 'I was wanting to see who the fuck they thought had done it!'

'As if!
They will only tell us what they want us to hear, Ridge Walker!
It will be blamed on whoever are the latest fashionable 'freaks of the week' for Westminster and Washington to use as scapegoats for what's really going on.
The BBC will not know who was responsible!
You must know by now after our referendum that the BBC cannot be trusted to give unbiased coverage of anything that affects the national interest, foreign affairs or more precisely the safety and security of the United States.'

Ridge was bewildered by the way Zakia spat out her last statement.

'But, you cannae be serious?
You're the *police* for God's sake!
You ARE the state!'

'Yes! I am!
But I'm also a human being with a brain in my head!
Of course I will always do my duty and uphold the law and all of that, but as I'm a policewoman and also a Muslim

126

woman, I'm probably one of the few people who can see through the smokescreen of the state machine and understand what the real agenda is!'

Ridge laughed and gave the astonished girl a quick hug.

'Thank fuck for that!
You're a proper rebel, girl! Welcome to the club!
Now can I have my phone back 'cos I want to see what they're saying even if it might be a load of old bollocks, it's all we have to go on for now, alright?'

Chapter 18

He'd miraculously drifted off to sleep at some point, his mind polluted with spectres from his past with the additional bonus of some new gatecrashers to the party. The Beeb had blamed the Lahore bombing on a splinter group of the Pakistani Taliban and Ridge had to grudgingly admit that the whole script did sound uncannily like the sort of thing Zakia had described earlier.

This group called themselves Jamaat-al-Jasari and they seemed to be an up and coming media savvy extremist group who had cloven away from the traditional Afghanistan Taliban. Allegedly the news media had been emailed by this group who had claimed responsibility for the atrocity in retaliation for some recent heavy handed raids on prominent Mosques which had been suspected of stashing weaponry and ammunition.

More chillingly, and also true to the script, they had claimed the position of 'most wanted local nutter group' by declaring their unwavering support for the Islamic State fighters in Iraq and Syria and pledging their allegiance to it's leader, their new Caliph. They had vowed that they would follow his command to the fullest extent in operations both in Pakistan and further afield. Each time a Western hostage had been beheaded they had posted their online support and promised complementary actions of their own although this had not yet materialised.

Ridge awoke suddenly to a poke in the ribs from Zakia and almost immediately the plane dropped into an alarmingly steep dive. Seeing his anxiety, she laughed and he caught that mischievous and thoroughly captivating twinkle in her dark eyes.

> 'Its okay, Ridge! We're just going through some turbulence but they said just to keep our seat belts on anyway as we'll be coming in to land very soon.'

He nodded with a sleepy grumpiness as the air pressure dropped and the foul stench from the toilets wafted down the centre aisle. There was no going back now. For better or worse, in a matter of minutes he would be in Pakistan.

The airport loomed out of the early morning darkness and they landed with the minimum fuss. *The calm before the storm*, Ridge wondered as he shuffled towards the rear door of the plane. Then it hit him and he almost choked. The rush of heat enveloped them like an invisible fog and his shirt stuck instantly to his skin. He found himself breathing more quickly, taking shallow half breaths as if he'd been punched in the solar plexus. The transit bus reminded Ridge of the packed old wrecks he'd endured for days on end in Guatemala and even though these were far more modern they were possibly even more heavily over-populated.

He'd been surprised and if he was honest, slightly pleased, to see that his little companion was also feeling the effects of their new strange habitat.

> 'Oh it's *so hot*, isn't it? I can hardly breathe in here!'

Zakia's face had lost its normal healthy golden colour and had now gone several shades of greenish white over the last few minutes to finally settle with a waxy sheen of gray. He realised he still knew next to nothing about the girl and he tried to think back to any conversations in which she had opened up to him about her personal life back in Glasgow.

He also tried and failed to remember her ever talking about her second cousin Nasreen, the main reason they were in this hellish airport bus. Perhaps she was even more nervous about all of this than him.

Then it struck him that she had probably less experience of living in hot and humid conditions than he had. So would it be he who carried her through this adventure? He wasn't sure if he could afford the luxury of a passenger this time, no matter how good that flashing grin could make him feel.

The airport itself offered no respite and Ridge had never seen so many people crammed into a single place. He recognised the architecture as being that particular style of brutally ugly concrete that had been so popular in the sixties all over the world and the intervening years had not been too kind to the place. The noise was deafening and there were seemed to be people standing on walls, climbing columns and even hanging from the light fittings. He could swear the actual walls of the main concourse were pulsing along with the laboured breathing of the accumulated mass of compressed humanity.

It was almost impossible to move until Zakia grabbed his hand firmly and pulled him seemingly in the direction of the baggage areas although Ridge was unaware of any signage relating to this at all. He felt extremely exposed as body after body rubbed up against him and he thanked his lucky stars he'd had the good sense to use a body wallet under his shirt. He thought back to poor Bert and how ridiculously easy it had been for the two Mexicans to rob them blind. He clenched his teeth and glared at anyone who caught his eye. He was a different man from that time. Older and meaner for sure, but any wiser?

The throng had thinned out as they approached the baggage reclaim hall and Ridge could see that Zakia hadn't been enjoying the experience either.

> 'Another year and we'd be in a brand new air conditioned palace of an airport! I can't believe I'd been so looking forward to coming to this place seeing as

it was named after one of my girlhood role models, Benazir Bhutto!'

The two of them were out of breath but Ridge could see that Zakia starting to wheeze a little harder than looked comfortable. 'You okay there?' She nodded and glowered at him before waving her hand dismissively, as if to try and make little of it.

'Yes... a wee bit... I just need my inhaler... that's all...should've had it on the plane...stupid really...be okay when we get the bags!'

The bags did miraculously arrive far faster than Ridge would have bet on and soon they were battling the crowds again although this time they each had the helpful road presence of a sturdy steel trolley armed with a large suitcase to barge through the turbulent crowds. Ridge knew they weren't actually in Islamabad itself but the adjoining sister city of Rawalpindi. In fact he'd thought that Rawalpindi had been the name of the airport but what did he know? He *did* know that this place was considered the poor relation out of the two and he looked forward to grabbing a taxi and heading to Islamabad for the safety and hopefully the air conditioned sanctuary of a western style hotel.

When he remarked as much he was met with an angry response from the now recovered girl although it hadn't done anything for her demeanour.

'A taxi!
Are you out of your tiny mind?
Didn't you learn anything from the information I gave you?
A taxi? If you just jumped into any old taxi from here Ridge Walker, you'd never be seen again! Do you understand?'

'But surely a taxi-'

'Did you leave your brain on the plane?
You cannot take a taxi or a bus over here!
Maybe a chartered taxi but even then you are still at a massive risk from being kidnapped!
Do you think the British will rescue you? Then who?
Look what has happened with Nasreen and then tell me what your hopes of being rescued would be.'

Ridge knew exactly who would rescue him if it ever came to it. How he would contact 'The Diamond Dogs' would be another matter and not for the first time over the last twenty four hours he wished he'd tried to get in touch with his old pal Thaddeus before he'd left the UK. It had been a while since they'd had any contact and he missed the reassuring presence of the big poofter. He toyed with the idea of telling

Zakia all about the crazy gang who had put their adrenaline charged lives on the line to save his skin. As he looked down at her, that sharply defined little jaw set hard, he thought better of it. A trolley swerved violently into them and for a brief moment they were flung together as mutual panic flashed between their eyes. He subconsciously put a protective arm around her only to have Zakia elbow him viciously in a soft area around his ribs.

'Just look out there, will you!
Do you have wealthy parents? No? Well they don't know that!
Here you are seen as valuable cargo just asking to be plundered.'

Ridge nodded glumly but couldn't help thinking that if he'd worried about, or even had been vaguely cognisant of, half of the perceived dangers when he'd parachuted into a Central American war-zone he might not have actually gone there and successfully completed his 'mission.' Sometimes you can just know too much right?

'Ignorance is bliss?' he offered.

'No, Ridge! Ignorance is certain death over here and the sooner you realise that the better. You were perhaps lucky over in Mexico or wherever you were but here we'll need all that luck of yours and a

134

great deal of planning, caution and patience if we are to find Nasreen and get her home safely!

Now look out for a man with a piece of card with your name on it. He's a registered driver with the British High Commission in Islamabad and he has instructions to take us to our hotel for tonight and to collect us again tomorrow for our appointment.'

It was only moments later that Ridge grinned as he noticed a disinterested looking man holding up a sheet of card with the legend 'Jonny Walker' emblazoned across it in thick red pen.

Chapter 19

It being a Saturday morning in Pakistan, he'd half expected the chaos of the airport to have continued throughout the city and so it came as a pleasant surprise to be met by wide roads and a general impression of modernity and calm about the place. Ridge had already been told that Islamabad was a new town although on a far greater scale than the grotesque examples back home. He'd often crashed at the family home of a college pal from Cumbernauld and when viewed through the eyes of an idealistic young island boy, the vomit of concrete that assaulted his senses had seemed a crime against humanity. Islamabad was an altogether different beast and far better for it.

He'd read that it had been built on a strict four kilometre square grid system and that each square formed part of a sector which again was rigidly designed so that each sector had an area set out for housing, business or green space.

He also knew that he would probably get to see just a small part of the city as most of it would not be deemed safe by Zakia and so he tried to absorb as much as his weary eyes would take in during the remainder of their now smooth and comfortable car journey. Zakia had fallen asleep against him within moments and he liked the feel of her warm body nuzzled into his side.

The hotel looked like a drab and dusty facsimile of an up-market hotel back home but despite this it was still a lot better than Ridge was used to and he gratefully fell through the door and onto the huge musty bed. He didn't smell too fresh himself and needed a shower badly and so summoning up his last ounce of energy he forced himself to stagger back up and see what delights the bathroom might hold.

'Wow…'

His head swam with the effort and he steadied himself against a wall. Judging by the fearful clatter, the air conditioning was already on at full blast but still the room was oppressively hot in all the far reaches and he struggled unsuccessfully to open any of the windows.

After briefly considering smashing a window with a chair, he collapsed into one and with the sun streaming onto his tired face he glared across at the cell phone lying alongside his jacket over by the bed. He still hadn't worked out what time it would be back home so he wouldn't alarm Orla when he eventually got round to calling. His plan had been to meet Zakia downstairs for food in a few hours but before he could formulate another thought, he'd fallen into a deep tortured sleep.

The clanking air-con played a discordant feedback loop to a jagged guitar riff being thrashed out by an all-woman punk band led by a scarily sexy-looking Zakia, her bare arms brandishing what appeared to his fevered brain to be a Fender guitar one minute and then a Kalashnikov the next.

He awoke to the gloom of imminent dusk and immediately knew he was in trouble. 5pm. *Shit*! He cursed himself up and down before staggering to the door, stuffing his phone in one pocket and slamming the door behind him.

Miss Zakia had gone out, he was politely informed at reception and so he had a sandwich sent to his room and went back up to wash and prepare for her wrath. Feeling a hundred times better after his shower he devoured the limp lettuce and ham offering and sublime ice-cold cola. The sky outside had become a dark orange and he stared out across the shimmering lights of the city, wondering if Nasreen was there and if she was safe. He'd spoken to Orla and everything sounded fine, the time difference less than he'd imagined it to be and she'd been relieved that he'd got there in one piece. Ridge didn't ask if she'd been watching the news, he figured that in this case ignorance really *was* bliss.

Just as he decided that the city didn't look that different to Glasgow at night, he noticed a huge swathe across the left hand side go black. Then another, and again, this time much closer to the hotel and then just as suddenly he was in darkness too. It was a power cut!

He was used to them on Sorsay, they were plagued with them every winter or whenever the weather acted up out of the ordinary. It remained a massive bone of contention the way the power companies were so willing to shut down the islands so readily, deeming the country folk less entitled somehow just because there were less of them. He'd always known he would have to invest in some considerable tech shit to be able to run his IT business from Sorsay once they moved over there. But here in a 'top class' hotel in a major city?

He waited a moment for the generator to kick in. Nothing. He stood up, peering out and watched to see if any lights were coming back on. Instead, another sector to the right also darkened. He now found it difficult to see anything useful at all and he began to edge his way slowly across the unfamiliar landscape towards the far wall, his arms outstretched in front of him. Finding the wall, he crawled fingertip by fingertip along the unfamiliar warm terrain in the rough direction of the door, cracking his shins on an unnoticed low table and knocking over a table lamp in the process. He stood cursing quietly in the gloom and then resumed his progress. The oppressive silence clawed at his neck and he gratefully clutched on to the door handle before yanking it open.

His eyes had accustomed to the darkness but out here it seemed blacker than ever. He was surprised to notice there weren't even any emergency lights on along his corridor and then that was when the first shiver of fear ran down his spine. He'd felt like this before, but not for some time. What if this wasn't an ordinary power cut? Images of the Mumbai hotel terrorist attack bounced across his cortex and he declaimed Zakia for making him watch those videos barely 24 hours previously. The whole building was heating up fast and his fresh clean shirt was already sticking to his back. It felt like the heat had begun sucking the oxygen from the building and instinct squeezed his chest tightly and he knew what he had to do. *Fuck this! I'm getting out of here!*

He inched his way along the corridor until he found the doorway to the stairs. He had no idea how many floors he would have to walk down. Five or maybe six? He couldn't work out any other way of doing it so he began the slow process of following the metal banister down the stairs while becoming more and more curious as to why he seemed to be the only person about. Did he miss that memo?

What felt like hours later he knew he'd hit the ground floor when he crashed into a store cupboard. After kicking over stacks of pails and groping several vacuum cleaners he at last found the door to the reception foyer and wrenched it open, relieved to feel the rush of fresher air on his damp clothing. He was heartened to hear the murmur of voices and then see the ghostly outline of other guests clustered around the desk, a few lonely candles affording a vague and tenebrous light.

By the time he carefully walked across the vast expanse of dark floor he could already hear the angry flow of complaints.

'What do you mean it's out of your control?'

'I am sorry sir! These power cuts do not last for long I can assure you!
Our generator is usually very reliable but today it has a fault that we are trying to rectify. Our top engineer is on his way but as you can appreciate the traffic is very slow at the moment!'

Ridge took a seat in the relative coolness near the entrance and wondered if Zakia had got back to her room. The tang of cigarette smoke drifted past and he felt his nose twitching. Right in front of him on the other side of the foyer, a cigarette machine sat redundantly with a church candle artfully placed on top. He glared at it and then made his decision. He glanced quickly around in the dim light and couldn't make out anyone remotely interested in him and so he made a dash for the street.

Chapter 20

He was out on his own! The first thing that struck Ridge, apart from the still stifling humidity was that the dark streets were almost totally devoid of traffic and this lack of machine noise helped lend the atmosphere an eerie almost brooding silence. There looked to be more people milling about the place than he'd noticed when they arrived earlier. He had been taken aback by the apparent car culture in the city which had reminded him more of the States than anywhere else. But now an entrepreneurial street vendor seemed to be doing good business selling candles from his tiny newspaper clad portable hut and Ridge queued up wondering how much a pack of cigarettes would cost.

After the claustrophobia of the long journey and then the stuffy hotel, coupled with the unmistakeable tension between himself and Zakia, the relief at just being outside and free was enough to make Ridge smile. He'd known he'd have to rein in his natural tendency to catch the eye of each passer by. He also understood the probable dangers of being out on the streets without a clue as to where he was headed but, if he was being honest, he had to admit that he liked it that way. He wanted to get a feel for this place, his way and there wasn't a damned thing anyone could do to stop him.

He spent a long time just walking, smoking and looking. His first idea had been to walk towards the west where he could see they still had power and he felt confident that as long as he kept remembering where he was on the grid system then he wouldn't get too lost.

This would have worked fine but after twenty minutes the power seemed to be restored city wide and seconds later the streets became snarled with traffic and he felt the scrutiny of lines of drivers as they sat in resigned stasis. It appeared to be quicker walking, *just like in Glasgow city centre*, he thought. The pedestrian traffic had mostly vanished and so he picked up his pace a little. *It's a Saturday night,* he kept trying to tell himself, *so where are all the people?* He had walked past a couple of reasonable looking hotels earlier on which had looked half closed but he had put that down to the power cut. But for the last thirty minutes he hadn't found a single shop, hotel or restaurant that had reopened.

Finding himself in a commercial zone he was startled to see large ultra-modern buildings bearing the familiar names of software houses and companies he had worked with or competed against when he'd been in the video gaming business. With their lower 'human resource overheads' it was an established fact that these guys, on this side of the world, were making all the play now, but even so, he was shocked to be confronted with the scale of the place. Is *this* the real revolution, he wondered and shook his head sadly and turned northwards again determined to find the real Pakistan. Where will he find Nasreen? Not in an integrated chip factory, for sure.

Inexplicably he began to lose his bearings and soon he was almost completely lost and had it not been for the hills to the north he would have lost his way altogether. He knew from experience that he could get roughly back to where he started from and so reluctantly he turned and headed directly south. He'd obviously veered off his original journey however as nothing seemed remotely familiar on the way back and he began to despair. It was hard work walking in the heat.

Large mansions loomed out over the tops of ornately shaped hedges and he hoped he might find some friendly ex-pats to cadge a lift from. Any thoughts of going knocking on doors were swiftly extinguished when he saw what looked like armed guards outside a couple of driveways and he crossed the wide avenue not enjoying the way they were continuing to follow his progress down the road.

He rationalised that the larger road must take him somewhere significant, which would make finding a safe taxi or even a hotel bar a lot more likely. He knew he could call Zakia on her mobile at any time but that was the last thing he wanted to do. The only thing he could think about now revolved around getting back to the safety of his room and ordering the longest and coldest beer in the hotel. But even more pressing was the need to do all of this before Zakia discovered his impromptu reconnaissance. That's when he saw the checkpoint up ahead, blocking the road.

He stopped without thinking why and instinctively turned around to give himself time to think whether this could be a good thing or a bad thing. But as he did so he heard that once-experienced-never-forgotten sound of a semi-automatic rifle being cocked in his direction and he knew that on this particular occasion his luck had run out.

He turned and jumped back a step. *Holy shit!* The army-style khaki Landrover must have come out of nowhere. He guessed they'd been tipped off by one of the security stiffs just a few moments ago and now he faced two angry young men in rent-a-costume military uniforms brandishing their rifles at him and gesturing him towards the vehicle.

As they roughly searched him, Ridge vehemently explained his tourist status and he continued to protest for the sixty second journey to the checkpoint where he was pushed against the flimsy wall of what seemed to be their base. To Ridge it looked no more substantial than a car park ticket kiosk back home. They told him to wait. Nervous excitement rippled through the hot night as the three armed men argued amongst each other as to what to do with him.

Eventually another vehicle pulled up and their obvious senior squeezed out in as dignified a manner as he could despite his enormous girth. As wide as he was tall and ignoring Ridge, he wedged a flat cap onto his greased head and ambled over to the group who only increased their clamouring. Despite his precarious position,

Ridge was reminded of the Sea Eagles he used to watch over as a boy on Sorsay and the way the hungry chicks would be when food hovered above the nest. He was that food now.

'Passport, visa or identification papers please!' the man barked.

'I haven't got any! You know that already, these muppets have already searched me!
I'm here on holiday for God's sake! From Scotland!'

'Then where are you staying?'

'Here!' Ridge pulled out his hotel key and cigarettes from his front pocket and waved the key fob in the man's face.

'Hello…!
It's got the hotel name on it, right there!'

The look on the guy's face was priceless and he took the key almost reverently from Ridge and turned slowly towards the others.

He roared various commands and within seconds one guy had shot off in the Landrover while another took refuge in the little booth, frantically dialling a number.

'It appears you do have a reservation, Mr Walker and I must apologise for the unprofessional manner in which my colleagues treated you this evening. However, it is my duty to inform you that it is an offence to attempt to pass a checkpoint without the appropriate documentation and unfortunately I must ask you to remain here for the time being until a Constable of the Capital Territory Police can get here to remove you into custody!'

Stunned beyond belief, he couldn't even mouth a reply before the man turned abruptly and rejoined the others. Ridge followed him with his eyes, unable to take in what had just happened. He watched the obese man release a torrent of abuse towards his unfortunate subordinates which failed to make Ridge feel any better. He'd been given a small plastic chair to sit on and he sat with his head between his knees and fumed quietly. 'One fucking day! I've been here one fucking day and I've gone and got myself arrested. What is she going to say when she finds out?'

But then he sat up and looked around. *If she finds out.* He had an idea. They were not even looking at him, the cause of their predicament. He could easily leg it over into those bushes and they couldn't all abandon their posts could they? And the wee chubby would

147

never catch him anyways! But they had his phone.

> 'Excuse me!
> Can I have my hotel key, cigarettes and phone back now please?'

> 'Yes of course! There will be someone here shortly but you may take your possessions with you by all means. Please sign here.'

Ridge had only just scrawled across the grubby clipboard, *why do they always have a clipboard*, when the guard snatched it back as a menacing looking black military truck screeched up in a cloud of dust. Ridge swallowed. *These guys looked a wee bit more serious. How the hell was he going to talk his way out of this?*

Two dark uniformed policemen jumped out the front and all the security guards stood to attention and saluted. Ridge stood up, aware that his legs were shaking and stepped cautiously forward. A brief one-sided conversation took place that he couldn't hear and then the atmosphere changed instantly. All eyes turned towards Ridge and within seconds all the men had the working ends of their rifles aimed directly at his head.

They screamed at him to turn and kneel and he meekly complied, thinking the unthinkable. After everything that he'd been through, could he be about to be shot just for taking a walk on a Saturday night? A walk on the wild side! He thought of Orla and the child he'd never know and how eventually for everyone, this was how it must be, when your luck finally runs out. He felt strong hands grab him and force his arms behind him and simultaneously his wrists were painfully cuffed as he was hauled to his feet.

Then he thought he'd imagined the word *'arsehole'* being whispered in his ear and before he had the chance to assimilate that familiar tone and body scent he was punched hard in the ribs and he fell forwards. Two pairs of arms then brought him back to his feet and there facing him, stood Zakia in a full on sexy-as-fuck black paramilitary uniform. Despite his predicament a huge smile broke across his face until she reached up and slapped him so hard he fell over.

'Throw him in the back seat with me!'

The two policemen dragged the bewildered Ridge over and into the vehicle and within seconds they were careering down the road at top speed. His aching head bumping off the bodywork, Ridge struggled to right himself and then he felt Zakia pulling at his wrists again.

'Ouch! What the fuck are you doing now? Jesus! What's going on?'

'I'm trying to take your handcuffs off you idiot! If you'll just sit still for a second!'

'So what was all that about back there? Did you have to be so fucking convincing?'

Zakia freed his hands and laughed.

'I *had* to be convincing, Ridge Walker. Your life depended on it!
But that was nothing to what I am capable of!
Remember this day. I don't want you to make a mistake like that again!'

She turned those piercing black eyes directly at his.

'You need to be utterly convinced that I *would* kill you.
If that was what it took to find Nasreen!'

Zakia then took his aching face in both her little hands and kissed him hard, her hot tongue probing deep into his mouth for a long time.

Chapter 21

He untangled himself carefully and slid out of the crumpled bed before padding over to the window. His hands were shaking as he lit a cigarette and stared out over the city, the early morning heat haze already shimmering as it had done the day before and would also do tomorrow. Some things never change. He slowly examined the cuts and bruises on his stubbled face and his fingers were redolent of her musk. He glanced back towards the wrecked bed and despite his anguished state he couldn't help but be in awe of that perfect brown back, every muscle defined but completely feminine, sensual like a panther.

He didn't know how they ended up in bed. There had been no 'get out of jail free' cards like drugs or alcohol involved but he'd allowed himself to be taken and for those few hot and sweaty hours he'd wanted to please her, to atone for his stupidity and to show her that he too had a physical capability although not perhaps in the same stratosphere as Zakia.

He felt so guilty now and he couldn't bring himself to call Orla at this, their mutually arranged time. He loved Orla with all his being and he would never have considered himself the unfaithful type. Having lost her once he did not want to ever make that mistake again.

But now look.

Her physical resemblance to Juanita was not lost on him either at this point. Small, wiry and brown-skinned. If he were a proper criminal then they would call that his MO. He *had* thought he'd loved that girl however and at that point he had been officially single too. He wasn't even sure he *liked* this girl and he was positive she had no longer term interest in him beyond the next hour or two. It had been a powerful release of the like he hadn't felt in an age and he acknowledged that it had been a long while since he and Orla had made love as passionately animalistic as he had just experienced, not that that constituted an excuse any more than having drunk too much beer.

He sat smoking and brooding about what would happen next, about the mission. *Mission! Ha! Emission might be a more prosaic way of describing their situation.* He seriously doubted whether they would achieve anything here at all now. He tried to push away all carnal images of Zakia and to conjure up instead the photographs he had of poor Nasreen potentially kidnapped and afraid in an alien land. The devil on his shoulder couldn't resist the opportunity to stick a knife in. Nasreen was also small and dark skinned. *Are you going to have to shag her too?*

He dialled. No answer! He walked carefully over to the bathroom and left a brief message saying everything was just fine apart from feeling the effects of the jet-lag and a touch of the 'trots' so not to worry if he didn't call back for a while. Too late he knew he'd made a

mistake in putting the light on and on his way
back to the window he saw the noise of the fan
had awoken Zakia.

'You up? Come on back here will you?
And pull that curtain across!'

'Naw Jake!
I can't, honestly. I'm done in!'

'I am not meaning that!' She laughed
from under the covers. 'I know you think
I'm some kind of machine but even they
can have parts that get worn out you
know! No, I want to speak with you
before we go anywhere out of this room.
We have a lot to talk about.'

Chapter 22

'You do realise what a foolish thing you did last night, don't you?'

'You mean before or after I got back to the room?'

'You know what I'm talking about! These civilian security guards cannot be trusted! If that fat superintendent hadn't come onto the scene you could so easily have been disappeared and then I would have been searching for two people instead of one.'

'What do you mean?'

'They get a pittance for those jobs and the kidnappers would pay far more than a year's wages for a British tourist like you. And of course nobody believes you are a *tourist* anyway. Like 99% of the American *businessmen* in Islamabad who are actually undercover CIA. So you must always remember you are a legitimate target for extremists and kidnappers and believe me when I tell you, Ridge, there are people vanishing from around here all the time, not just the high profile cases you read about in the British papers.'

'I'm sorry. It won't happen again, I promise.
What were you doing last night anyway? Cutting about with those army boys?'

'Not army, Ridge.
Actors!
Lucky for you I just happened to be doing some poking around myself and I'd hired these guys as protection and to give me a little authority in my investigations. I know the power of a good uniform after all! And sadly I also know how little authority a woman has over here and so it was a natural move really. Two of the 'soldiers' are in fact real policemen and I had already told them what I did for a living and so when the call came through about you they told me immediately.'

'But how would they…'

'Because!
Because I had already told them about you! *And* that you had gone AWOL and that I was worried about you!
Yes!
We were out looking for you, okay! Just don't get too many grand delusions! I was concerned and I'm glad you're safe and that's it. Don't expect any further welcome home parties next time.'

155

Zakia jumped up in the bed, letting the sheets fall unashamedly from her firm body, her dark nipples standing proud of her small perfectly formed breasts.

'Now let's get something to eat, I am one ravenous girl!'

'Ravishing!'

'That's enough of that! We have a lot to do today. We have to leave this place quickly as it's probably not safe any more and I've organised us an apartment for rent for the next two weeks but we need to make a few changes first.
So! Food first!
Then apartment, then some innocent tourist sightseeing before we get settled in and then tomorrow you have your big interview!'

They ate breakfast in the hotel for speed and took a chartered taxi over to the East of the city. He swore some of the streets looked familiar but he thought it better not to remind Zakia about any of that. It turned out that he had in fact been correct.

'This is the sector they call the Diplomatic Enclave and it's the most heavily guarded area apart from maybe E

156

sector where people like us would
normally stay but I just couldn't swing
that I'm afraid.
Even here a brown face like mine
wouldn't get through the checkpoints
without a visa whether I had a passport or
not!
We're going to stay in an ex United
Nations flat, once I've checked it out that
is! Come on! We're here!'

Ridge was pleasantly surprised to sail
through the checkpoint without having to get out
the air-conditioned cool of the taxi as Zakia
displayed her papers and a moment or two later
they arrived at a collection of immaculate white
modern apartments of the kind you'd get in
holiday complexes the world over.

Two young soldiers were waiting, both
looked British and they actually saluted him as
they approached. Zakia quickly asserted herself
however and very soon Ridge was an irrelevance
at best.

'The apartment will be fine ma'am.
But as you had thought, it will need to
have some security modifications made
and we can have the work completed by
1600 hours.
You will need the following, ma'am.
Shatterproof film over the windows,
standard operating procedure, I'm afraid.

Two extra dead-bolts on the door and a complete new steel door in the bathroom and a steel swing shutter for the window so as to afford you the comfort of a 'safe-room' should you need it.'

'Very good. And the guards?'

'Yes ma'am! I am pleased to say that I've sourced you a reliable pair of guards, two brothers in fact. They do work with us all the time and you'll have no trouble with them, I can vouch for that. They will be in place for 1600 hours also.'

'Blimey!' Ridge remarked to Zakia as they walked back to the waiting car. 'That's a bit over the top isn't it?'

Zakia glared at him. 'Do you even know what day it is today?'

Chapter 23

The midday sun was unrelenting and the man could see darker scabs of dried blood appearing like weals across their thin backs. He knew he was asking a lot from them in this modern age with all its easy ways and corrupting influences but it was for their own good, he understood that, and they would thank him in later years, just as he'd thanked his elders.

The smell of blood was everywhere around them now and as they grew closer to the main procession at the centre, the swelling crowds made progress slower and he was having difficulty keeping the spectators out of the way of his young charges. He didn't mind at all the closeness and mingling of the crowds in these too narrow streets as he disliked the idea that this was a show in any sense of the word. It should not be a joyful event or anything like a festival. There were already far too many of these licentious abominations in the Western world. As if to emphasise his feelings he flexed his right shoulder and the sunlight flashed off the blades as he felt his flesh rent open once again.

'Uncle, can we rest soon?'

'Rest?
Did the young Husayn rest when he was forced to fight to save his family?

Remember, *a single tear shed for Husayn washes away a hundred sins*.
You want to have this instead?'

He waved his *zanjeer* menacingly in front of the skeletally thin teenager and the boy quickly stepped back into formation and began to flagellate himself with the small chain. The man observed his tiny frame wince with pain and he felt great satisfaction in his certain thought that the boy would remember this day for a long time to come.

'So! What's all the fuss about today then?'

Ridge had jumped into the car feeling vaguely like an impostor after having been saluted by the new security guard in his white painted kiosk. He'd nodded back in a poor copy of the way he'd seen members of the Royal Family do a thousand times on television, hoping he'd not offended the guy in any way.

'It's the day of Ashura today!
Remember on the plane I was telling you about the month of Muharram where they have lots of different religious anniversaries and processions all over the place? And there have been some nasty incidents of violence and bombings in the

160

past? Well, today is the biggest one for the Shi'a community, who are only a small minority and so later on we're going to have a look seeing as we're here. It's always been a contentious issue, you know, a wee bit like the Orange Walk back in Glasgow? If we stick to the main procession where there's bound to be other Westerners everything will be fine, but stay close to me and don't look at anyone the wrong way whatever you do!'

Ridge had nodded without much enthusiasm, remembering how terrified he'd been once as a lad when he and his Dad had got caught up in a Loyalist March over in the Gallowgate. As he stared out at the sweltering sunshine, he realised just how thirsty he felt and he couldn't shake the image of a cold can of Irn Bru from his mind.

But they had spent an enjoyable couple of hours doing the tourist thing and having fun just like any other young couple on holiday might do. Ridge saw Zakia really open up and underneath that policewoman's harsh facade he could begin to see glimpses of a confident young girl revelling in new experiences and happy to have broken free of the shackles not only of her profession and gender but also the heavier expectations of her community, even if only for a brief while.

161

They toured the various sectors, each one very like the other apart from the ones where the overseas residents had had an influence. They visited a very well laid out but less than exciting market which had been smaller than ones back home and Ridge was generally unimpressed with the city as a cultural experience. He related tales of his experiences in Chinatown, San Francisco and the chaotic markets he'd been to in Mexico and Guatemala. They had both noticed that most people travelled by car and it reminded Ridge of Smalltown USA more than what he had imagined Pakistan to be like. He'd expected poverty and beggars on every street corner and not car dealerships and car parks the size of Hampden Stadium.

The Faisal Mosque was the only time they had to walk more than a hundred feet from their car and Ridge had at last thought he'd found the pandemonium he had been looking for. Beautiful and ornate with tall jagged white towers pointing skywards from each corner, the stunning architecture had been intended to make the mosque look like a desert Bedouin tent but to Ridge it looked more like a 1980's Star Wars Starfighter. It had become stifling hot by that time and he found it harder to get his breath. The crowds were immense and sombre but thankfully there wasn't the crushing pressure that he feared. Small children were passing around sticky sweets and the only sounds were the shrill peals from kids with plastic whistles and the low wailing calls from the mosque itself which they couldn't get anywhere near.

He had told Zakia about the Software Technology Park he stumbled upon and he asked if she knew what had caused the power outage the night before as he could imagine that would be a major headache for computer companies. She didn't know any more than he did but told him not to judge Pakistan by Islamabad standards. He found out that she'd been born in Glasgow but her parents had come from Quetta close to the Afghan border and in a region considered a no-go for Westerners nowadays.

> 'But no.
> I have no family there, the last of my grandparents died when I was eleven and that's the only time I've ever been over until now. I remember it being very different to this.'

Ridge saw a cloud of sadness cross her face for a moment and he squeezed her knee gently. 'Any chance this driver can take us somewhere cool for lunch?'

An agreeable hour later, lunch had impressed Ridge and he could see Zakia had begun to enjoy herself too although she was loath to admit she liked the colonial splendour of what she mockingly called 'Little Beverly Hills.'

163

They'd crossed over the massive Margalla Road which seemed to split the city in half and driven up into the Margalla Hills through barbed wire watch towers and a series of checkpoints to a beautiful hotel overlooking the city. Behind them in the distance, purple as heather in the misty sunlight, Ridge could see what he subsequently found out was the foothills of the Himalayas. He thought of his brother Gavin as he always did at times like that and his heart squeezed hard as he remembered the many happy hours they'd spent tramping the hills together until that fateful last day.

Zakia had allowed him a quick visit to the bar and he gladly took the opportunity to drain a cold beer in the time it took the barman to put together a gin and tonic and a long glass of natural lemonade. On his way back to the outdoor tables he was barged into by a dishevelled and overweight giant of a man with flaming red hair and a complexion to match.

'Steady pal!' Ridge exclaimed good naturedly and the man lifted his huge head to mutter an almost inaudible reply before stopping for a second. Ridge clearly saw him doing a momentary double-take before the head lowered and he crashed on through the bar.

'Just met one of the genuine old Empire chaps I think!' Ridge laughed as he set the drinks down and licked the spilled drink off his bare arm. 'It was weird though. Almost like he'd

164

recognised me or something! Didn't catch his
accent or anything.'

Zakia stared at him for a moment,
unsmiling. She glanced at her watch and stood
up abruptly causing Ridge to jump.

'Look at the time! Come on! We'll never
see the rest of the procession from here!'

He grabbed a half glassful of gin and
chased after her.

Chapter 24

The first thing Ridge noticed before they even got close to the main procession was a row of tiny ambulances and a huge white marquee with a red cross crudely stencilled on the side. 'Oh shit.' His heart sank.

'No Ridge, it's not what you're thinking. Let me show you something. Come on!'

Zakia grabbed his hand and he let her pull him deeper into the throng of people, their driver electing to stay in the cool of the car.

'Look!' She pointed towards the centre of a long and slow moving procession of men and women, all dressed in beautiful but dark coloured traditional clothing. They were silent and strangely pre-occupied looking. Then he thought he saw what Zakia had been meaning. Ridge squinted against the sunlight, disbelieving at first, but he could see what looked like a whole section of bare-chested men and boys who seemed to be covered in blood.

They pushed a little closer and the true nature of the horror became apparent. Some of the men had blood all over their heads and as they walked, they would intermittently cut their scalps with a small sharp looking curved dagger of the kind Ridge had only ever seen in old Sinbad films. Others were whipping their own backs and shoulders with what looked like black

166

feathers on the end of a rope but, as he saw more clearly, he realised that what he'd thought were little feathers were actually tiny curved blades and the black colour was actually layer upon layer of congealed blood. He saw young boys barely into their teens, each with something like a bicycle chain which he would swing up and behind his head to lacerate his back and shoulders. And all of this was happening in complete silence.

'What are they doing? And why?' Ridge asked, to nobody in particular, unable to mask his shock at the hellish vision.

> 'It's not as bad as it looks, Ridge.
> I've heard about this and some of that red stuff is dye for effect but they do it for the remembrance of the death of the alleged grandson of The Muhammad who the Shi'a believe died in a battle between good and evil. For these men it is a time for sorrow and respect and for self-reflection.
> That is why there is no music or brightly coloured clothing.
> They are trying to show the rest of the world that there is still a place for religious justice or piety as a counterbalance to the terrible injustice and corruption in the world at large.'

'Wow! Pretty far out way of expressing yourself.' Ridge exclaimed as he snapped a few photos of the surreal parade. Just then he saw a member of the procession lift up an iPad and capture his own photo memory and Ridge chuckled as he quickly caught this incongruous moment for posterity himself.

'So what are the ambulances for?
In case they take the self-abuse a wee bit far?'

Zakia gave him one of her most scornful looks.

'No stupid! If you look a little more carefully you'll see that long queue of people there.
See? They are all giving blood.
Just like we do at home but in this case this is just their way of showing respect to Imam Husayn by shedding a little blood but without all that that pain and drama and also to do some good in the world too.
And there will always be a need for blood in this country!'

Further behind he could see a bear of a man carrying what looked like a twenty foot plank of wood across his shoulders. Spread across this beam at intervals of a foot or so were burning fires like more dramatic versions of the

small ornately made silver fire buckets he'd
noticed on the hookah pipes back in Glasgow.
This time each of them had been welded onto the
end of a metal spike with the height of each
spike rising along towards the middle of the
beam and then falling to the other end so as to
give the appearance of a huge flaming triangle.

'Woah! Look at that Jake! Can you see it
from down there?'

'Shut up!
No, I can't, there's just too many tall
people in my way.'

Here then! Climb onto my shoulders,
just for a wee minute!'

'Okay! But quick then!'

He bent down and to the amusement of
the people closest to them he helped Zakia to
climb onto his shoulders, her diminutive size
allowing her this temporary impropriety.

'Wow! You're right. That is amazing!'

Thinking of another possible highlight
moment, he pulled out his iPhone again and tried
to pass it up to her. 'Take a wee video will you?'

'No chance. Let me down will you?'

'Aye in a minute.' Ridge zoomed in across the heads of the crowd. He panned carefully along the procession and satisfied that he'd got enough of the spectacular scene he began to pull back over to the right where he saw a man pointing directly at him. He slid his thumb and index finger to open the zoom to maximum and found the man again.

There seemed to be another smaller guy with him, looking down at a tiny slip of paper and then up and over towards him again. They both looked agitated compared to the other people around them and the little guy started jabbering and pushing at the other man who pointed directly at Ridge and then began to push his way through the crowd straight towards them.

For a surreal second or two, Ridge watched all of this as if in a dream. Everything seemed to slow down and go blurry as if none of what he could see really mattered at all. He shivered the length of his body as a faint but familiar sound of bagpipes filtered though his consciousness like a siren call from the past. The sound of adrenaline.

He ducked down, sending Zakia flying onto the unfortunate men standing in front of them. 'Hey careful,' she yelled before regaining her cool and somehow managing to land cat-like on her feet. 'What's the deal?'

'Quick Jake! Move! *Now*!'

He grabbed her arm and yanked her hard in behind him as he shoulder charged into the nearest surprised spectator who fell backwards cursing him in Urdu. Most people moved adeptly out of his path and catching the seriousness of his voice Zakia quickly sped up and they made good progress towards the edge of the crowd. Ridge scanned behind him but saw no sign of the men and he looked ahead to see how far they were from the car. No sign of that either.

'What's going on Ridge?'

'There are two men after us! I picked them up with the zoom and when they saw me they made a definite beeline for us, no doubt whatsoever!'

'What did they look like? Have you got them on camera?'

Ridge looked at the petite woman beside him in a mixture of admiration and confusion. He shouldn't have been surprised by how quickly and coolly she'd appraised the situation but still he thought it a little odd. But now wasn't the time to start weighing up her behavioural idiosyncrasies and so he pulled her in behind a police Landrover and peered cautiously over the high front end. He couldn't see them but he started to panic as to what the hell they looked like anyway. In a sea of brown faces he couldn't even be sure they *were* even Pakistani.

171

He hunkered down again and fished in his pocket for his phone.

> 'Aye! I should have them but maybe only for a second!
> At least we seem to have lost them for the-'

The day turned into sullen night like the flick of a switch. It only dimmed for maybe a second at most, reminding him of that eclipse back in the spring. The same unreal sensation. Orla had hated that brief moment, feeling like her entire life would now be played out in a bleak monochrome. This time Ridge thought it felt even more sinister. Pitch-black eerie silence. The world seemed to shimmy sideways before an ear-splitting tornado of dust and glass enveloped everything and Ridge and Zakia both instinctively grabbed for each other.

The Landrover lifted off the ground and thumped back down narrowly avoiding them and a huge rush of heat poured through the underside of the vehicle. Ridge had pulled Zakia in between his legs and they held their heads down and tight against each other for what seemed like forever until he felt the sharp sting of shrapnel jagging into his upper body and then the warm splatter of something wet and spongy across his arms and neck. He clung on to Zakia until he heard her screaming in his right ear although she sounded a long way off.

He opened his eyes to see her terrified face soaked in blood and mouthing a language he couldn't comprehend. He peered around them and his brain rebelled at the horror. There were torn and bloody pieces of human bodies everywhere he looked. Behind them, a whole row of little shops and offices had been devastated with their frontages ripped off completely and small fires burning along the rooftops. Then the pain kicked in! He knew the backs of his legs must have been burned for sure and his backside in particular felt worse than when he'd sat on a wood burning stove at a party on Sorsay, drunk as a skunk.

'Are you okay?' He felt himself shout the words rather than heard them but he could see her anguished face nodding in that manic rocking way, when the conscious mind has left for another place. He dreaded standing but knew from experience that it wasn't going to get any easier and he had to move quickly before his fight or flight response weakened. The thought of that half finished gin swam in front of his eyes and it might as well have been in another lifetime.

'Right then! Are you okay to move?'

Ridge gritted his teeth and slowly pulled Zakia to her feet. She seemed to have been largely protected by his body and he hoped he'd borne the worst of it. Although they'd both escaped comparatively lightly, he realised, as they surveyed the devastation around them. The little fleet of mini van ambulances were now being pressed into a far more serious role than anticipated and Ridge could see the shock on the faces of the poor Red Cross workers as they tried to console those among the wounded that they could do anything for.

They had only taken a few steps when Zakia bent over and was violently sick all over her own feet. He held her hair off her face as she retched and retched whilst gently steering her away from the severed head of a young man, the eyes still open and staring up at him in astonishment. For a horrible moment he thought it was one of the men who'd been coming for them and it was at that point he first worked out that they'd probably just survived a suicide bombing. Could all of this carnage have been on account of them?

It was unthinkable. He guessed his hearing was beginning to recover as he began to be aware of the now constant screaming of the wounded and the background wail of the hopelessly underprepared ambulances.

There was no point in trying to be inconspicuous. They were hurting and soaked in blood, just like every other wretched soul who'd been watching the procession just a few short minutes ago. Ridge clenched his jaw tighter still and hobbled onwards away from the devastation as the pain became more persistent.

His most immediate problem seemed to be the backs of his legs which were tightening up for some reason forcing him to walk in a half stooping position which meant he couldn't properly see where he was going.

'Any sign of that fucking driver anywhere?'

'Let's stop for a minute and I'll try to call him' she shouted back. He stood crouched and watched helplessly as Zakia tried to operate her cell phone but her hands were shaking so much she wasn't getting anywhere. Then she looked up at him in bewilderment and he realised what else was wrong.

'There's no reception, Ridge! The network is down.'

She burst into tears and he held her as best he could before she pulled away from him, suddenly standing straight and setting that beautiful little mouth into its trademark hard line. 'But it can't be far from here!'

True enough, they rounded the next corner to see the car and driver where they'd left him. He ran over and helped Ridge over and into the back seat.

'Thank God!' I was only going to wait another minute!

I did not want to leave the car as it would surely have been commandeered for the wounded. I will take you to the Shifa, it will be much more satisfactory than the general hospital.

We will need to make a call once we find reception again. I would imagine the local mast must have been close to the blast area.'

Ridge passed in and out of consciousness over the remaining twenty minutes and he barely remembered being stretchered into the hospital. But a couple of hours later and heavily medicated, he was able to shuffle back out of the beautifully equipped international hospital and into a carefully cushioned taxi back to their apartment. And this time Ridge felt that he'd earned his salute as Zakia helped him walk through the entrance.

Chapter 25

Zakia understood that to say they had been incredibly lucky would be the understatement of the year. She had returned almost completely unscathed barring a few scratches and bruises. Ridge had bruised his 'dignity' somewhat and the tightening in the legs had been down to a couple of massive blisters each over a foot long which had been quickly dealt with at the hospital but were proving excruciatingly painful.

He'd been told to watch they didn't become infected and to drink plenty of clean water. He'd burned his arse as well as his legs which meant sitting was awkward and so they'd managed to borrow a tall 'poser table' from the hotel bar and since there was apparently lots of water in beer, Zakia had sanctioned a crate of lager to be transported up as well, 'for the pain.'

She knew she probably owed her life to her crazy friend. As they watched the aftermath of the attack on prime time television she felt a strengthened bond that only comrades in arms will ever understand and although already an accomplished and capable police officer, it still felt new and strange to her. She would never have admitted it to the man standing awkwardly in front of her, but it wasn't that unpleasant a feeling either.

He stood and drank fast but talked faster, a cigarette hanging constantly from his mouth as they worked out what to do next. They had both thought it vital that Ridge attended the High Commission the following morning as planned but to be safe he would leave a couple of hours earlier than scheduled and Zakia had suggested they changed drivers as a further precaution.

The death toll had reached forty already but there had been so many hideously wounded by the home-made bomb that the fatalities were set to rise over the next few hours. No-one had claimed responsibility yet which was not unusual in Pakistan but they had agreed to keep the television on low just in case there were any updates.

Ridge had called Orla as soon as he got back and was relieved that she had been entirely unaware of the whole thing. He downplayed his injuries, telling her that they'd only been nearby and that it just a run-of-the-mill event in this part of the world. She'd planned to leave the island for a couple of assignments back in Glasgow but he'd persuaded her to chill with his parents for a few more days. There were so many unanswered questions at the moment and he knew from bitter experience how murderous evil could travel continents faster than juicy gossip.

Could this be connected with him being in Pakistan? Or even be a revenge attack for their previous adventures further west? *Less likely*, he thought but he didn't dissuade Orla when she said she might try and contact her brother to see if he knew anything that hadn't been reported in the media although she was sure he'd have already set off for Chile.

Ridge didn't want to alarm her any further but he'd also decided to speak with Thad if he could, perhaps with a little help from the Foreign Office guys in the morning. He needed all the help he could get right now and Thad had never let him down yet but he couldn't help laughing as he imagined what his handsome friend would have to say about his red and tender backside.

As Ridge had not quite managed to retrieve his phone from his jeans pocket by the time the bomb went off, it remained fully functioning and the pair of them had played and replayed the fourteen second video a hundred times already. The footage clearly showed the two men for the briefest of moments but Zakia had been dismissive about the likelihood of the police getting any ID from it. He graciously accepted that she held the valuable insider knowledge on such matters after she scathingly referred to all those high tech US TV shows where they seem to be able to locate anyone anywhere on the face of the earth just from a grainy photograph.

But when she had asked if they could keep it from the local plods until they could work out who they could actually trust around the place, Ridge was secretly pleased about that. He was in total agreement about the issue of whom they could rely on and he didn't want the footage getting accidentally 'lost' in a file forever.

     If he was able to get hold of Thad, the first thing he would do is to get that video to him *muy fucking pronto* and then he'd really show Jake how good their tech could be. With the military muscle and financial clout of Thad's dad plus the massive favour bank that he now had with the Yanks he felt sure that they would nail these guys from the video alone.

     They talked on for a while just for the sake of talking but once they'd got it all out of their system and the painkillers had ganged up with the alcohol, Ridge began to fade fast. Zakia helped him carefully arrange his bedding before slipping quietly away as he mumbled 'Thanks Jake…' He crashed out instantly, face-down on the bed with a thin cotton sheet draped loosely across his tender body and a creaky but powerful free-standing fan playing directly over him.

     In the next room a sober but equally tired girl could not even consider the idea of sleeping. Like Ridge, her mind had been racing with all the ramifications of the bombing.

     But she had problems of her own.

     She'd been amazed that neither Ridge nor Orla had suggested what, to her mind, had been such an obvious line of inquiry. Of course it hadn't been Ridge the man had been pointing to at all!

     It had been her.

She was the one sitting on his shoulders, higher than anyone else in the crowd. She'd been incredibly stupid, letting her guard down like that. She of all people should have known that they'd be expecting her to come to Pakistan at some point. They would have a mole at the police department for sure, and they'd have a spy at the airport too. And then Ridge's little stunt the night before would have alerted them to her presence in Islamabad even if they had slipped up on the airport side.

She should never have climbed onto his shoulders like that. She would have been far better wrapping her toned thighs a little tighter around his neck the night before and finishing him off there and then. A nice way to go. She fancied that there were a great many men who would pay her good money to die like that.

But then he had gone and saved her life.

She was under no illusions that if he hadn't pulled her in between his legs and sheltered her from the blast, her tiny frame would have been catapulted through the front windows of the shops and they would be picking off fragments of her flesh from the grimy walls for days to come.

She sighed. It would still make a lot of sense to walk through there and smother him right now. It would probably be kinder too. She could be out the back of the hotel and away. They'd not suspect her and assume she'd been kidnapped.

In a perfect world, she could have had the police post her as having died in the explosion. It seemed to have worked well for Mr and Mrs Walker, up to a point. But she knew that it could never work in her case due to a number of reasons. Firstly, the local police would never wear it because they were already all over her like a rash due to the fact of her being a woman holding the rank of detective. It was inevitable that her boss back home would have been informed by now and so she certainly faced a serious disciplinary when she returned, if she was lucky. Obviously, it didn't look good from their perspective. Why would a career path detective lie about where she was taking a holiday and then find herself caught up in a bombing incident in a terrorist hot spot on the other side of the world?

To get the Pakistani authorities to agree to such a story would only compromise her reason for being there in the first place due to their police department being as leak free as a colander. And for the same reason, to fake her death would only work if they people she wanted to deceive actually bought the story which she sincerely doubted and so it would all be pointless

And on top of all that; despite their precautions, she was experienced enough to know that the British authorities would have a damn good idea who 'Andrew Walker' really was and what he'd been up to his neck in before. So basically she was fucked.

Or was she?

As the dark night slowly transformed into day, so her prospects began to brighten and her mood lifted. She'd no doubt that her original cover was blown and so her position was now weaker than she'd anticipated it to be at this stage. She'd lost the element of surprise. And that was going to make her job harder. No, it only meant that it would be harder for her to stay alive. There might well be more people trying to kill her but she knew she was far better than they could ever comprehend so perhaps the odds were only even now. The job remained the same. She might even have edged an unexpected advantage, despite everything that had happened today, as she decided she had found a better ally in Ridge Walker than she could have hoped for. His luck was the kind that didn't wash off.

All she had to do was fulfil her mission and get back home as quickly as possible. No-one need ever know what had really been going on and so if she just continued with the original plan she'd return with Ridge and be hailed as a heroine.

A heroine who'd obviously fucked up a little but there was no way the police could sack her for it and perhaps they'd take her a little more seriously after that and give her a job with the big boys. And then just think what she could do! Her eyes gleamed in the early dawn light as she pulled open the bed sheets for a quick nap.

Chapter 26

'Jesus wept!'

The pain had not abated for long during the night with Ridge spending most of the long hours alternating between freezing to death and being boiled alive depending on whether he had the fan on or off. Every time he would begin to get half-way comfortable then his bladder would start complaining. He swore off alcohol for the millionth time in his life and decided that once they got back home to safety, he would commission a study to further understand how you can drink six cans of beer but then pee out twelve cans worth later.

The bruising had taken effect now and he stood admiring the kaleidoscope of colours all the way up his back when Zakia walked in.

'Look at you, Rainbow Man!' she laughed and then slipped him the gentlest of kisses on the side of his cheek, before he had time to react. He blushed and hoped she wouldn't notice.

'I'm pretty sore too but the bruises don't seem so bad on my skin. I'm a rainbow girl all over anyway! As you well know!' she winked at him. 'Are you ready for your early detour? I thought we could try and get breakfast up on the terrace over in 'E for Elite' sector?'

Three hours later Ridge was gratefully leaning against the public counter at the British High Commission in Ramna 5, not much more than a mile from their apartment. Zakia had found him a walking stick and although he'd initially liked the idea of it he felt too much like some comic Chaplin figure and he knew he didn't look quite right.

They had arrived in plenty time to make sure he would be first in line and as he glanced back along the short queue he'd hoped his legs wouldn't shake so bad when he had to walk past them all. The building was magnificent in a modern sophisticated way but the marble floor was perilous for a wobbly Ridge.

Eventually a smiling face appeared and informed him that the Deputy High Commissioner was expecting him next door and would he please follow her. The tall and elegantly attired woman was obviously embarrassed at his apparent disability and as she slowed down her gait to match his, she explained that as he had a previously arranged appointment it hadn't been necessary to queue up in the public area. She ushered him into another grand room about the size of a tennis court and he sat gingerly onto a soft upholstered chair along a side wall. He preferred to be able to see both the door and the massive desk behind which he imagined the posh twat would want to interview him from.

The room was super-chilled and Ridge admired the huge antique fans whirling gently above him. He deduced that they were purely decorative like a lot of the beautiful furniture in the room. *Like the job too*, he snorted quietly.

Only minutes later the door crashed open to a cacophony of voices rising and falling as a large white man bowled his way through a revolving group of Pakistani men and women all thrusting papers at him and vying for his attention. He suddenly stopped dead, his head looking to the floor and then he swivelled his neck so as to take in the sight of Ridge sitting patiently waiting, his mouth agog at the sight. Then the man walked a few more steps and the flurry continued around him. He stopped again. Up came his huge arms as if he was attempting to take flight.

'OUT!
Right now! If you will!'

The frantic gesturing subsided and the four aides slunk out, their shoulders and heads drooped in what must have been a routine despondency. Ridge couldn't help feeling sorry for them although the whole scene had such a comic air about it, he couldn't quite believe what he had witnessed. If someone had come up to him and politely told him he'd entered the theatre rehearsal room by mistake then he wouldn't have questioned it at all. It reminded him of a grand dinner he and Orla had once attended during which there was scheduled to be a 'murder mystery event.' He had won tickets to the dinner through work and they hadn't known a soul beforehand. Milling about in the bar prior to going in to dinner he'd had a series of increasingly ridiculous conversations with different people before he realised that they'd been actors playing out their roles for him to judge after the meal.

The man stood over his desk with his back to him, his enormous cream jacket crumpled and shapeless, and he appeared to throw a heap of papers down and sweep others to the side with little care or administrative aforethought. Feeling embarrassed that the man hadn't yet acknowledged him Ridge felt voyeuristic sitting there and he wanted to cough or do something to remind the guy that he was still there. His backside was killing him and he had a legitimate need to stand up so he made a point of rattling his stick against the chair leg before he struggled to stand up. *I'll give him ten seconds, but then I'm off,* he fumed to himself.

The man turned his attention towards him.

'Ah! Do please forgive me!
Monday morning chaos, what can I say?
Please come over and pull up a chair.
Mr… ah…, Walker isn't it?'

He clocked the stick and Ridge's slow pace.

'Oh! I see. I do beg your pardon.
Please take your time, and here let me
pull this out a little for you.
There. That's it.'

Ridge sat in the big heavy chair a little
harder than he'd intended and couldn't avoid
wincing. The man regarded him shrewdly for a
moment and then Ridge jumped in surprise as he
realised he'd seen the guy before.

'My name is Ross. Logan Ross, Acting
High Commissioner, at your service.'

'Good morning, Mr Ross. My name is
Richar… I mean *Andrew* Walker and
I've come over to Pakistan to help find a
friend of the family…'

Ridge went through the carefully
rehearsed story, taking his time; all the while
feeling like this huge bear of a man had already
heard everything that he said. He also felt
himself warming to him for reasons he couldn't
fathom.

Logan Ross for his part sat unmoving,
not taking any notes and not lifting his gaze from
Ridge's face even for a moment. He wasn't
much older than himself, Ridge guessed
although he had that kind of well upholstered
soft face which was more difficult to age. His
impassive features gave the appearance of

absorbing every last fact without a blink of a question or a moment of disinterest. He reminded Ridge of a large and ever faithful dog. Ridge decided he must be either one of those idiot savant genius types or more likely, just an idiot. But he definitely wouldn't have wanted to play poker against him.

Ridge kept on with his monologue, although he'd said everything that he'd intended and then he got the horrible feeling that the other man was keeping quiet just so Ridge would say enough to hang himself and so he brought his story to an abrupt conclusion. '…and then the bomb happened.'

'Quite!
A horrible, horrible waste, as always.
I witnessed the whole thing myself, albeit from a distance thankfully. I'd spent the day up in the hills as I usually do at the weekends. Reminds me of the hills of home, I suppose and-'

By this point Ridge had already learnt two valuable lessons about Mr Ross. One was that he was Scots, well disguised posh Scots, but he knew the type.

'You're a liar, Mr Ross!
You were in the bar all day, I saw you there!'

'Oh! I do believe that I've been busted!

Well yes! I *was* a little worse for wear yesterday.
Family birthday, you know how it goes?
Not much else to do over here to be honest. I don't remember bumping in to you but then I wouldn't have known you yesterday now would I?'

He was doing it again, but despite the fact that he was a lying bastard, Ridge couldn't help liking the guy and he decided to change tack and see if maybe they really could work together and find Nasreen quickly. All of a sudden he wanted to be back home and hear lots more Scottish voices, posh or otherwise.

'So where are you from?'

'From? Oh I see! Yes! Kindred spirits aren't we?
Speaking of which, I bet you could do with a wee snifter, eh?
A nice cold G and T on the rocks perhaps?'

'Bit early for me Mr Ross, but go on then, you're a scholar and a gent!'

'Splendid! Call me Logan, please.'

Ridge sat up a little more and smiled at the man in genuine surprise. He could get on with this guy for sure. His jaw dropped further as

Logan swung to the left side of his desk and pulled out a fully functioning mini bar from where he plucked two crystal glasses, a bottle of Bombay Sapphire and a bucket of ice.

'Perk of the job you see!
Now that I'm *Acting* Commissioner.
When I was merely the deputy it was my job to go and get the blasted ice!
Slainte, Mr Walker!'

'Call me Andrew… ah fuck it!
Call me Ridge!'

'Ridge Walker it is then! It has a great ring to it don't you think?
Cheers!'

'Get it up ye!'

'Quite!' The man laughed for a moment before his face fell and he slammed a huge paw on the desk, making Ridge jump and his legs rub painfully on the chair.

'Now!
Sadly, I have to cut short our chat this morning as I have to go and look at dead bodies and console some relatives. We lost three local staff members yesterday, all native, but still extremely harrowing. Hence this 'self-medication' to be perfectly honest. I find gin does an

admirable job of dulling the smell of death, what do you think?

   We could continue tomorrow at the same time and in the meantime I'll get my team to begin some preliminary enquiries and we'll see what we can dig up from the visit of that Saad fellow. Although the bugger never did me the courtesy of a visit, but nevertheless. Drink up old boy! What doesn't kill you makes you stronger!'

   So before he knew it Ridge was back out in the public area again with at least an hour before Jake was due to pick him up. He called Orla but she'd left Sorsay and her mobile wasn't picking up so he'd guessed she was enroute, the West Highlands having notoriously poor cell phone reception. He assured his old mum that everything was going well with the IT project and that he'd be home soon. He toyed with the notion of going walk-about but he really wasn't able for it plus he'd had his fill of excitement. Emboldened by the swiftly consumed gin, he decided to try his luck instead.

   There was no-one queuing at the counter and so he hobbled over, putting it on ever so slightly.

   'Excuse me, good morning! Mr Ross, the Commissioner told me to come and talk to you,' he peered at her name badge, 'Jacinta, isn't it?

Yes, he said you would be the most sensible person to ask.'

It was the same woman who'd taken him through earlier and he smiled as the woman gave herself a little congratulatory quiver like the Mallard ducks on Sorsay after you'd tossed them some unused fish bait.

'Mr Ross said you could let me have the use of a private room and a laptop for a few minutes, so that I can send a photo of my poor missing wife back to the authorities back in England. We were caught up in that awful bombing yesterday, just terrible.
So they can get back to him before our next meeting here tomorrow at eight.
I'll only be a minute or two, I promise!'

As he spoke he could see her expression swing between professional concern and heartfelt sympathy and he gave her his very best sad eyes look until he saw the scales swing in his favour.

'Yes, of course sir. It was a black day for all of us.
I hope you find your wife soon. Please come this way.'

Chapter 27

He knew only too well that this was a crazy idea. Using an official British Government computer was just asking for trouble but he figured they'd not be expecting anyone to do this and anyways he knew lots of ways of subverting the most common surveillance programs. *This is my domain*, he whispered as he began to hack into the Foreign and Commonwealth system to search for anything that might be useful to his quest. He also instructed the system to download any files relating to him or Orla dated in the last year.

While he was waiting for these files to finish transferring to an encrypted cloud server, he tried to find out where Colm might be by using any of their coded email addresses he could remember and he used a similar coding system to put up a warning flag to Thaddeus wherever he was in the world.

Between them, they had devised an intricate system of communication that even Orla was not fully aware of and by bouncing emails and posts through various Social Media sites in a certain order the net result was that signals could be sent that bore little or no correlation to the actual subject matter of the messages which were conveyed.

The codes between Thad and him were always based on Bowie lyrics, their mutual adoration of David Bowie being one of the main things that had cemented their initial friendship.

So the final and most important message that he hoped Thad would soon be seeing, read; '*Battle cries and champagne, just in time for sunrise,*' from one of the classic older albums. Thad would interpret this as; 'I am now engaged in a violent situation and I require your input within the next 24hrs.'

Both Colm and Thad also knew how to access the server which would soon hold the new data and he'd also transferred the video from yesterday's bombing for them to have a look at. Thad would know what to do with it and so would his amazing multi-millionaire dad, who Ridge had named previously as 'the man who can' due to his considerable military connections. It had been Thad's dad who'd supplied the jet helicopters that had saved their bacon in Guatemala.

With any luck Ridge would know that the two men had received his messages when he checked in tomorrow at the latest. He should then find a secure number for each of them and before using either one he would buy two throw away mobiles so that there could never be any linkage between them. He laughed to himself wondering which of his two best friends had the most to lose by being associated with the other. A former British spy and international assassin turned family-man and vineyard owner or a rampantly bisexual international model with a taste for cross-dressing mercenaries. Tough call, he thought.

Just as he powered down there was a polite but insistent knock on the door and he guessed he'd used up his goodwill gesture. He pulled open the door and gushed his thanks to the woman. The entire operation had taken only nine minutes. Good old military complex networks, works a treat every time. *Beat that Google*. His only problem now was he still had ages to wait for Jake and he had no friends who were going to want to come out to play with him around here.

He asked the redoubtable Jacinta if he would be causing her any further trouble if he sat and waited for his cousin in the foyer as his legs were troubling him due to his injuries and he didn't feel confident walking outside on his own just at the moment. He knew she would agree and he settled himself down for an hour or two of boredom interspersed with the odd checking on the mobile.

Apart from the insistent rumbling from his stomach, the foyer had become very quiet and completely deserted. Ridge was beginning to fade away himself when the whole building was plunged into darkness. This was becoming tiresome! But they *must* have generators here? Then he felt the dull vibration of a power surge and weak greenish emergency lighting began to seep its way into the large room. Barely enough to see by, Ridge waited patiently for the rest to kick in. After ten minutes and feeling like the last man on earth, he hobbled over to the public counter and leant on the bell. A door opened

from the end of the corridor and he could see
light streaming in around the silhouette of a tall
woman.

'I'm so sorry, I forgot you were there!
We're closed now until the power is
switched back on!'

She must have suddenly remembered his
predicament and so she clicked down the
corridor so as to be able to speak without
shouting.

'You will have to leave the building I'm
afraid. We have some power but not
enough for the public areas and it's very
unpredictable at best.
But some of us girls are going across the
road for a cup of tea in a minute.
They have a most excellent generator that
never wavers.
You're more than welcome to join us if
you like?'

'I will thanks. That's very kind of you.'
He smiled although in the back of his mind he
was thinking, *okay so now I'm a charity case*!

He ended up camping out at the café bar
long after the office girls had left to go back to
work but by then he'd felt safe enough to go it
alone. Jacinta had been most useful and it was

great to have been able to ask questions without there being any hidden agenda.

They called the power cuts 'load shedding' and it had been a common problem throughout the city where they were continually trying to balance a system where demand always exceeded supply. No-one appeared immune to the cuts not even the Diplomatic Enclave. Ridge decided that must be why everyone seemed to favour security guards at their properties rather than fitting alarm systems.

He gauged from listening to their conversations that most of the population were fairly well off compared to the rest of Pakistan and that the government jobs were highly sought after despite the obvious security concerns. Logan Ross was well thought of among the girls but he was pretty sure he could detect that 'mother hen' tone from some of them when they talked about him although everyone was very careful not to speak out of turn. He did learn that there was a decent phone shop around the corner which all the girls had used in the past and so when the power came back on he took the initiative and made his way slowly round. Qualifying as the most taciturn customer of day he quickly purchased two cheap pay-as-you-go mobile and sim card deals.

Back at the café, he soon became disinterested with their airy chat and he drifted off into his own troubled thoughts, consulting his phone as often as he could without drawing too much attention, whilst enjoying the luxury of a quality wi-fi service. He'd spoken briefly with Orla who had still been in bed as he'd forgotten the time difference. She was back in Glasgow and had set up various freelance writing projects to keep her mind from worrying about him.

He sat and watched the bustle of life around him and thought about the baby and how much his life was going to change over the next few months. He leant over in pain as the acid of regret pumped into his stomach.

As the girls left, he assured Jacinta he'd be fine on his own and he managed to last at least quarter of an hour on his own before he ordered his first beer. It was shortly after that when he received his first coded message reply. It was from Colm!

Struggling to maintain his composure Ridge copied the contact number onto one of the new mobiles and immediately scored the screen across with a sharp piece of grit. This would now be Colm's phone. He glanced around him to see if anyone would be in earshot but by now he'd become part of the furniture and there was no-one paying him any attention whatsoever. He dialled the number wondering where in the world his brother-in-law might be.

Colm picked up on the second ring.

'Where are you?' His voice was terse.

'Islamabad. I'm fine really but there's been a bombing and-'

199

'Ye can stop right there, so ye can!
What the fuck was I after telling ye?
So who's looking after me sister?
And her about to have your feckin' baby!
Jesus H Christ…'

The phone went dead. Ridge sat there for a minute, waiting for Colm to call back. Then another minute and then he realised that there wasn't going to be a call back. He'd never really fallen out with Colm and to be honest it wasn't something anyone in their right mind would want to do anyway. He knew what Colm was capable of and most of the time that had been a comfort, but now he wasn't feeling quite so sure. It was at this point that Ridge realised just how alone and afraid he was feeling and how much he had been looking forward to hearing the normally calming and practical advice from the closest thing to a brother that he had left.

He looked around him. Everything else remained just as it had been a few minutes ago. But he didn't feel the same. He was shaking and he felt sick. Had he made a big mistake coming here? He'd certainly pissed off Colm and on the face of it, he admitted that he had been pretty selfish putting his life in danger when he didn't have to. It wasn't like the last time he'd found himself in mortal peril. That time he'd been an innocent abroad and had just been in the wrong place at the wrong time.

This time he had chosen to come here. For money. He tried to paint the picture in more romantic or heroic terms but even he had to admit that much as he wanted to find Nasreen, he wouldn't be sitting in this humid café if he hadn't been paid ten thousand pounds a fortnight ago.

The Colm phone pinged and he jumped so hard he almost put his back out. Unfamiliar as he was with the new device he guessed it was a SMS message. Praying that it wasn't just a welcome message from the service provider, he snatched it off the table and read the contents of the small screen.

> *Sorry - Spoken O - AOK*
> *Will lk at homework + call ltr*
> *R u secure?*

Ridge was so relieved that he had to blink through his tears as he replied.

> ? Sort of. Café waiting for Z. V late.

> *How lt?*

> 3 hrs

> *GTFOOT now!*
> *Ltr x*

Ridge stared at the screen. Colm obviously didn't share his optimism that he was in a safe place. He started to shake again and decided that what he needed most was a drink. A proper one this time. Then if Jake still hadn't turned up at that point he would 'get the fuck out of there' and chance getting a taxi back to the apartment.

Aware that his nerves were starting to get the better of him, he glanced around carefully, fearful not to attract any unwelcome attention. He downed the fastest gin ever and then tried to stop his left leg from jiggling manically. But it was no use. He knew what he had to do. He signalled for a fresh drink and when the barman came over he flashed him a ridiculously huge tip and asked, as casually as he could manage, if the guy could phone him a recommended taxi to take him to the Blue Zone.

He had already peered out a window but the black night only served to aggravate his unease. He tried to work out what could have happened to Jake. She had seemed so capable that night back in Pollokshields but ever since he'd got to know her better he'd also seen a vulnerable side and yet there had also been something else puzzling him but he hadn't worked that one through yet.

Just then his normal phone went off and he felt his body relax instantly as he put the phone to his ear.

> 'You're a wee bit late for lunch you know! Just as well I've had a whole bunch of office girls to keep me-'

'Ridge! Get out of there! Right now, I mean it!'

'What's happened? Are you all right? Where are you?
You're the second person to warn me in the last 5 minutes!'

'Listen I'm okay. I can't say where I am but I'm fine.
But you must go and hide somewhere!
Do NOT go back to the flat!
It's trashed and the day guard is dead, neck broken!
I'm sorry Ridge!
You're on your own for now, got to go. Bye…'

'Sir!
Your car is here. Just out there. Please hurry sir.'

He stood up and slung the rest of his drink down his neck. Where to go? What the hell was he going to do? He stumbled to the car and fell into the back seat.

'Good evening sir.' The driver was as polite as the last one. 'It's turned out a beautiful evening again. Where to tonight, sir?'

'Take me to the Monal please!
Thank you.'

He sat back into the seat, wondering why he'd even said that. But it was the only place in the continent of Asia where he might find someone who could help him. Logan Ross!

Chapter 28

Orla sat and stared across the flimsy wooden table at the bullet headed oaf she was supposed to be 'interviewing.' He'd been staring at her tits for ages now and he'd not even clocked the fact that she'd put down her pen in a silent protest at the utter garbage that spewed from his slavering gob.

She was seriously starting to wonder if she'd ever be ready for the outside world. It had been such an effort getting out the door even, her enormous belly now too big to squeeze out the storm doors of the flat without having to open the right hand side. Normally most people keep the right hand door permanently locked and so they've only got to slide the bolt from the left hand side after closing the flimsier inner door. Of course, Ridge being paranoid Ridge, they had installed a solid steel inner door that would withstand a hell of a lot more than any wooden storm door and so rendering their one superfluous.

But it was only since he'd swanned off that she'd been unable to get through just the left side. Again it wouldn't seem a big deal to most ordinary folk to have to open the other side but of course the storm doors have their bolts at the top and the bottom. Because of her swollen tummy she couldn't reach the top one without dragging through a chair from the kitchen and then she still had the bending down to the bottom one to contend with. And she hadn't seen her feet in weeks now! So, this morning, by the time she'd managed to do all of that, she then had to go back in to the flat for a pee.

It had been fine just sitting in the flat at her laptop. She was getting on well with her novel and the writing assignments were arriving in her inbox with a satisfying online thud. But recent events had set her back, she knew they had. Despite going through a far worse experience than her, Ridge seemed to have moved on more quickly and be coping a lot better. She had begun to feel settled and content with their new quieter life and above all she craved a safe and secure future for the three of them. So why did she now feel trapped in the past?

At long last he's noticed. She forced her mouth into a thin smile as Tommy Taggart pointed a tattooed paw towards her fluorescent biro sitting in obstinate defiance on the desk, next to her iPhone.

'You've stopped writing hen!
Are you no interested in what I'm trying tae tell ye?'

Orla wasn't the slightest bit interested in what he was saying although she did find him fascinating in the same way that modern generations continued to have such a morbid curiosity for monsters like Hitler. She looked at her phone and lied through her teeth. Blame the hormones, but she didn't need this shite in her life.

'You've got to move with the times Mr Taggart!' *Aye! In more ways than one.* 'My wrist has cramped up for the now. I'll take some further notes in a while but rest assured, I'm after recording every single word that you're saying, so I am!'

'Oh! Right ye are then. Are ye no supposed tae ask permission afore ye dae stuff like that?'

'I thought I had Tommy, right when I came in, so I did. But anyway, I would have assumed that a man so well versed in the world of the media would have expected me to do that anyway! Can you please carry on with your spiel as I'll be after needing a visit to the ladies soon enough!'

'So, as I was saying, tae take from that great and often misunderstood man, Mr Enoch Powell, we're just 'throwing a match onto gunpowder' the now, with all these new fangled immigration policies. Thank fuck, excuse the language, but thank fuck we didnae go for yon independence nonsense.

Let me gie you a direct quote from the
man himself.'

Orla groaned inwardly as the man pulled
out a small piece of card with a photocopied
paragraph glued on by inky hands. Improper use
of a Post Office copier, no doubt, she thought.

'Aye. So listen tae this, written in 1968
mind;

Those whom the gods wish to destroy,
they first make mad. We must be mad,
literally mad, as a nation to be permitting
the annual inflow of some 50,000
dependants, who are for the most part the
material of the future growth of the
immigrant-descended population. It is
like watching a nation busily engaged in
heaping up its own funeral pyre. So
insane are we that we actually permit
unmarried persons to immigrate for the
purpose of founding a family with
spouses and fiancés whom they have
never seen.

See! We huv' tae be mad! Look at
America! Riots in the fuckin' street!
Sorry, but it's a fact is it no'? They're
going off their heids over there every five
minutes 'cos some white polisman shoots
a black guy who was going tae grab his
gun off him?

208

And there are thousands of them flooding intae Europe every week!
You just dinnae see it, dae ye? I'm on the streets delivering the post every day and I see whit's going on and I hear whit folk are saying, honest working folk like you and me!'

Orla felt her face flushing hot.

'Don't include me in this Tommy! I do not particularly agree with your views and anyway I'm trying to write an unbiased piece here that's after giving both sides of the argument.'

'Fair point, hen but I'm telling you there's going to be trouble over here an' all, but this time it'll be us causing the rammy! I swear that afore that bairn in yer belly grows auld there'll be a war, a Crusade and we'll all be made tae pay for this stupidity!'

'I think you're being a little dramatic Tommy aren't you?'

'Dramatic? Do ye ken that in some parts of England they're already talking aboot havin' Sharia Law 'cos there's mair of them than us?'

'I really doubt if that…' Orla paused as her phone began buzzing angrily cross the desk. 'Excuse me, Tommy! I'm so sorry! Give me a minute will you?' Orla picked up the phone and took it over to the far side of the empty hall.

It was her next door neighbour.

'Fiona? What's the matter?
I'm working right now, so I am and-'

'Aye I'm sorry about that hen! But I just thought that you should know, like, after what you'd been saying the other day an' that. I'm not being nosey you understand but there's been two men at your door. They were chapping your storm door for ages. I though they were Jehovah's, when I saw them through the glass, dead smart an' that, but then when I went out to get a better look, just getting some milk from the shop, you know, I nearly got the shock of my life!
They were about ten feet tall and black as coal, so they were!
Right handsome too if you really want to know. Lucky girl, I thought, they could bang my door *all day*, so they could.
So, do you know who they were?'

Orla held on to the wall for a moment, feeling a wave of heat race up her back and around her neck. She only knew a few handsome

210

black men and if they had been looking for her over here in Scotland, it could never be good news. She had to get back to the flat as fast as she could waddle. It was time to wind this cosy chat up fast.

'I'm sorry, Tommy but there's been a problem at home and we'll have to either continue this another time or if you prefer I could just take a good closing statement from you. Something memorable, but please not too incendiary if you don't mind.'

'Aye nae problem hen! You were just going to tell me that this stuff could never happen in Scotland. Well it has already happened. The Muslims have already infiltrated the police and the judges and that's why they're too scared to do anything about all these gangs terrorising the streets around here!'

Orla decided to go in for the quick kill. She leant forward and looked him directly in the eyes.

'I am no particular fan of either the police or the judiciary, Mr Taggart, but I seriously doubt if you are living in the same world as the rest of us!'

Tommy had been enjoying himself up to this point and he'd always fancied Irish lassies with that wild red hair. And the fucking melons on this one were a real sight for sore eyes. He'd got her riled up that much that he could see the milky white skin around her cleavage growing redder by the minute. Now she was leaning that far forward he thought one of them might be about to fall out! Snooty as fuck, mind you. Wouldn't be so high and mighty if she knew what he knew! Fuck it! She was pissing him off now and if she wanted a real show stopper he'd fucking give her one!

'Is that thing switched off? Good. Keep it that way will you. Now lean a wee bit closer cos' I don't want anyone to hear this!
It's you who is living in a different fucking world. This is strictly off the record right, between you and me only. You think you're so fucking high and mighty with all your middle-class morals but do you know who yer fucking hero husband is in cahoots with? Naw! I didnae think so! You'll no be so fucking cheeky when that wean of yours is asking who his fuckin faither wis and why he isnae…'

Tommy jumped as the girl's bonnie face turned ashen and her chair bounced across the dusty wooden floor. Green eyes flashed bolts of

212

vicious fury down on him before she turned and stormed out of the building, the notebook and pen lying abandoned in front of him. He looked down at them and blinked, several times, not knowing quite if he'd done something monumentally stupid.

'What did I say…?'

Chapter 29

Standing at the far end of the long bar, Logan knew he'd spotted the bewildered looking lad long before he'd had a chance to notice him. He was staggered that he'd got through security tonight as they had, all of a sudden, become very particular about who they let in. On his instructions, *naturellement*. So he'd jinked behind a wooden column festooned with vines and then ducked down below the bar top, to quizzical looks from a pair of over stuffed matrons in over priced outfits. Despite his ludicrous situation, he couldn't help smiling as he overheard them agree they had seen him a lot worse.

Safe for now, he then made his way down the treacherous steps to the dimly lit back bar which was always deserted at this early hour. He preferred it that way and it had become his unofficial fiefdom. It might be a far cry from the grandeur and style of London but it was all he had. He spent most of his free time, which was considerable, drinking in this bar. What was the line, drinking to remember, drinking to forget?

The boy would find him soon enough. He took a long pull at his glass and considered the strange case of Mr Walker. He had smelt something fishy about him, that much was obvious, but at the same time, the boy didn't fit in to any of the usual categories. He wasn't a conniving Yank to start with and Logan still couldn't work out what his angle could be, which had piqued his curiosity immensely. And when you became trapped in a Petri dish environment like this place, microscopic examinations of each other's idiosyncrasies and motivations coupled with rampant speculation had become a daily pastime amongst all the ex-patriots. When you threw in an unhealthy strain of intrigue to the mix, then a fresh specimen like the callow Ridge Walker made for one of the rare stimulations that made life bearable, almost.

The official line from on high was that he should help the chap as much as was practicable, without compromising the FCO position, but once the poor fool realised he was on a wild-goose chase, Logan had been ordered to pack him back off to GB with great speed.

And he had found that so very curious. Never in his fifteen months out here, had he received specific instructions about a named individual who wasn't either on the official wanted list, and therefore fair game in anyone's book, or part of the establishment, which he patently could never be in a million years. The man was a badly spoken oik, brought up in the sticks and he reminded Logan of a character from one of those awful druggie films so beloved of the chattering classes. Yet despite all of these fundamental shortcomings, Logan had felt an unspoken bond between them and notwithstanding his official remit, he had already made up his mind to delve a little deeper into this case and maybe do something really useful for a refreshing change.

So he was well aware that Andrew wasn't his original name and that he'd somehow been involved in something big over the pond. Logan had been told to keep the Yanks as far away from the chap as possible without being obstructive but in his experience he knew if they wanted to talk to him they would and there was precious little he could do about it. As far as he could work out it wasn't a witness protection situation and young Walker hadn't been suspected of any real criminal behaviour but he detected the unpleasant whiff of something Irish about the case and this had him fascinated. If he was honest, he knew very little about Irish terrorism barring what he'd seen on the television news back in the school common room.

But he knew about people. And most Brits would have been on the next flight home after yesterday's horrific violence, speed-dialling the BBC. Not sitting across a desk from him first thing the next morning, bruised and bloodied, but apparently still keen to go back into the ring.

Logan looked up to see him struggle down the slippy stairs. *Seconds out*.

Chapter 30

Ridge had almost given up when he noticed there was a lower floor at the back of the building, the more subdued lighting giving it a strictly 'off limits' feeling. Out of sheer desperation he literally caught hold of a passing waiter in a pristine pressed white jacket. 'Excuse me but is that part of the same bar? I'm looking for a good friend of mine, Logan Ross, do you know him?'

The waiter brushed his sleeve and eyed Ridge up and down in a nano-second. After hesitating for a single second more, he waved dismissively towards the stairs. 'Yes sir that will be fine. He lives down there.'

'Logan? Hi there!
Listen can I buy you a drink?'

'Of course! Sit. I'll take care of it.'

Ridge slumped down gratefully as Logan raised a pink hand and waved two fingers momentarily towards the bar.

'I'm so glad I found you, I need to ask a favour if possible.'

'Well then, you're very lucky indeed!

I'm only in for a spot of dinner. They do a splendid mixed Thali here! You're welcome to join me of course.
Now ask away!'

Ridge told him about Zakia being late and her call about the apartment. Once again he saw little evidence of anything happening behind those jowly features but before Ridge had even finished speaking Logan had his phone to his ear and an enormous plasma screen was flickering to life on the wall in front of them.

Ridge sat in silence, exhausted by the combined pressure of humidity and emotion as the local news flicked from story to story without any mention of a murder that afternoon. The footage was principally a rehash of the bombing with gruesome pictures of injured spectators in hospital. Ridge had to turn away, feeling nauseous, then he remembered he'd not had a lot to eat in the last two days. Food might be a very good or a very bad idea.

'I see. Fine. Yes…
Right then, keep me informed of any progress will you?
Yes! Top priority on this one. No, only me. Whatever.'

Logan's big green eyes had widened a little during the call but his voice hadn't given away any trace of emotion. He turned to Ridge

218

and this time there was a vague pallor to his complexion.

'I'm very sorry, Ridge, but your information does appear to be spot on. One of our best security freelancers has been found dead and it seems his neck had indeed been broken. There are reports of further violence on the outskirts of the city and I'm awaiting further details.
I don't know how to tell you this except to tell you the truth. It looks like your lady friend has been kidnapped!'

'But she…, I don't think… Oh shit! Listen Logan, I've not been totally honest with you!
Zakia's not my girl friend or anything like that. She's a cop and I'm being paid to help the family find Nasreen.
I'm a fucking *bounty hunter*!'

Logan waved for more drinks and gave an additional hand signal that worried Ridge until the man smiled and thumped a huge hand onto his shoulder in a gesture that he probably thought was comforting but would have nearly buried him into the ground had he not been bracing himself.

'Of course you are, old bean!

219

And I have not been completely honest
with you either.
Shall we go through and eat?
They'll keep these seats for us, rest
assured.'

Despite his anguished state of mind,
Ridge found himself to be starving and he
hoovered up everything within reach on the table,
giving the far more ample man a showing up.
They downed a couple of large Indian beers and
Ridge was relieved to see Logan had dropped the
whole British Empire act and had reverted to
what was probably his natural state, resembling
more an avuncular and eccentric boffin.
        They switched back to the bar and Logan
had the staff bring over a blue bottle of gin and a
bucket of ice. It looked like it was going to be
one of those nights but Ridge didn't know what
else he could really do and so he allowed himself
to slip into relaxed inebriation. It was only when
he realised he couldn't read the breaking news
along the bottom of the 60" screen that decided
it was time to slow down. His new friend
obviously had an enormous capacity for the
demon drink and it was fair to say that he'd been
out of practice lately.
        It turned out they had more in common
than either would have cared to admit only a few
short hours ago. With their defences lowered
they had both exchanged their sad story of a lost
sibling, each one in similarly tragic
circumstances.

Logan had said how much he had
genuinely liked to go hill walking and although
brought up in suburban London he had been
installed at a boarding school near Perth and had
gone walking most weekends. His family had
connections with His Grace The Duke of Argyll
and they'd often sailed past Sorsay on their way
back down to Inverary Castle. As he guffawed
with laughter, Ridge told him how the islanders
referred to the Duke as 'His Disgrace the Plook
of Argyll.'

Ridge told how his brother Gavin had
died on the harsh scree of Ben Cruachan and
how he'd felt helpless to save him, even
breaking his own leg in the process of an
unsuccessful rescue. He blamed himself for not
seeing the signs that his brother had been
dabbling in drugs, the cause of his death. Drunk
enough to speak his thoughts without the normal
social filters, he muttered that was maybe why
he felt compelled to involve himself in these
ridiculous situations.

Logan nodded compassionately and told
Ridge about how he'd lost his older sister, only
four years previously and how he'd also gone a
little off the rails afterwards.

'Ha! Did you just say *not seeing the signs*?
Those four words, my friend have come
to define my whole wasted life.
She'd been such a bright kid!
We both were I suppose, but the
difference between us was that Elspeth

221

had applied her intelligence and worked her socks off. She'd got a first from Oxford, as had I, but then she went on and completed her accountancy papers and had a high flying job with a merchant bank in the City. Whereas I just drifted into the Foreign Office like my father although I had vague aspirations of entering the Commons at some stage. We'd all been up in your neck of the woods for Hogmanay.
Stobo Castle. You know it?'

Ridge spluttered his drink. 'Know it? Oh aye I know it, but only when I've heard words like Madonna or Brad Pitt mentioned in the same sentence!'

'Absolutely, old bean!'
And so anyway, Elspeth had been driving back down South with her prat of a friend, Adrian, in her spanking new Jaguar XK8. They'd had the top down as it had been a glorious morning apparently, although I was still fast asleep when it happened. She'd been sitting behind a lorry on the A9, you know how frustrating that can be? The lorry signalled that it was safe for her to overtake and so she pulled out directly into the path of a wood lorry. Killed outright!
Poor Adrian will be in a wheelchair for the rest of his days.'

Ridge did feel bad but he also remembered that when his father taught him to drive, one of the absolute 'cast in stone' lessons was never ever to trust the 'safe to overtake' flashing indicator signal from a driver in front. It had wiped out many unwary tourists in the Western Highlands, particularly those with left hand drive cars.

He watched Logan down four fat fingers of gin that would have floored many a rugby player and he sat quietly as the other man continued talking, more to himself than anyone else.

'And so that's when I began my little 'drinky poo' problem, I suppose.
Just after I had to identify my first dead body.
I still think of her every time I do it you know!
After that I tended to get so drunk I didn't know what I was doing half the time and people would tell me I was a real 'hugger bugger.' But don't be alarmed! I try not to do that now as that's what got me into trouble.'

Ridge threw a couple of ice cubes into his mouth and crunched them hard in a desperate bid to sober up.

'I'd go to all these expensive West End clubs and get completely smashed. Unfortunately when I got too drunk I never passed out or became sick, I just carried on drinking even more and so more often than not other people would have no idea I was so out of my head until I did something monumentally stupid.

Like the night I put my hand up a young woman's skirt and she screamed the place down. I don't remember much about it but in my drunken stupor I'd thought that she'd been giving me all the right signals and that she'd be coming back to my place!

But she was the daughter of a Cabinet Minister and so naturally it was all over the Red Top papers and I ended up being shipped over here! It was only my family connections that prevented me ending up in court and losing my job completely. Four months after I arrived, the top job became available and so here I am, exiled in Islamabad!'

Just then a phone went off in Ridge's jacket. He thrust a hand in and stroked he screen. No scratch. It was Thaddeus! He grabbed it and turned to move off.

'Important?' Logan gestured to leave instead as it was obviously easier for him to move around. He made a hand gesture to indicate he was going to the toilet and Ridge mouthed 'Mother' back at him and gave him a thumbs up sign.

'Thad! Is that really you?' Tears trickled down his face as he tried to get a hold of himself.

'Hey dude!
Can't leave you alone for a minute? What the fuck?
Half expected you to be up to your ears in diapers round about now.'

Ridge gave him a thirty second précis of the situation as he saw it, anxious not be overheard by his new friend, just in case.

'Ok amigo! You gotta find this girl, Zakia. Real fast, man, you know what I'm sayin' right? What kinda back up have you got?
Just one guy? The head Brit?
Okay, I guess he should have some muscle over there. Ridge you gotta use this guy and get some more feet on the ground. Where are you now, are you secure?'

'I think so, Thad but I don't think anyone else-'

Ridge never got to finish his sentence as behind him the huge floor to ceiling window of jet black perfection shattered in a deafening cascade of glass shards. He'd caught the initial moment in the reflection from the large TV but his alcohol-slowed reactions were not fast enough to prevent two dark skinned men from stepping through the falling glass and pulling him back out into the stifling darkness. He struggled hopelessly until one of the men squeezed hard around his throat and held a vicious blade up to his terrified face.

The manic looking eyes told him everything he needed to know and he allowed himself to be dragged through the undergrowth towards a car parked in the shadow of a tall coiffured tree. Lying up against the side of the car he could see the large form of another man, his head bent over listlessly and his hands bound in front of him. Logan.

Chapter 31

The man holding Ridge by the throat pushed him across the back seat of the car and Ridge gurgled in pain. The other man had gestured Logan up with a pistol and as Ridge struggled to right himself in the gloom of the car he heard the loud crack of a bullet and he feared the worst. His equally surprised captor turned to meet the head on charge of a 260 pound drunken Scotsman in full flight. The two of them crashed on to Ridge's legs and he cried out in agony at the same time as trying to somehow gouge the face of his kidnapper.

But Logan had this all under control. In a massive show of brute power he pulled the man out of the car, right up into the air and wrestled him into a half Nelson hold before dragging him across the narrow drive way. Ridge fell clumsily out looking for the other guy who'd been packing the revolver only to find him spreadeagled on the ground with his head at an unnaturally jaunty angle. Seeing the gun he scooped it up and strained to see where Logan had gone.

He heard sounds of tussling ahead and as hotel staff began to filter out and one had the presence of mind to train a torch onto the proceedings, he could just make out Logan and the kidnapper rolling across the rough ground. They were moving too fast for Ridge to get an accurate shot and then to his astonishment he saw the kidnapper rise up into the air and accompanied by a savage roar which seemed to emanate from the bowels of the earth, he saw the man fly through the air into the darkness of space. Ridge stumbled over as fast as he could manage, thrusting the gun into Logan's massive paw.

'Quick! Come on! Before he tries to get back up again!'

Logan let out a heavy sigh and laughed.

'Thanks old bean but I don't imagine he'll be getting up again Ridge!
The drop over the side of that wall is at least a hundred feet!'

And sure enough, as the crowd of excited staff and guests spilled across the gardens and to peer over the wall, Ridge could just make out, with the help of many torches, the mangled body of a man far down below, his blood smeared across jagged rocks and seeping into the dry earth of the Himalayas.

'Bloody hell Logan!' Ridge hugged the big man hard. 'Remind me never to get on the wrong side of you again! Where did you learn to do that?'

'I wasn't always like this, you know! I once trialled for the Under 18 Scotland squad you know, good prop I was, back

228

in the day. Remind me to tell you the story of when I wrestled a bull at the Inverary Games on my 21st birthday! But let's go before this gets too complicated. The boys here will cover for me! I was never here this evening so that would make things rather awkward for you I fear. Anyway, I know where you friend is being held! These idiots didn't imagine that a buffoon like me would understand Minglish!'

'Minglish?'

'A mixture of Urdu and English! A lot of them speak like that around here.
Did I tell you I got a First in Languages? Come on! You better take the gun and I'll drive. Let's hope there are not too many checkpoints tonight!'

Logan drove erratically down the narrow hill road. Considering how much alcohol the man had quaffed, Ridge was fairly impressed although still nervous about that deceptive two foot wall on the right hand side.

'Are you sure Zakia is there? And shouldn't we get some back-up?'

'I am not positive but I think I know where they've got Nasreen because that's where they were taking you. I was not

229

going to be hurt, just warned off. You might not have fared so well however although any Westerner must be worth something in ransom potential.'

'Thanks a lot' Ridge hadn't meant it to sound sarcastic and Logan laughed again. Despite the danger Ridge could see it was obvious Logan was having the time of his life.

'No. I really mean it Logan. Thanks for all of this. I don't know what I would have done without you.'

'Forget it old bean! I have wanted to do something like this ever since I got here! It's not like they can ever demote me from here, where could they send me after this? Besides I am not the pussy cat you think I am. I have always loved a bit of danger. Did I tell you what my nickname was at Oxford? Rogan Josh! Get it? Logan Ross, Rogan Josh? I would be the first to admit that I've always loved a good hot *Ruby* but it was also because I was such a tearaway always getting into hot water and up to high jinks!'

High jinks! Ridge still couldn't get his head around this wrestling beast of a man and his old fashioned turn of phrase. It was like Downton Abbey meets The Rock!

230

'What did you hear about Jake, I mean Zakia?'

'Well, I'm not sure to be honest. It didn't seem to make so much sense, that part. But I definitely heard them talk about her at the same time as they were talking about us and the girl, Nasreen.'

'So where are we going?'

'It's no big secret, old chap. There's a huge and ever growing slum over in Rawalpindi which is infamous as a haven for terrorists mainly because the police and authorities are too afraid to go there. Unless you know your way around it's like a warren and when I first visited when I was still keen and eager, you know, wet behind the ears, they just disappeared down rat holes whenever they saw me. Like vermin.
Don't get me wrong!
I don't mean that in a racist sense at all. Part of my legacy when they eventually find me lying dead in a drunken heap will be the huge improvements that I've helped to negotiate for the inhabitants of the place.
They are not all bad people. Where do you think all the people who service our pampered lifestyle actually live? They

can't all afford to rent an air conditioned apartment in F sector?'

Ridge could see an armed checkpoint ahead and as Logan slowed to an abrupt halt and then revved the engine hard, he felt his shirt stick to his back.

'Logan! What are you doing?'

'Don't worry old bean! I've got this. Our main problem right now is the car. But in a few minutes it will probably be the only thing that guarantees our survival. This might hurt I'm afraid!'

Just as Ridge was about to ask what he meant, the sky turned all kaleidoscopic for a second and then he felt the warm comfort of darkness overcome him.

It was the deathly silence that reawakened him, immediately followed by a hot current of pain flooding down his spine and he jack-knifed uncontrollably across the back seat.

'Argh! Jesus!'

He tried to sit up and realised his hands were bound behind him. That was when he realised that he couldn't see properly either. He knew he was still in darkness despite the flashing spirals dancing across his straining eyes and he could feel the oppressive heat of his own breath bouncing back across his face. He guessed that he'd been knocked out and covered with a blanket and judging by the sandpaper caress of the rough material every time he moved his head, he must have picked up an open wound.

'What's going on? Logan? Are you there? What the fuck's happening?'

'Sshh! Keep quiet Ridge!
You've got a bag over your head. I bashed you I'm afraid and I've got you tied up into the bargain! You have to trust me. If you don't listen to me very carefully you won't see daylight again. Things have changed over the last few hours and you must do as I say. I promise that all of this is for your own good and it's the only way you or Nasreen will ever survive.
Do you understand me?'

'Not really, but go on!'

'That's a good chap! Now, I'm going to take the bag off for a minute and I want you to sit still like a good boy and not attract any attention. Got that?'

Ridge grunted and then suddenly he could breathe and see again. He squinted at

Logan who did his best impression of sheepish before smiling nervously.

'Right! It's curtain up old bean! We've both a part to play if we are to make it to the final scene. Okay?
You're to play act my prisoner. I'm going to deliver you into the hands of the Jamaat-al-Jasari and then leave you there as their prize!'

'But what-'

'Wait! Let me continue!
This is the *only* way we'll resolve this situation and I promise you within a few hours we'll be toasting our success with a nice cold gin.
The only way that I could have penetrated this far into their stronghold is by pretending you were my captive. They know me here and they like me but that only goes so far. To find exactly where your friend is we need to have a Trojan horse. That is you old bean!
Once they allow me to leave I'll return with reinforcements and we will get you out. I promise this is the only way!
Now. I couldn't help noticing you've got a wide selection of phones there. I need you to tell me exactly what they're for and who'll be at the other end. There's no point in you lying to me about this and

obviously we don't want to allow these phones to fall into the hands of the enemy.'

'How do I know I can trust you? You could be doing all of this to line your pockets!'

'Now, do I look like a man who is worried about money?
I know we've formed a bond here, Ridge Walker, as unlikely as that may sound. I've exchanged confidences with you this evening that no-one else in Pakistan has ever heard.
You have to believe me. Sometimes in life we just have to take a leap of faith. I have faith in you Ridge, to do the right thing.
What do you say?'

'Do I have any choice?'

'There is always a choice, old chap. Every morning, as I unscrew the top off the gin bottle I tell myself that.
Now quickly! Tell me everything that I need to know!'

So Ridge gave Logan the briefest summary about whom and what Colm and Thaddeus were and what they could be capable of. He also added what he thought they'd do to him if he ever betrayed them. Logan took the phones reverently and hid then within the capacious pockets of his blood stained jacket.

'Tally ho then! Into the belly of the beast!'

Chapter 32

The narrow streets were bumpy and twisting and they were travelling little faster than walking speed. Every time he peered out through a tiny rip in the bag, he'd see the flickering of fires, tended by shadowed faces and pairs of eyes looking up with a moment's curiosity before turning away to resume their tasks. Curiosity killed more than cats down here. Ridge was terrified but he grudgingly admitted to himself that he did trust Logan and that he did feel exactly the same way about their short friendship. He just wished there could be another way other than him being delivered to notorious terrorists as a captive.

He was also extremely worried about the 'rescue' as he'd seen too much footage over the last week of abortive rescue attempts where the kidnap victims meet a grisly end. On the plane he'd read about one particular case which had touched him as he'd remembered speaking to a couple of the islanders back home who'd actually known the victim. And people from Sorsay never usually knew anybody!

She had been from neighbouring islands, one of the Inner Hebrides he couldn't remember which, and she'd been working as a medical aid volunteer worker before being captured. The rescue attempt had gone hideously awry and she had been shot and killed by American Special Forces personnel.

Just in case of any mishaps he'd given Logan instructions to phone Orla and to tell her how much he loved her and to try and forgive him one day.

'Okay Ridge, this is it.
I'm taking the bag off now so keep calm and don't do anything sudden.'

As the handbrake was being applied, men with guns appeared out of the gloom and surrounded the car. They were only boys most of them and Ridge noted that there were eleven of them but only nine had a weapon. *That means they are short of funds,* he reasoned. So less likelihood of him getting killed? He gulped and hoped so.

Logan got out first slowly, the pistol in his right hand which he showed openly and then used to gesticulate towards Ridge to climb out his side. 'Stand there, don't move,' he whispered.

The older of the men signalled the others and they quietly made their way along the narrow rutted track. The smell was catching the back of Ridge's throat and he tried to swallow down the bile that wanted to leave his body. *Nothing like sobering a man up like the end of a rifle,* he decided, as they seemed to arrive at the base.

Nondescript, shabby and littered with kitchen waste and debris, the base was less than inspiring. Before he could say anything further to Logan, Ridge found himself being ushered away and down a narrow corridor into a makeshift bedroom. There he saw the girl who he assumed was Nasreen, handcuffed to a long chain stretching across the middle of the room and sitting on a filthy mattress. She was stroking a mangy looking dog and barely acknowledged him as he was led in and shackled to the same chain.

He sat away from her on the roughly finished concrete floor but quickly had to raise himself up onto his hands to relieve the pressure on his still painful burns. 'Do you mind?' he whispered as he shuffled on to the far end of the mattress.

The girl didn't even look up and he wondered if she was the girl from his Glasgow neighbourhood.

'So, did you get the train from Pollokshields East or Pollokshields West?'

It was an old joke back in Glasgow and it certainly got a reaction but not the one he'd hoped for. The girl broke down in tears and put her head in her hands.

'Hey! It's going to be okay, I promise you!

I've come to get you out of here! It might
not look like it but this is all part of the
plan, you'll see.'

'Piss off! Do you think I'm stupid or
something!
I don't what kind of games you think
you're playing but you can fuck off with
your Glasgow shite!
You're worse than her!
I bet you've never even been to Glasgow
in your life!
Why should I believe anything you say?'

'Because Masood told me to tell you he
loved you and that, no matter what, he
wanted you to know.'

Nasreen gasped and for the first time
since he'd entered the room he saw a spark of
life in her tired eyes. She wiped away grimy
tears and beamed at him.

'Really? Really, really? But what about?
You know?'

'Don't worry! It's all under control.'

'Oh! I so want to speak to Masood and
say sorry for all the trouble I've caused
and how I'm not and never have been a
terrorist and I didn't run away because of
the arranged marriage and that he was

240

right about Shahid and that I've been such an idiot falling for a man like him and now he wants me to marry him and of course I said not a chance and so now if I don't marry him when he returns he said he'll have me married off to one of his men. He was-'

'Wow! Slow down, it's okay!'

'But he's going to make me be a jihadi bride!'

'That is not going to happen Nasreen, I can promise you that…'

Ridge stopped talking as a huge row exploded in the first room and he heard chairs being flung and different raised voices all arguing at the same time. He could have sworn he heard a girl's voice but then some of these guys were so young their voices probably hadn't broken yet.

For a split second he'd thought that perhaps help was arriving but he told himself to get a grip. More worrying yet, he saw by the fearful reaction from Nasreen that this kind of stramash didn't happen that often.

One of the men came rushing in and went straight for Ridge. Nasreen had already turned away bracing her body for a beating and so he

241

fully expected he was in for the same kind of treatment. But instead he looked down and saw the man unshackle him from the chain before trying to pull him onto his feet. Ridge was easily twenty pounds heavier and for a second he thought about wrapping the chain around the man's neck but the look of utter desolation on the face of the girl took the wind out of his sails and he saw that it would be a futile gesture at this point.

He allowed the man to drag him out and on looking back to give the girl a reassuring smile, he saw she'd already dropped her head into her hands and so he just left her there, feeling somehow ashamed that he'd already failed her.

They chained him up in a smaller room further away from the main area but this time with no mattress, no dog and no-one to talk to. He propped himself against the corner and wrapped his arms around his aching legs trying to stop them slipping on the dusty floor. He was so tired. He needed to rest. He laid his head down just as he'd watched Nasreen do and shut his eyes. Then a key turned in his brain and the words he'd just heard came echoing back – *you're worse than her* – what or to whom was she referring? An awful thought began to coalesce in the darkest recesses of his confused brain as he drifted off into a fitful sleep.

Chapter 33

He was in a field hospital. It was 1917. The nurse was gently re-bandaging his head and he thought she was the most beautiful thing he'd ever seen. She'd been off duty all afternoon; there had been a lull in the fighting. He knew she must like him too as she'd sat for hours at the side of his bed as he finished his watercolour painting, his way of thanking her for writing in his treasured autograph book. She was French and he only knew a few words but still he could see love in those eyes and he laboured long and hard to try and distil her essence onto the page. He pointed to the finished picture and she stood up, the evening sunshine illuminating her beautiful long tresses. He imagined for a second what she might look like naked and then he blushed.

But she shook her head and scowled at him. Lifting a hand to her furrowed forehead, she pulled at her hair and he saw with a shock that it had been a wig and her real hair was short and ugly. She ripped off her nurse's tunic to reveal the rough grey and black uniform of a German soldier. He opened his mouth to say something but his throat was too dry and she just turned her head to the right and then he saw an orderly bring in the most delightfully aromatic tomato soup he'd ever known. It had been such a long time since he'd had real tomato soup but then he began to feel all strange and dizzy. He

tried to stay awake for he so longed to taste that
soup.

'Ridge! Wake up!
It's me! Sshh!
Keep quiet, I've brought you some soup.
It's real Heinz tomato soup!'

'Jake?
What the fuck?
Are you okay? How come you're-?'

'Sshh! Eat your soup and I'll tell you!'

Ridge took the proffered spoon and
began to scoop the still warm soup into his
mouth, taking a few attempts before he had
compensated for the fact that his wrists were
chained together. His head was spinning and he
wasn't sure he could cope with any further
complications.

'Listen! I've got these guys thinking that
I'm a regional commander!
From Balochistan!
I think there's a big job coming up and
they've got an ambitious new boss who's
trying to impress the leaders. He sounds
like a real charmer. He's got them all on
eggshells as they're just waiting for a
grand visitation from the Caliphate, over
from the Tribal Areas. I've just been

waiting for the right moment to get away with Nasreen. They are all dead nervous of showing up this new jerk because of his reputation. He's the one who nearly blew us up! I was trying to keep you out of this Ridge but now you're here you can help me and between us we'll stand a better chance of overpowering them. But we've got to pick the right moment. You look lousy by the way, what happened to your head?'

'My head? You wouldn't believe it, honestly. But how did you find these guys and more to the point how did you convince them you are one of them?'

'They're not the brightest! I saw them go to the apartment; you know how good I am at that stuff, right? But this time I was too late to do any good. I figured that you'd be next if I didn't do something.'

She lifted up the wooden bowl closer to his face to make it easier for him and he slurped greedily.

'I listened to them talking all the way from the apartment, through the woods and back to their car. I could hear what they were saying and I picked up on their nervousness and inexperience. The oldest man here is only twenty two! I hotwired a van and followed them all the way here. I know that there happens to be a high ranking fiercely tough female terrorist operating out of the border area from all that stuff we read on the plane and so I just planted the seed and let their imagination do the rest. I had hoped that someone might come to my aid but I didn't expect it to be you, no offence, but now this means we are both in danger.'

'So why don't we just make a run for it now before this *Shaggy* guy or whatever his name is, gets back? Surely we've got better odds?'

'How do you know about him? What did Nasreen tell you?'

'Nothing really. But you must've spoken just as much to her, haven't you? You're family for fuck's sake!'

'Of course! But any extra knowledge could make the difference between life and death, Ridge. Trust me! I'm good at this stuff! I know this Shahid has an arms base nearby and that's where his crack troops are. We're safe from them here, he won't pull them away for anything and it would be more than his life was worth if the police got hold of that. It would have been one of them who was with him at the Ashura bombing, the one that blew himself up!'

'How could you know that was him, have you seen him yet?'

'No Ridge, I haven't seen him but I've told you already. I listen. I'm a good listener. But you're tired, we're both tired. Get some more soup down you then try and sleep. I'd better not spend to long with you or it'll raise suspicion. See you in the morning!'

She kissed him on the head and tiptoed off. Maybe he was just tired but this wasn't making a whole lot of sense to him. He was glad that Jake was alive but he was mightily confused as to what kind of a game she was playing and just as when he had at that first meeting outside his flat, he was feeling more than a little wary of his elfin friend.

Chapter 34

'Would you listen Mam, I'm not dressing
up because I'm not bleedin' going,
alright!'

'Don't you take that tone with me, young
lady!
After everything you've put us through!
I thought you of all people would show
some respect for all the poor people who
died so as we could live free.
For the love of God, that's all I'm asking
of you!'

Orla groaned and leant against the wall
by her bedroom window. She could see the local
lads playing a quick game of football before
church. They were all especially smartly dressed
for the Remembrance Service and with the blue
sky and fresh autumn sunshine it made quite an
attractive pastoral sight. She held her swollen
stomach for a second. 'There's another wee
nipper who thinks he's playing football an' all'
she said, more to herself than to her mother who
was sitting on the edge of the bed tutting like an
agitated hen.

'Come away downstairs then and I'll get
us all a nice cup of tea.'

The little goalkeeper had already scuffed the right knee of his trousers and he was being so careful after that that the ball just sailed past him every time. Stupid really, he thought, playing football in long trousers. Black ones at that.

Then Sean dummied Malachy and sent a beauty of a volley towards him and the goal. But a serious wind came out of nowhere and the boy marvelled as the ball sailed higher and higher, right over his head. *No need to worry about that one*, he was thinking and he swivelled his head right back as he followed the ball until he was blinded by the sunshine.

But then the sun disappeared for a moment and he saw the rest of the boys, who were facing towards him, all look up at the sky behind him. As he turned he heard the terrifying noise of machinery like a thousand tractors all crashing their gears at the same time. He looked up to see a massive black shape burst out of the sun and then he promptly fell over backwards with the shock. Struggling to find his feet, he screwed up his eyes and tried to protect his face from being whipped by the sandy soil of the goal mouth which had become fiercely airborne.

The boys grouped together in awe at the side of the football pitch as a huge black helicopter slowly descended in front of them.

'I'm after telling yous! It's a fookin' Transformer!' cried Malachy, his arm over his face as the air was filled with dust, stones and the weekend's accumulated sweetie wrappers.

249

Seconds after the helicopter had landed and with the rotor blades still whirring viciously, a door must have opened on the far side because through the dust and chaos, the boys could see three black creatures emerge on to the football pitch. Two of them came around the back of the machine towards them while the third made its way across the road over to the nearest row of houses.

The two nearest to them proceeded to stand shoulder to shoulder as if to defend the machine from the terrible danger posed by the wee boys. Each of the huge men was dressed in identical black camouflages with a black beret and wraparound sunglasses. To complete the terrifying picture both men had skin which was as black as the inside of Mrs Mac Laverty's cavernous coal shed. None of the boys had ever seen a black man in their life.

'Naw!' said Sean, his voice cracking with emotion.

'They're fookin' aliens, for sure!'

The third man strode briskly across the road, checking the house details corresponded with the data on his hand-held device. Satisfied he had the correct target location in sight, he removed his sunglasses and his beret, smoothed back down his thick mane of gleaming black hair and set his muscular jaw from impassive to relaxed and smiling. He knew from experience that the first four seconds were vitally important.

It was the target's mother who answered, but he when he looked down, he saw the same fear and the same questions in her watery eyes.

'Good morning, Mrs O'Dowd. Please forgive this intrusion but may I speak with your daughter Orla? I am an old friend of her's and her husband's.'

When Orla poked her head around the door, gripping on to it as if the ground was going to fall away from her feet at any moment, he was struck once more by how beautiful she was. He fixed his most appealing professional smile and opened his arms like a welcoming uncle.

But the girl didn't move. Her eyes scanned his for any clues to the purpose of his visit. She had already been crying, he could see that of course and he quickly held out his hand for her to accompany him outside, for privacy.

She reached out tentatively, before recoiling in terror.

'Ridge! He's not… he isn't… is…'

'No Orla! He's not dead!

251

That's not why I'm here.
But it is bad news I'm afraid.
Real bad.'

The wee boys were still standing there, just as mute and motionless as the two black automatons guarding the helicopter, when there was a commotion on the other side of the road.

The boy saw old Mr and Mrs O'Dowd hugging that queer daughter of theirs who used to beat them up playing Tig not so very long ago. They were also in their Sunday best and the boy smoothed down his own matted jacket self consciously, knowing he was going to be totally for it in half an hour, but right now not caring a tinker's cuss about stuff like that.

He watched as the biggest of the black bastards then took Orla's arm and led her across the road and they disappeared behind the helicopter. Just then the massive rotors began to flex and roll and the two guards peeled off to the right and round to the door of the machine.

As the boys stood open-mouthed, the helicopter began to rattle and roar and the boys were forced to cover their ears as the raucous intensity of the jet engine start-up became too painful to bear. Then just as quickly as it had arrived but even more noisily, the helicopter lifted into the azure sky and vanished into thin air.

'They've fookin' stolen her!
They've stolen our Orla!'

No sooner had the dust begin to settle over their once immaculate school blazers, did the boys begin their huddle, swapping versions of what they were going to boast about tomorrow at school.

Only Mr and Mrs O'Dowd were left in the end. Standing there in their finest clothes as if that alone could have somehow atoned for the terrible misdeeds of their wayward daughter.

Chapter 35

Logan sat alone in his untidy bedroom with only a small bedside light to see by. He'd hardly spent any time in the tiny apartment for weeks, with the hotel allowing him to crash there any time he'd gone over the score which had been practically every night of late.

He kept no alcohol whatsoever in the place and that had been one of his main rules to keep reasonably sane. It was, in fact, his only rule to be fair. But he was glad at this precise moment because he was so scared he could have put away a whole bottle of gin without pausing for breath. But that wouldn't do anyone any good now would it, he scolded himself.

If he was completely honest, he was very scared yes, but he was even more excited and given the choice between this or sitting up at the Monal doing the Times crossword he knew where he'd rather be.

So here he was, awaiting an imminent visit from the assassin relative of a man he barely knew who had managed in the space of twenty four hours to have transformed Logan from a bad tempered but harmless drunkard civil servant to a double murderer and potential hero of epic proportions. Even he found it hard to believe.

He'd been impressed with the calm and methodical way Colm had interviewed him over the phone. For that was what it had felt like. Logan got the impression that this was a man who wasn't too keen on surprises. Colm had asked him how many good men he could trust in an awkward or military situation and by that Logan had implicitly understood he meant 'trust with your life.' When Logan had hesitantly replied 'none….,' there had been a considered silence. Then Colm had said, 'Good. That shows me you are not a fool and certainly not the fool that you portray yourself as. A man who doesn't value his own life would be no use to me!'

Logan wasn't sure whether to be pleased or insulted. But one thing he'd been secretly very happy about over the last few hours was that after a long time in the dark woods of self despair, he finally felt as if he truly did have a reason to live. Now sitting here he knew that instead of the numbing comfort of gin sloughing through his soft body he had exchanged that for the fire and electricity of survival!

The front door rapped twice. Jeepers! He hadn't even heard anyone approaching! Logan cautiously went to the door and peered through the security spy hole. The door rapped again, harder this time, impatiently even. He unlocked the door and stood back.

Chapter 36

Colm stepped in out of the stifling heat and saw a large but out of condition man in a crumpled linen suit with blood stains all down the front. Satisfied that the blood was someone else's, he nodded to the man and shook his enormous hand. This was a man I can work with, he thought. He threw down his large black rucksack, looked around at the messy room and ran a hand through his thick red hair.

'Jaysus. You've had a break-in then? Were they after leaving you a kettle? I'm parched!'

The two men sat and talked quietly for only an hour or so before Colm had to crash. He'd been on the go for too long and he knew it wasn't going to get any easier when he walked back out there. He'd scouted the vicinity of the apartment for a good while before he knocked on the door and he was satisfied that there was no immediate threat. Logan had agreed that had anyone asked a neighbour, they'd genuinely have said they thought he'd moved out weeks ago.

Colm knew Logan was scared and although the big fellow must have some hidden talents to take out two terrorists single-handedly he also knew from experience that when civilians like him are scared witless they don't take in information too readily and when the brown stuff starts flying they go and forget it all anyway.

No, there was only one way to do this. Boy's Own adventure. Nice and simple. Walk straight in the door, no fucking about, less to go wrong. He'd got Logan to arrange a meeting just before dawn with two security personnel he'd vouched for, ex-military, salt of the earth types. The men hadn't been told anything about what was required of them but when Colm had taken the phone and asked them to bring every pistol, rifle, grenade or explosive charges they could lay their grubby hands on, totally off the record, and not to talk to another living soul on pain of death, Colm reckoned they'd have a pretty good idea that they weren't being asked to park cars at the Commissioner's garden party.

Five hours later, the two men, Taff and Duncan, had arrived and Colm was pleased to see they'd brought a small arsenal with them. He wasn't going to ask them where it had come from. The three of them talked quietly while Logan was left to struggle with the Kevlar vest which Colm had lent him earlier. The bewildered Commissioner had been like a young boy at Christmas when Colm had disgorged the high tech equipment from his capacious rucksack. The bullet proof vest hadn't been intended for Logan but the terrorist nest sounded cramped and the likelihood of ricochet injuries would be high. The vest was obviously too small but Colm had assured him it would be better than nothing.

The basic premise was that since Logan had been perceived as a good friend to the both the impoverished inhabitants of the slum and also the terrorists, if he was to be seen transporting *another* Western kidnap victim then who would want to stop him.

This time it would be Colm wearing the black hood and the other two men were to conceal themselves in the car, drawing straws for the less attractive proposition of the dark and cramped trunk. The men had passed around crumpled photos of Ridge and Nasreen. Instructions had been to minimise collateral damage but almost in the same breath Colm had warned that there would be no back up team, this was unofficial and they wouldn't be in a position to take prisoners. Once out and away they would be extremely vulnerable to being harried all the way out of the slum area and so it was vital that they were in and out quickly and cleanly with maximum speed and minimum upset.

Taff turned to Duncan, punching him on the shoulder.

'Just like you SAS lads eh? That's what your wife was telling mine anyways. That you'd be in and out so fast she wouldn't even know you'd been there!'

Colm tried to keep a straight face as he snapped a live magazine into an assault rifle and checked the lines.

'Nice gun lads, Heckler and Koch to be sure, but I'm not after seeing one like this before?'

'It's an HK53 sir, cut-down from the 33. Both me and Spunky here, we were with the close protection squad boyos in Helmand before we got out.
They're great guns these are. Pack more punch than a MP5 so they do, real champion! Only got the two here unfortunately, and the pistols.'

'That's fine Taff.
I've got my old Browning 9mm, wouldn't be without it so I wouldn't.'

He remembered back in Mexico, when Ridge had joked about Colm and his treasured Browning and that he probably slept with it. Colm had agreed immediately that he always did unless he was doing his 'sleeping naked hanging upside down up a tree' routine. He knew that Ridge would have no answer to that and to this day he doubted whether his brother-in-law ever believed him. But he alone knew the truth and he swore by the beneficial effects of his unusual habit particularly the way he could slow his heart rate down to 40 beats per minute.

'And lads, I've got a wee present for you two if you're up for it. Have a look at these. You ever used them before?'

The men continued to discuss the ordinance they'd be using and it was a few minutes before Colm noticed that Logan had been standing in the background very quietly. He was experienced enough to know what it meant when men went suddenly silent, especially civilians who weren't used to the nerves before an op. It meant they were terrified and the expression 'scared witless' was chillingly apposite in these circumstances. He needed to be able to rely on this man and so made it his mission to put the big man at his ease.

'You okay there, Logan? Ye'd think they were after talking about the accessories on a new car rather than weapons for killing people, right?'

Logan nodded.

'I bet you never thought that you'd have bumped off a couple yerself eh?
And all on yer own too.
At least this time you know you have some real professionals with you this time. Jeezo, a wee bit of training and you'd be putting us all out of a job.'

Colm didn't think it would help Logan's confidence if he was honest enough to tell him how lucky he'd been to get out alive.

'I wasn't quite on my own. I had Ridge with me after all.'

'Now you've got something there, Logan! There's something jammy about Ridge, so there is.
I don't know what it is or how he does it but we've stepped through the mouth of hell and back, so we have and we're still here. He saved my life, if the truth be known and I don't mind telling you that! So if anyone could survive in that place, it'll be him, I've no worries about that and as long as you throw yer lot in with him you'll be fine!'

Logan hesitated for a moment, and Colm could read the signals. He knew that the civil servant was still in turmoil. Someone had once explained the feeling to Colm as being in a mental tumble-dryer, strangely exhilarated but nervous at the same time.

'So what would you like me to do old chap?
Just stay out at the car? Maybe turn it for a hasty exit, perhaps?'

Colm looked at him carefully and then at the limited weapons left on the kitchen table. 'Have you ever handled a weapon? A pistol maybe? I could really do with a fourth man to be honest.'

'A weapon? Of course!
By Jove I nearly forgot about it, it's been
so long!
Wait until you see this!'

He disappeared into another room and
they could hear furniture being shifted and
cupboard doors creaking. The three men turned
back to the weapons again and Colm outlined
what he had in mind for them.

Shortly after, Logan burst into the
kitchen brandishing a huge shotgun, his eyes
wide with excitement. 'What do you think of this
beauty then?' The others dived for the floor.
'Oops! Sorry!' He pointed the gun at the ceiling
before stretching out to allow a red faced Colm
to take it from him and check if it was loaded.

'Jaysus Logan! Don't do that again
alright? But what's this?
She is a real beauty to be sure! Yours?'

'Yes, of course! Only used once I'm
afraid. She's a Robertson. Proper British
gun, you know.
Not like that Spanish rubbish! That's
French walnut too.'

Colm held the gun lightly in one hand.
Perfect balance, light for a double barrelled

shotgun. He held it up and squinted down the barrel. 'Nice lines too, must have cost a packet!'

'Perk of the job!' Logan beamed. 'I sometimes have to go on hunts up north, with important guests, that sort of thing. We hunt Ibex mostly.'

'So you can actually use this thing then?'

'Of course I can old bean!
I've been on shoots ever since I was a young boy. Bagged my first brace of grouse by the time I was twelve, I'll have you know!'

Colm nodded and smiled at the assembled men.

'Grand!
Gentlemen I think we have our team!
Listen carefully, this is the new plan.'

Chapter 37

The intense heat building up in the back of the car was suffocating him as he fumbled for his boot knife in the dark. Taff initially had had his reservations about this job and about that upper-class twit Logan, but he'd been impressed with how the man had accepted everything without a word of complaint. Even when he had watched Taff puncture several holes in the bodywork and lid of the trunk before squeezing himself in along with his kit. *And that is precisely what I'm going to do any moment now once I've wriggled my knife up here.* He tried to relax and slow his breathing down, just like he'd been trained to do. He'd rather live long enough to see daylight this morning but right now he wasn't too worried about dying in combat. Unless he did something drastic he would either suffocate or be poisoned by exhaust fumes.

The checkpoints had been the only aspect of the mission that worried Colm as they were the one thing beyond his control. They could be such an unexpected complication, depending on who was on patrol at that point and what had been going on around that time. He was thankful that both Logan and the silent Duncan seemed to be known to the security guards on duty that morning and so despite his initial concerns they sailed through without arousing any suspicion. He did notice on glancing back that Duncan had a hand over his compact Sig Sauer automatic pistol. The kind of guy he needed on a job like this. One that didn't believe in taking any chances.

Before long they had reached the outskirts of Islamabad and already the traffic had thinned and the quality of the road had deteriorated significantly. Logan positioned Colm so as to give the impression that his hands were handcuffed behind him and then covered his head with the black cotton bag. Colm had taken the precaution of cutting two small eye holes so as to be more prepared for the sudden brightness. And there should be a considerable amount of brightness if everything went to plan.

Logan had opened the trunk of the car for a minute to check Taff was still alive and then help him don his SF100 respirator and ear defenders. Getting the thumbs up from Taff, Logan then pulled the lid down and tied it with a thin plastic cord so it looked closed but wouldn't prevent Taff from charging out. Duncan pulled a tarpaulin over himself and lay in the footwell and just before they set off he smiled as he heard Taff cursing furiously through the fabric of the seating.

And so for the second time in as many days, Logan found himself driving a hooded kidnap victim down the narrow streets of the Rawalpindi slums although this time there was a lot more quiet conversation going on which he was grateful for as it took his mind off his heaving innards and shaking hands.

'Now keep me informed of everything you can see Logan, these wee holes don't let me see a whole lot, to be honest. I need constant information from you.'

'Okay, it's really quiet. There's hardly anyone about compared to last time, do you think they know we're coming?'

'Impossible, Logan.
We only knew what we were going to do a half hour ago ourselves! Now keep yer eyes peeled and listen very carefully while I go through it just the once.
The boys will go in first with you and me behind. Their job is to penetrate as far as they can as quickly as they can, then Duncan will throw the Flash Bang's or stun grenades to you. They will go off with a blinding flash, so they will, and they'll let off a bang that'd wake the dead. It's over 150 decibels right enough, which is plenty loud enough to destabilise the balance function of anyone unfortunate to be in the same enclosed space.
This means that Ridge, Zakia and Nasreen will need to be helped out of there as they'll be too dizzy to walk on

their own. That will be one of your jobs,
okay?
If you reach into my middle right pocket
there, you'll find a couple of ear plugs.
Not brilliant but they'll stop you going
deaf, so they will!
Got them? Grand.
Now, when we first arrive I want you to
turn the car around as quick as you can
then be out and handy with that big
fuckin' gun of yours!
Remember 'The Italian Job?'
Well we might need you to *blow the
bloody doors off*, okay.
To be honest, there'll probably not be
any need for it but on top of the grenades
it'll be good to have the shotgun for
effect more than anyone else. The poor
wee bastards will think the world has
fallen in on them by then anyway.
Just promise me one thing. That you'll
not be after shooting any of us in the
back! But if anyone comes running at
you, don't hesitate!'

Logan nodded, his throat suddenly dry.
Then realising the futility of that gesture, he
coughed hard and got enough spit to reply.

'Got that!
Stand back.
Shoot any solid objects that get in the
way and anyone else running at me.

Help the others out. Splendid!'

Then he saw where they were and swallowed hard again.

'Colm! We're here!
This is it!'

Chapter 38

Half asleep and his first panicked thought had been that a helicopter had crashed through the roof. The Clutha Bar disaster was still fresh in the minds of most Glaswegians and the city was still waiting impatiently to find out why a police helicopter should fall like a stone through the roof of one of the city's busiest live music venues killing and maiming so many people.

But then he recognised the sound of gunfire and guessed that at last Logan had come good. He struggled to his feet and began wrestling with his shackles and that was when the second bomb must have gone off. A pulse of white light fought all the way down the narrow corridor to his dark room followed by a deafening bang. Momentarily blinded and with his ears ringing, Ridge staggered and dropped to his knees as the whole building seemed to lift off the ground and then settle in a cloud of dust. The meagre string of electric bulbs had been fried and he couldn't see a thing. His guts tightened and he hoped the terrorists hadn't detonated a suicide attack.

After a frenzy of shouting a third smaller bomb exploded but this time he was ready for it. However he didn't expect a soldier in breathing apparatus to crash straight through the wall followed by a tsunami of shrieking and gunfire. He thought he heard Zakia scream in terror and as the man made straight for him he held up his hands as best he could in helpless surrender.

'You Ridge Walker?' The soldier roared through his respirator as he looked down on him and a shaft of cold white light pierced through the smoke with surgical precision. Ridge nodded as the man drew out a black knife and broke the lock on his shackles with a single blow before grabbing his arm and yelling 'Come with me!'

The dark corridor was dark and Ridge fell over a wet and bloody corpse, his hands floundering in a warm liquid as he attempted to find his feet. The soldier hauled him up and pushed him on ahead into the worst of the smoke and dust. Then he saw Colm standing impassively as usual and the two men hugged each other, oblivious to the maelstrom around them.

As suddenly as the noise had begun it had abated and Ridge allowed himself to be led out. He was relieved to see Nasreen leaning against the side of a car being sick and Logan beside her, his hair thick with grey ash and standing straight up making him look like a cross between Boris Johnson and Johnny Rotten.

Where was Zakia? His heart began to sink as he realised she wasn't among the living and through the relentless ringing in his ears he could make out the faint skirl of bagpipes once again. He thought how he was going to have to tell Masood that she was gone and that her cheeky smile was no more. A second soldier appeared dragging one of the men who'd been guarding him. The man was terribly thin and Ridge could see that one of his legs had been badly broken below the knee, the white of the bone contrasting vividly with the blackness of his grimy skin.

'Logan! HERE QUICK!' Colm bellowed.
'Ask him where the others are!
There must be more of them than this for sure and find out where is the girl Zakia?'

The man was obviously in a lot of pain yet Ridge couldn't afford to consider his suffering as he was suddenly consumed by the hope that his little friend had not been killed after all and he urged Logan on to find the answers. But the weakening man could barely talk and as he pulled out a blood stained piece of paper his head fell backwards into the arms of one of the soldiers who only seconds later passed a hand down gently over his eyes.
    Logan stared at the scrap of paper and then up at Ridge, shaking his head.

'Colm! There's another location! Deeper in. The girl is there but we'll never find it. Even this poor chap had to use a map. Here! Look for yourself, it's damn near impossible to make out!'

Logan was shouting like he'd gone deaf. Must have been the blast, Ridge decided and he staggered over to the car and took a long drink proffered by one of the soldiers. The man smiled but Ridge knew what the man had just done to save his life and he just nodded his thanks. He remembered Zakia going on about an arms dump and that's where the top fighters were based. He wanted to try and find her but he knew there would be little appetite from anyone else. They had Nasreen. Job done.

'There is another base! I heard Zakia talk about it. This was just a holding spot for keeping Nasreen and I. But the other place will be heavily guarded Colm, that's where they keep all of their explosives like what they used for the bombing the other day.'

Logan stared at Ridge, a fresh panic creasing his red face. He stood up and handed the slip of paper to Colm who immediately turned away, his phone at his ear. Taff and Duncan looked at each other and some unspoken agreement must have been made as they began preparing to leave. Logan was yelling at Colm's back. 'It's too dangerous! And I don't think that…' He stopped shouting as Colm held up his hand in a sudden warning. Colm pointed to his ears and Logan made a childish face for a second before removing his ear plugs.

'You go back Logan, if that's what you want to do!
Guys? What about you?'

For the first time since they'd met, Duncan spoke.

'We're with the Commissioner. Our job is done.'

Colm knew there was no point in trying to negotiate. When a man says as little as Duncan, you had better pay attention when he does speak.

'Taff? Can I have your pistols?'

'They're yours. Best of Welsh luck to you sir! Beats the Irish every time!'

'Logan. Give that shotgun to Ridge will you? We'll bring it back safely I promise you.'

'Absolutely old bean! My pleasure! The shooting season doesn't start for a while anyway. Here Ridge, I've only got half a dozen cartridges I'm afraid.'

'And Logan. The vest too. Give it to Ridge, will you?'

They exchanged brief handshakes and Ridge said he'd see Nasreen back at the Consulate very soon. Her eyes thanked him but he could tell she was still in a state of shock.

'You sure about this Colm?'

Ridge looked carefully at his brother in law as the two of them turned away from the burning building and stepped out into the unknown. He saw a look in his face that he'd seen before and it scared him then just as much as it had the first time. For a red headed Irishman, it was strange the way his eyes could look so black at times. Colm stopped him and looked around slowly before putting a hand on his shoulder.

'Ridge. If you'd wanted to go back then you've just missed the last bus home. Do you want to find your friend or not?'

Ridge gulped and started walking alongside him. He knew there was something else going on here. He knew what Colm was like.

'Yes of course I do! But I don't get why *you* do.
You've never even met her have you?'

'Ridge. There's got to be more going on here than us just rescuing one wee girl!

274

Sure I want to find her. An' I want this to be over for you, sure I do.
But we have a chance here, to do something beyond that. This Shahid fellow will be there too. He isn't just your run of the mill wee eedjit, now is he?'

'Jesus! You're doing a fucking homer aren't you?
You can't even come to the aid of your own bastarding family without making money out of it! I can't believe that you'd-'

His throat was being squeezed so hard he barely registered that his feet were off the ground. He vainly tried to bop Colm on the head with the shotgun but his vision was going all silvery and he didn't seem to have full control of his body any more.

'YOU brought me here!
Don't you *ever* forget that!
There are far more important things in this world than money!
You should be after knowing that by now boy!'

They walked on in silence, little brown faces nervously watching them from the shadows, staring at the guns and at the look on the taller one's face. Ridge felt as if he was

275

accompanying a ghost along this dusty track. Yet he didn't feel scared any more. You didn't need to fear anything when you had Death by your side.

Chapter 39

The heat had become unbearably sticky. Ridge wondered if they were walking in circles and he was starting to doubt if the scrap of paper was actually a genuine map or not. Their progress was painfully slow and each time they stopped for Colm to hold up the map to catch any available light and try to match it to where they were standing, Ridge could feel a panic rising up in his guts. He felt sure they were lost in this confusing warren of tin shacks, narrow crossroads and stinking culverts and everywhere he looked he saw the baleful eyes of barely dressed children sitting in the filth, silently watching their every move.

Colm hadn't spoken since their altercation twenty minutes before and Ridge was too tired, scared and confused to make the first move. On one hand he knew that Colm wouldn't put him in mortal danger without a good reason and Ridge had seen how much he'd been looking forward to becoming an uncle, more than Ridge had expected for such a man's man. So then why would he risk the life of the wee child's father? But then, in situations like this, he could be so markedly different, like a man possessed.

Looking at his face right now, less expressive than a block of granite, Ridge doubted that domestic family concerns were high on his list of priorities right now. So *was* there a hidden agenda? Or was this how the true professionals went about finishing a job? Ridge still only knew sketchy details of Colm's murky past, working undercover for the British during The Troubles, but the one thing that had been obvious even to a rank amateur like him was that Colm was a survivor. Nothing was left to chance. He dotted all the i's and eliminated anyone who crossed him. Somehow, he had risen out of the mire and made a life for himself elsewhere and so Ridge determined that he would once again put his trust in this man.

The narrow pathways had widened without Ridge noticing and he felt a hand press his chest. 'Hold on,' Colm whispered. 'I think we're close, very close.'

Chapter 40

Ridge crouched down behind a burned out car and peered through the shimmering haze to where Colm had pointed. The whole area ahead had widened considerably and it looked to Ridge like they had found an improvised roundabout which encircled a loose arrangement of tin shacks and abandoned vehicles, some of which had somehow been stacked one upon another. He felt like he was in the middle of a stage set for a low budget dystopian movie.

Colm passed him his military grade binoculars and now as he could see a lot better, Ridge was looking at two distinct islands, one in front of the other. The second one further back was lower in profile and had what appeared to be a chicken wire fence enclosing it. Both of these islands were covered by camouflage netting and Ridge realised he was looking a double roundabout and there were so many rubber tires scattered around that it reminded him slightly of the 'banger racing' their dad had taken him to, over on the mainland, when he and his brother had been excitable wee boys.

Colm slipped the phone back in his black flak jacket and turned to pull Ridge closer, his eyes shining.

'Right then!
We know that there are two areas ahead, both populated with enemy fighters. I now know we're after looking at four in

the rear bunker and eleven in the closer
one including one woman or child.
That'll be yer wee friend so it will!
And from what I've been told it looks
like she's in an area on her own right at
the back so I reckon she's been rumbled
and they're holding her captive. Probably
until the big chief arrives and I wouldn't
give much for her chances when that
happens!'

'How do 'we' know all this?'

Colm pointed upwards and smiled.

'Eyes in the sky, so we have. Eyes in the
sky!
So it's good that Zakia is separated from
the others but we still need to act fast
alright!'

Ridge nodded, not fully understanding.
All fear gone now and full trust restored in this
infinitely resourceful and endlessly surprising
man.

'Same as before Ridge.
Full frontal but we'll need to be a wee bit
more canny so we will, I've only got one
of these and cricket was never my strong
point!'

Ridge turned to see what looked like a
dusty green lemon. Colm answered the question
before he'd even mouthed the words.

'It's a fragmentation grenade. M67. Nast
wee fucker but very effective. Got it from
Taff, a present from our Americans
friends back in Islamabad so I believe!
The real trick with this is to throw it in
just the right place.
Can kill up to fifty feet but I've seen
damage done at over five hundred so it's
not a toy, sure it's not! But sure, you'll
know all about that, won't you?'

Ridge had been blown up by one of
Colm's grenades in the past. Stolen and then
used against them during a fierce battle with a
Mexican drugs cartel in which there had been
heavy casualties with Ridge being fortunate not
to have died. But even though his left shoulder
had also been shot to smithereens and it still
pained him to this day, he was right handed and
had always been a good thrower.

Growing up with the World Stone
Skimming Championships on a nearby island
might have had something to do with that.
Originally just another excuse to get pissed on an
otherwise dull Autumn Sunday, the
championships had grown into a well publicised
tourist magnet drawing media coverage from all
over the world. All the wee boys had become
expert at skimming the small slate projectiles

across the flat black water of the abandoned slate quarries.

'I'll have a go Colm if you'd like. I'd feel safer throwing one of your grenades, that way I'll know it won't go anywhere near me!'

'Unless you drop it ye eedjit!' Colm laughed.

'No, yer fine! I'll do it, sure enough, but I'll need you right up by me for cover okay, so no time for shrinking violets! You got that?'

'Cheeky bastard!'

Colm gave him a rude hand gesture and then turned away sharply, his phone at his ear within seconds. Ridge couldn't hear any distinct words but he got the ill-tempered gist of it. Somebody wanted Colm to do something that he didn't want to do. In Ridge's experience, this wasn't normally an easy thing to achieve and as an uneasy sensation gripped his heart like a cold dead hand, he crouched down impatiently waiting for an end to this nightmare.

It struck him that Logan still had all three of his mobile phones but then, still thinking of Sorsay, he had the absurd thought that this was probably a good thing considering how easily he could get killed by an ill timed phone call.

His maternal great grandfather *had* been killed by a phone call in a way. Archie had been a manual labourer on the railways in Ayrshire and as was customary in those days he'd been working his shift as normal even though his wife had been taken into hospital to have their second child.

And so half way through another hard day, digging the unforgiving flint earth, a fellow worker had shouted over to him that when he'd just passed the offices they'd said to tell Archie to get to the office phone as soon as he could. Apparently the man had yelled his congratulations and that he was now the father of a bouncing baby girl. Poor Archie had been so excited that he'd thrown down his spade and run across the railway tracks, straight into the path of a heavy goods train.

So in the space of one short hour the world had welcomed the youngest member of his clan and despatched one of the oldest.

Ridge glanced across the dusty wasteland towards the two bunkers. A lot could happen in the next hour. Most of the people over there would most likely be dead by then and there was always the chance that he would be joining them. He was acutely aware that he himself was just about to become a father and that perhaps he was trapped in a generational 'Groundhog Day,' destined never to see his newborn child. But then, as he felt Colm's hand on his shoulder, he decided that no, he wasn't going to let that happen to him. Not today.

Colm pointed across the wide space to their left. Marginally closer to the bunkers, it would afford them a far better view of the rear one. Ridge was nervous about crossing such an open space but as Colm pointed out, no-one appeared to be on sentry duty and as far as he could tell their presence hadn't been noted yet.

'But don't go counting on that for much longer,' he said, without a glimmer of a smile. 'Quick, let's move!' Ridge jumped up and chased Colm's shadow across the rutted dust track, feeling the full force of the midday sun on the back of his neck. They'd begun to appreciate just how precisely the loose assortment of wrecked cars had been placed and this was helping more than hindering the pair of them as they could now see right past the first bunker into the front entrance of the rear one.

'This must be their forward position that we've just taken over,' Colm whispered.

'They can't have anticipated any attacks or got wind of our earlier stunt and that suits me just fine! Now it's time for the real fireworks, and don't be giving me any grief 'cos I've about had it up to here already!'

'What do you mean?' Ridge asked cautiously.

'Well, it must be obvious to you by now that we're not quite on our own now, yeah?'

Ridge nodded, but only because it seemed the appropriate response. He remained as clueless as before but wasn't about to let on.

'We've got the Yanks up there, watching every move we're making. They turned up just *after* we rescued the wee lassie.'

He turned and looked Ridge straight in the eye.

'Ye don't think I'd have gone into this with just yourself to help me, do you? No offence! But Orla would fookin' kill me if anything happened to you now, ye daft wee prick!'

Ridge knew the relief must have washed over his face as Colm laughed quietly whilst he knelt and quickly checked the two Sig pistols before handing one up to him, butt first.

'Right, time is getting on so let's get this party started, okay?
What I want you to do is this. I'm going to start carefully peppering the forward

bunker until we get a reaction and then when anyone is stupid enough to come out, I want you to use that big gun of yours to take them out as quickly and accurately as you can, no matter what else is happening. And when you see what is gonna happen you'll see why I'm so sure they'll be like turkey's voting for Christmas any time soon! But keep down just for a wee minute more will you?'

Chapter 41

He wasn't sure what Colm had in his hands but it looked like a small torch, like the expensive ones he favoured on his treasured old mountain bike. Colm leant carefully over the jagged edge of what had been a car roof and glanced up at the hazy blue sky. Intrigued, Ridge peered around the side but still he couldn't work out what the hell was going on.

Just then he thought he saw a bright reflection from the second mound and he pulled back nervously, hearing Colm cursing him under his breath. Not knowing how Colm could even have seen him from there, he sat still for an agonisingly long few seconds but nothing seemed to have happened and so he poked his head out again. This time he could see the same light bouncing off the few available reflective surfaces and he clicked as he realised two things. It wasn't him that Colm was talking to and that it was Colm who was controlling the bright light playing across the bunker.

Colm ducked down and quickly grabbed Ridge, pulling him inwards just as the first missiles hit. Realising that his brother-in-law always meant business, Ridge had guessed that the tables were about to be turned.

But this was unlike anything Ridge had ever experienced. The previously dependable and solid surface that he had always known as Earth disintegrated as a bass kick from hell literally turned everything loose under foot.

Ridge gasped as his insides juddered and he floundered helplessly onto his back as above them the sky flashed bright white then crimson before black clouds of smoke and debris choked their battered lungs. He felt himself being roughly pulled up on to his feet.

'Come on!' Colm shouted, his grey ash face only inches from Ridge and his mutant red eyes gleaming hideously as they scanned his own. He fumbled for the shotgun, his ears buzzing, as the ground reverberated again for a few seconds as yet another explosive detonated deep in the crater where the second bunker used to be.

Already Colm was firing his Browning with fast and lethal precision. He'd also been deadly accurate in his premonition that the sudden destruction of the arms dump would cause utter chaos and Ridge might have felt some small pity for the men who were getting picked off so efficiently had a bullet not ripped into his chest knocking him onto his back, his shotgun pointing up towards the menacing mushroom cloud polluting the sky above them.

He lay stunned for a brief moment, fingering the dent where the Kevlar vest had stopped the rifle shot. Aware of how lucky he'd been, he thought of Orla and the baby and then of Jake over there in the eye of the storm. He jumped up and gave himself a shake.

This was a serious as it was going to get. Ridge crouched over a section of blackened metal and brought the gun up to his shoulder. It sighted far better than the ancient shotguns he'd used all through his boyhood and he tried to blank out the mayhem of smoke and noise. He closed his left eye, the grime making both eyes water uncontrollably and he fought to regain his composure, breathing out slowly and focussing on the first target he could find. He'd squeezed the trigger before thinking about the consequences and when he saw the black shadow of a man crumple to the ground it made him feel sick to his core.

But there was little time for sympathy. The bullets were flying in both directions now and as there didn't appear to have been any damage done to the first bunker, Colm's turkeys had seemingly recovered their poise and were now proving to be resilient fighters.

Ridge feared that despite assistance from above, they were still heavily outnumbered and he couldn't see how the two of them were ever going to be able to overcome the increasingly fierce resistance from such an open position. They were being strafed continuously and Ridge knew that the opposition had an exact bead on their position as each time he tried to look over the parapet there would be the resulting flurry of bullets exploding all around where his head was going to have been.

Ridge glanced up at Colm who was still firing steadfastly in a controlled rhythm, albeit more slowly than before. Colm must have seen the panic and confusion in his eyes and he crouched down beside him.

'Almost there, Ridge!
You've just got to keep it going for a wee while longer!
I'll be after chucking this in a minute, so I will, and then it will be all over, for sure!
But when I do, Ridge, I want you to stay back for a wee bit okay?
Until it's safe. No point in us gassin' you now is there?'

Ridge stared at the grenade, his eyes wide with terror. He saw his brother-in –law look up anxiously at the black sky as if he was deciding if the weather was going to brighten up for a wee bit of fishing. He wondered who was at the other end of the phone which Colm kept pulling out and what good any more bombs were going to do when Jake was trapped just a few metres away through the smoke and flames. Inside that cauldron of death.

He worried that he was going into shock because he began to feel distanced from the noise which had all of a sudden seemed that much more muted and indistinct. He just looked up hopelessly as Colm snapped a fresh magazine into his Browning before jamming a second pistol into his belt at the small of his back.

'Come on! I need you to cover me!' Colm yelled down at him. Ridge got up gingerly as if in a hypnotic trance and shouldered the shotgun. He felt a hand briefly grasp the back of

290

his neck and then Colm was gone. Ridge fired and another black shape dropped out of sight. Weaving his way through the smoke like an apparition, Colm was keeping his body low to the ground and Ridge panicked that he might shoot his brother-in-law by accident. He took a deep breath and fixed his eyes on the bunker and waited for movement.

Colm had vanished. Ridge wanted to know where he was but knew he couldn't afford to take his eyes off the bunker for even a second. If he lost his marker and one of them got Colm he wouldn't be able to stand it. Not after everything they had gone through.

Then out at the periphery of his vision, he saw a black shape rise and fall again into the dust just before the whole surreal scene in front of him became momentarily painted in the coldest of white light. In that hideous second he saw the terrified faces of the men frozen for ever in a macabre reminder of the pointlessness of war like a too-sharp photograph from the trenches of the First World War.

Then he realised that he too must be visible and he ducked down just as the blast wave rolled across the wasteland. His ears were ringing painfully and as he jumped back up he saw the sky had become streaked with red lines and he realised they were flares like the ones he had seen many times over the sea, back on the island. Taking advantage of this extra light and not questioning where they had come from or what they were for, he let off a couple of shots without aiming specifically at a target. It was then that he noticed the black spiders.

Chapter 42

The man dropped silently onto the hot dusty ground and traversed across the open space with a nimbleness that belied a man of his size. He was the first. This might not have been the only Black Ops sortie that these men had taken part in over the last few weeks but it was definitely the most leftfield. So because of that, he had felt it incumbent on him to lead the charge. The men were all highly trained killing machines and they didn't ask questions. Not any more. They were to be well remunerated for their services, yet more anonymous bank transfers into numbered accounts in overseas locations.

They'd all served their country proudly and then found themselves returned to a nation which had become morally bankrupt, financially impoverished and desperately short of any consideration for the rest of the world. Unceremoniously dumped onto the unemployment scrap-heap and deeply suspicious of the motives of their political masters, the vast majority of the Vets had drifted back overseas into quasi-official military units like this one. Scratch that. Not like this one. There had never been an outfit like this, of that he was goddammned positive.

He watched as the others fell to earth, virtually invisible to the untrained eye. Dressed in Special Forces black fatigues complete with infra-red goggles and laser sighted carbines they would not have looked out of place in a CGI rendered futuristic battle scene. He signalled his wing man and the order was quickly relayed through the team.

They had a very simple mission objective.

Retrieve three high value assets and eliminate all others, with extreme prejudice.

Colm had frantically dug himself into the unyielding dry soil and he waited until the first wave of ghost troopers passed by him, receiving a cursory nod from the closest of them. There was a brief and lively exchange of gunfire and even to his experienced ear it could have been mistaken for Chinese fire-crackers, so short and intense was the noise. As he prepared to advance, Colm nearly jumped out of his skin as a large black face appeared out of the smoke, white teeth gleaming under the goggles giving him a look of a giant mutant insect. The soldier lifted Colm clean into the air and for the briefest of moments the two men hugged amid the chaos like lost brothers reunited once more. Seconds later the huge bear like soldier turned and disappeared through the smoke towards the now much quieter bunker.

Colm looked behind him and waved to where he knew Ridge would be hiding and then he chased after the soldier, anxious to be among the first into the bunker. Just in case.

Still there was sporadic gunfire and as Colm drew closer he saw that the perimeter of the bunker was encircled by the black-clad troops, each one crouched down on one knee in an identical pose, their laser-sighted rifles pointed accusingly inwards towards the centre of the target area like deadly spokes.

Then there was the eerie sight of hands in the air, tentative at first then thrust up high through the dense carpet of smoke. The signal went back and Colm felt himself being pushed by a soldier and taking his cue, he dashed forwards, knowing full well that his lion-hearted young brother-in-law wouldn't be far behind. The soldiers wasted no time in throwing the survivors to the ground, hands searching efficiently for booby trapped devices and so Colm pushed further into the compound choking on the acrid smoke. He heard Ridge calling for him in the distance, just as he stumbled into the low-roofed central area to be met with the pointy end of a M4 Carbine.

Immediately in front of him were two men, both injured and one bleeding seriously and only barely conscious. The other man could not have been more animated and his eyes flashed madly around the room as if he was somehow still expecting to escape from this. But the person brandishing the assault rifle at Colm was a woman and Colm quickly recognised her from a photo in his back pocket, just as Ridge confirmed this with an involuntary exclamation.

'Jake?
What the-'

'Don't move Ridge! I will shoot him! I'll shoot you all if anyone moves a muscle.'

'But, what are…?'

'Zakia!' Colm shouted.
'Put the gun down!
I've got twenty marines behind me, you might get me, for sure, but you can't kill us all.
It's all over!'

Chapter 43

Ridge stared at Zakia, seeing but not understanding. He realised with horror that she wasn't joking. She had that tiny furrowed brow that indicated she was in turmoil and which up until this point he had thought to be cute. Her eyes were ferocious and black and yet he noticed the gun which was still levelled at Colm was being held as still as a heron waiting to pounce on the water's edge back home, a million miles from here.

Ridge heard voices behind him and he guessed the Special Forces guys were just about to crash in and he couldn't let that happen. No matter what his eyes were telling him, he couldn't believe Zakia would harm him or his family. Then he heard a deep American drawl instructing the men to pull back. The voice was strangely familiar and reassuring as if from a childhood dream. It was all getting too weird. He had to do something. He stepped forward.

'Jake! What are you doing?
These guys are on our side, you're safe now.
We're all safe!
We can go home now!'

'Ridge, shut up!'

Zakia didn't take her eyes off Colm as her words spat fury at Ridge.

'We can't go home!
There is no more *home* for us, don't you
understand?'

Ridge saw the panicky man become even
more nervous and then he spoke for the first time.
His voice was high-pitched with fear and seemed
at odds with what he was actually trying to say.
Something else didn't seem to fit the situation
either. He had a Glaswegian accent.

'Boo! I can sort this, just put the gun
down!'

'Boo? Did he say? What is…?'

Before Ridge could find the right words,
they became superfluous.

He saw Zakia turn to look at him for a
second, a mixture of affection and then anger
crossing her contorted face. Her gun arm swung
around towards the other guy and just as Ridge
grasped what she was going to do, it was all too
late.

Colm became a blurred apparition in
front of him then he was still again. But there
had been a short subdued sound, almost like a
drip of water from a certain height and he saw a
tiny red hole appear in the centre of Zakia's

298

beautiful little forehead, all creases gone now and she fell, lifeless, to the ground.

Ridge sprang to catch her, not caring about the danger from the other guy and as he clasped her head to his chest, the hot tears pouring down his face, he looked up in horror and revulsion as Colm strode through the mayhem to shake the young man's hand strongly and usher him quickly out.

As if things couldn't get any stranger, he then felt a strong pair of arms encircle both himself and the stricken girl and as he lifted his wet face he saw his old friend, his best friend in the whole world, Thaddeus!

Chapter 44

'Thad? What are you doing? Are the Dogs here? What's going-'

The handsome giant placed a huge hand to Ridge's mouth and pulled him closer.

'Ridge, my friend, there's a lot I have to tell you but right now I've got someone else to show you, so you have to get up, right now.
Come on. This girl is past help now, amigo, but there's a girl outside needs you now more than ever!'

Ridge gently laid Zakia down on a discarded pile of jackets as uniformed men streamed into the crowded space and he allowed himself to be lifted up and pushed towards the front of the bunker.

'Girl? What do you mean?' Ridge saw that familiar gleam in his mischievous friend's eye. 'You don't mean that-'

'I surely do, old buddy.
Orla!
But we'd better be damn quick 'cos you don't wanna know what's just about to occur out there, that's for freakin' sure!'

Ridge felt as if he was slipping ever-faster down a never-ending flight of stairs. He was descending deeper into a ghastly black world where nothing was absolute, nor as it should be. A hellish parallel existence. First the horrible death of Zakia and then his big friend appearing out of the nightmare, like Banquo's ghost, only to be warning him that something wasn't right with Orla who for some strange reason was here too, instead of being safely home in Scotland!

Colm was nowhere to be seen but there were people in uniforms running around in the confusion of dust and smoke that was being whipped up by the noisy rotors of at least three helicopters. Through it all, the smell of death was all-pervading. Thad had encouraged Ridge into a run now and he practically threw the confused Scot in through the gaping maw of the farthest away helicopter.

And there she was!

His beautiful wife Orla!

Surrounded by worried looking soldiers, she was half lying on the floor of the aircraft swaddled in bullet-proof jackets and something was definitely not right. He felt his heart beating through his chest as he rushed over to her, the words tumbling from his lips as he sank to his knees and clutched her to his chest.

'Orla! What are you doing here? Are you okay, my love? Have you been injured? Why are you here? What's going on?'

'Injured? Of course I'm bleedin' injured! You did it to me you dozy eedjit! I'm after havin' a baby can't you see? Now tell these fookin' bastards where the nearest half-way decent hospital is will ye?'

Chapter 45

Seconds later the noise made it impossible to talk as the huge rotors began to spin in deadly earnest and the helicopter rose up through the black smoke of burning tires and back into the warm light.

It was all that Ridge could do to hold Orla's hand tight and he just smiled inanely through his tears as she writhed in obvious discomfort. The noisy engine had abated just enough for basic communication and Ridge had worked out that they were headed for the Shifa International hospital where they would be met by Logan. Ridge wasn't sure where Colm had gone but he thought that Thad must have been in a second aircraft which had left around the same time.

They were only in the air for a few minutes and as Ridge peered out onto the tarmac, he was amazed to see another black helicopter sitting waiting for them with Thad and a group of soldiers still in their black Ops gear standing guard. The immediate danger obviously wasn't over yet, he realised. Although now he had far more pressing concerns much closer to hand.

Orla was breathing fast now and her grip had become vice-like. They'd transferred her onto a stretcher which made it awkward for him to disembark from the helicopter and he had to stumble alongside like some human life-support device.

Thad was grim faced and still carrying an assault rifle as he nodded briefly and helped the others to escort them speedily into the hospital. Ridge was very worried now as he assumed Orla must be in real danger and he cursed himself again for putting her in this precarious predicament. He still had no idea what the circumstances of her sudden appearance in Pakistan meant but all he could think about now was the impending birth of their child and that they would all survive this dramatic situation.

That was before they got told about the bomb. Thad was striding behind the speeding stretcher, conspicuous in his once black uniform. Now blood and grime splattered, he was totally at odds with their now sterile clinical environment. He towered above the scurrying medical staff in their pristine whites and on first seeing him they all gasped in momentary horror at this futuristic gun-toting storm-trooper who refused to be herded away from his wounded friend.

The trolley bed crashed through the doors of the theatre and at that point both Ridge and Thad were barred from entry.

'But, my wife!' Ridge screamed as Orla shouted his name back through the still swinging doors. 'Just give us one moment,' the nurse held up a resolute hand. 'You can come through shortly. We haven't got a lot of time, I'm afraid and you'll just get in the way. Of course you can be there for the birth but right now we have to make sure both mother and baby are fit enough to proceed. Do you understand?'

Ridge nodded helplessly and Thad led him over to a waiting area just as two other troopers came stomping along the corridor, wielding their guns. They saw Thad and gestured for him to come over. A brief conversation ensued and Ridge saw Thad's face drop and he got that sinking feeling again. He dragged himself back onto his feet and began to walk over to be met by Thad's enormous outstretched hand which stopped him like a sledgehammer to the chest.

'Sit down, Ridge! Please?'

He went back over and slumped into a tiny plastic chair wondering what was going on, not for the first time that long day. He looked up at a clock and was amazed to find that it was only early afternoon.

Thad came over a minute later and sat beside him. His eyes had welled up and he had never been very good at hiding his emotions despite his tough guy image. Ridge used to say it was because he was a stereotypical screaming gay but he soon got tired of that after Thad would dangle him out of ten-storey windows by his ankles.

'That was Logan on the cell phone a minute ago. Lucky for him he's on his way here by car and he left Colm and the asset, this Shahid guy, back at the High Commission. I'm sorry Ridge, but the Commission just got hit.

Hit bad.

I guess they were trying to get this guy before we could get him out. Colm was waiting to hear about Orla.

There's nobody left, Ridge. It was a suicide car bomb.

The whole place is destroyed.

I am so sorry.'

Chapter 46

He sat for what seemed like hours. His
eyes smarted from the unforgiving glare of the
bright lights reflecting the clinical efficiency of
his surroundings. He tried shutting them but then
the discordant and unrelenting noises seemed to
attack him with the vicious precision of a
surgeon's scalpel. Doors would slam and
torrents of confusion would flood through the
corridors frightening him out of his exhausted
half-sleep, time after time. Angry voices accused
him of crimes unknown and above them all he
could hear his chief inquisitor Colm screaming,
'Was it was not *you* who brought me here?'

Thad had disappeared somewhere for the
umpteenth time, still trying to find out more
about the attack on the High Commission. Ridge
also suspected that he would just want to have
something to do apart from just sitting and
waiting. There had been a steady stream of
ambulances but they'd heard that so far there had
been very few bodies recovered from the rubble
of the once beautiful old building.

There were complications with Orla too
and Ridge had still been unable to see her and
although the staff had been sympathetic to his
situation they had been equally firm in
forbidding his entry. He was just managing to
keep a grip on this emotional roller-coaster ride
but his face was wet with a mixture of tears and
grime, his red eyes testament to the anguish
within. He looked anxiously around for his big

307

friend, glad that he had chosen to wait with him but sad that he, along with everyone else he loved, was enduring yet another suffer-fest on his account.

He couldn't stop thinking about old Archie and the revolving doors of life. Here Ridge was awaiting the birth of his first child, what was supposed to be one the best moments of his life but he knew that as soon as Orla saw him she would know something was wrong and would immediately ask where her big brother was. What was he to do? He knew that whatever else, the most important thing to him was that both Orla and the baby would survive this and if that meant he had to sit here tortured for a while longer then he was prepared to endure. He wondered how his great grandmother must have felt; nursing her beautiful wee baby girl for the first time only to be told her young husband had tragically died as a consequence of the birth.

Thad appeared back having divested himself of his intimidating uniform and he now looked like a regular Yank overseas with his freshly pressed chinos and a sailing shirt struggling slightly to stretch across his strong physique. His thick mane of lustrous black hair was shorter than when Ridge had first met him in San Francisco but with his high cheekbones and full lips framing that inflammable smile, Thad still emanated the powerful allure of an intensely sexual animal underneath his veneer of carefully cultivated metropolitan sophistication.

308

'Where'd you get the clean clothes?' Ridge asked enviously.

Thad laughed for the first time since they'd met up again.

'Well, let's just say that I had an interesting experience in the Doctor's compound and not being boastful but I think that somewhere in this hospital there will be a young surgeon with a big smile on his face most of today!'

'Slut!' was all that Ridge could bring himself to say, and despite himself, he felt his face painfully realign itself into an impudent smile.

But then he saw the mirth leave the face of his handsome friend and he turned to see the medics rushing towards them, surgical gowns flowing and clipboards in hand. Ridge jumped up to confront them.

'How is she? What's happening?'

The two doctors looked tired and Ridge understood that they'd probably had a longer day than even he'd had. He tried to restrain himself but there was too much at stake here and he saw his hands go out to grab the nearest startled man, only to be expertly intercepted and wrestled away by his physically superior friend. 'Sorry dude!' he apologized, as Ridge sank back down, pole-axed not by any material force but by the worried demeanour on the doctor's face.

'I am so sorry that you've had to wait out here for so long! It's has been most regrettable but we are very short of staff today what with the terrorist attack and everything. But I am pleased to tell you that there is no problem with the baby except that we will have to perform a surgical operation and we intend to proceed immediately as long as you have no issues with that.'

'Surgical? What do you mean?'

'It is nothing to worry about, sir. It will be a routine C-Section that we will carry out and there will be little risk to mother or child, I can assure you most sincerely.'

'Can I see her? Does she know what's going on?'

'Yes, of course! She has asked for you and her brother.' The doctor passed a less than subtle glance over to Thad before returning his poker face to Ridge.

'Will it just be you then, sir?'

Ridge nodded, his mind racing with the joy and the horror of what was to befall his beautiful wife this day. He turned and hugged the massive frame next to him before chasing after the two doctors who'd already headed back at a fierce pace.

The long corridor was warm and airless and Ridge felt light-headed and dizzy as he struggled to decide what to say to Orla. He was desperate to see her and above all he wanted this birth to be happy and safe but he wasn't sure if he should be celebrating the new life of his son with a cruel act of familial betrayal.

'STOP!' He yelled and lunged for the nearest of the two doctors who sprang back in alarm.

'Wait! Sorry!
I just need to ask one quick question before we go in. Does my wife know about the bombing of the High Commission?'

The doctors looked at each other in a shared disgust and they shook their heads silently as if to say 'What an irrelevant question for an expectant father be asking at a time like this,' before they shouldered open the door.
There she was, beaming over at him and looking more beautiful than anything he'd ever seen in his life. He knew then what he would do.

He would lie. He would lie like the bastard he was.

Chapter 47

He slammed his fist into the powdery wall and groaned, more with pure frustration than with any admittance of physical pain. Personally speaking, pain was fine by him. He knew where he was with pain. Giving or taking, it used to be pretty much all the same to him. But these days he had softened a little. More than a little. Where it came to those he loved, an endangered species at the best of times, he had a firm and fast rule. No-one gets within a fucking mile. But in the last 24 hours he'd seen his rule broken one time too many.

Although he was a virtual stranger to the others in the room they already had wind that something bad had happened as immediately prior to checking the structural integrity of the building with his bare hands, he'd tested one of his many throw-away phones quite literally and two of the people sitting at the nearby table were still picking out fragments of plastic from their hair and clothing.

They'd been in complete lockdown and incommunicado to all outside forces for the last few hours in a deliberate plan so as to be difficult to find by anyone, friendly or otherwise. Right now, Colm wasn't 100% sure just *who* he could trust and in that situation he always preferred to lie low and watch which way the wind was blowing.

Having just spoken to Thad he now knew that the latest forecast was a particularly foul stench blowing straight towards him. That, he could deal with, as he always had done in the past. But it was his wee sister and her lion-hearted eedjit of a husband he was most worried about and so he'd given Thad a clear and unequivocal instruction.

'Thaddeus, just cut the jibber-jabber will ye and listen very closely to what I'm after tellin' ye. I don't want you to be more than an inch away from me sister until you hear from me again!
You got that?
Are ye quite sure now?
Say it back to me now, just so we're clear, alright?'

Until he'd called the big ex-marine, Colm had been oblivious to the fact that there had even been an attack on the High Commission and if he'd needed proof that the two Americans with him were the genuine article, it was the way the colour had ebbed so dramatically from their faces that finally convinced Colm. Either that or they were the best actors on the planet surpassing even his own considerable thespian abilities. Although he could see an opening for a little role playing now, he decided. He'd allowed the senior of the two men to borrow one of his cell phones and judging by the strangled look on the guy's face it

314

looked like the call he was making was serious and so he cautiously allowed him to leave the room to talk. So it was now or never. Time for a reprise of *The Phantom* in all his terrifying glory.

The poor guy didn't stand a chance. Before his brain could comprehend what was happening, Colm had sprung over his desk, relieved him of his side-arm and pushed him hard up against the wall. With one hand around his throat and the other slowly squeezing his testicles ever more tightly, Colm wanted the quivering office worker to understand implicitly two very important life lessons. That he should have remained back in his safe cubicle on the fourth floor at Langley was a given and he'd also immediately grasped the fact that here, in the field, in his domain, Colm was the undisputed daddy.

Colm had an idea.

'You got a family?'

'Just married a few-'

Colm gripped harder and his face contorted into a dark snarl.

> 'Well let me tell ye, family means the feckin' world to me!
> And if ye ever want to have any of yer own, ye better be after giving me the right answers here, so you will!

Now who the bleedin' hell is *he* and, so help me God, ye better tell me the truth this time!'

Without letting either hand relax for a second Colm still managed to send an accusatory stare towards the young man slumped and handcuffed in the far corner.

The elephant in the room.

Chapter 48

Colm relaxed his grip to allow the man to breathe but kept his right hand in position so as to ensure the man never strayed from the universal truth that honesty is always the best policy.

Although in this game, honesty was a commodity in short supply at the best of times and Colm acknowledged silently that he was as guilty as the next man. Or the next, supposed-to-be-retired, dinosaur relic from a vicious and carnivorous past.

He had been lied to by the powers that be in the past. Lied to, betrayed and hunted like an animal. But he'd adapted fast to that situation and evolved into something more terrifying than they could ever have imagined in their worst nightmares. That was why he was so angry right now. Because he'd never thought that they'd willingly taunt the beast again.

He decided to give the youngster the benefit of the doubt. He was American. He'd probably still been in kindergarten during The Troubles and perhaps he really didn't know who he was dealing with. Realising also that the other man would be back soon, he tightened his right hand once more.

'What's yer name, son?'

The man tried to wrench his head free in order to speak but Colm was not for relieving him of any discomfort just yet. He mumbled nervously. 'Frank... my name is Frank.'

'Okay Frank. So who is this guy and why was I asked to kill the girl?'

Frank's eyes betrayed his racing thoughts as he scanned the room madly as if expecting assistance to emerge from the grimy paint-peeled walls.

'I have no idea... I just-'

Colm growled and flexed his strong fingers tighter around Frank's damp throat, feeling the accelerating throb of the terrified man's pulse. He started to choke and Colm released the pressure, just enough to let him speak.

'The asset was to be protected at all costs, that's all I know... the girl was a new threat... but I don't have any intel on her, we thought she was one of yours, until... until you-'

'Until I was given unequivocal orders to terminate her prior to my attack on the second hide-out. She was going to take him out for sure anyways but we didn't know that then. Or did we? Up to this point she had been considered a friend to my family and so I need answers and fast!'

Colm registered movement from the shackled man and he stared hard into his tired face before his head sunk down onto his arms on the desk. If there had been a flicker of emotion it had quickly passed and the mask was there once more. The mask of a pro like himself? Somehow it didn't seem to fit. Nothing about this whole sorry mess seemed to fit, and he didn't like that.

Sensing that he was running out of time, he tried another approach and released Frank and allowed him to sit. Pointing the gun directly at the 'asset' who remained oblivious, he looked at the terrified youngster and knew he was on to a winner. He cocked the pistol.

'He's one of ours! He's CIA and he was bringing in serious intel on the meeting with Jabba the Hut, the tribal leader. That's the mission objective to capture him or failing that to take him out.'

'So where the fuck is he? And was it his people who blew up the High Commission? And why is laughing boy here still in cuffs?'

'I really have no clue. I guess it was their bomb but we just got here and you saw the chief's face when he made that call!'

Colm gut kicked hard and he realised the chief had been away for more than a few minutes. There was no time for pleasantries. He reached into a hidden compartment under his shirt and extricated a small piece of plastic.

'You want some gum, Frank?'

Frank looked both astonished and then relieved as he nodded and reached out for a piece. He didn't see it coming and Colm had his arm pulled up behind him and had smashed his head face first into the desktop almost splintering it in the process. The prisoner jumped up in horror, Frank's nose having splattered blood across his own face. Colm already had the keys and he kicked the chair back and dragged him onto the prone Frank. In seconds, he had searched the man removing his belt and shoes.

'Okay *Shahid* or whatever yer name is! Move and I'll fuckin' kill you!'

He then rubbed the 'gum' and affixed it to the corner of the room. Seconds later the wall exploded and Shahid was roughly dragged out through the dust. Out on the street, Colm extended his gun arm and pointed it to the nearest car, gesturing the driver to vacate. There was no argument given and within thirty seconds he had the car turned and headed for the safety of the hills.

320

But the car had travelled no more than a hundred yards when Colm sensed rather than saw an air-to-ground missile streak past him and then the ground shook with the force of the explosion. He rammed the throttle and didn't need to look in his rear mirror to know that their 'secret' location had been raised to the ground. He thought for a brief second about that new bride back in Virginia and then his own beautiful wife before swivelling around and smashing a fist into the nearest flesh he could reach.

'Hey! That hurt you know!'

'Strip!'

'What?
I'm not bugged, pal, honest!
I'm on *your* side!'

'Fuckin' strip or I'll leave ye here for the jackals to rip you into pieces!'

The rest of the journey was spent in silence barring the howl of an overstretched engine and the sounds of ripping cloth as Colm tore the man's clothing with his teeth as he wrestled the car through the dusty streets. They were lucky to avoid any patrols and he crashed through the perimeter checkpoint so fast that if there had been anyone on duty they wouldn't have stood a chance in catching them.

Chapter 49

The light was fading fast as a white legged man was dragged into the forest his hands tightly bound and his modesty covered by a soiled car rug. Utilising a handy length of tow rope, Colm quickly tossed it over an overhanging branch and motioned Shahid to stand underneath.

'You're kidding, right?
You're going to fuckin' hang me now, is that it?'

One look at Colm's face should have been enough for the young man to know how serious he was. He must have clicked though as he darted to one side and attempted to throw the travel rug over Colm's head, matador-style before scampering gingerly into the dusk. He'd got ten feet before Colm calmly shot him in the back of his right knee and Shahid dropped like a stone, passing out instantly.
Within five minutes the blood-stained body was hanging upside down and Colm rabbit-punched him in the guts to bring him around. Retching and arching his body the man cried out in sheer terror.

'Please don't kill me!
I'll tell you whatever you want.
I can help you, honestly!'

Shahid's arms were now tied behind his back and he writhed like a worm on a hook which only made his position more uncomfortable by the second.

'My head's gonna burst, here, pal! Are you fucking mad or what?'

Colm pulled out the CIA issue revolver and placed it against the beleaguered youngster's forehead.

'Let's get this straight from the start. I'm not after being yer pal, okay, but I am fookin' mad right now, so I am, so if you really want to see daylight I suggest you shut the fuck up and let me think rationally.
Any more whining and I'll just be sticking a bullet in you to get some bloody peace, so I will.
So just relax, alright. Hanging upside down is good for you anyways and if ye keep still ye might no bleed so much either.
Me? I'm after going for a kip.'

At this point Shahid would have taken odds that nothing could have surprised him ever again until Colm then deftly scaled the tree above him. He watched astonished as Colm seemed to have found a safe berth a couple of metres above him and he swung his legs over a branch and allowed his body to hang down motionless. Shahid couldn't get his upside-down vision to work right but he was convinced that the crazy Irishman had gone to sleep.

Somehow despite the excruciating pain he must have drifted off because the next thing he was aware of was the sound of wood being arranged underneath him as if to make a fire.

'Whoa! What are you doing?
I told you, I'll give you whatever you want… please … you have to see reason!'

Colm laughed coldly.

'Ha! Reason is it. I think we've gone a long ways past reason, don't you think?'

He sat down against a tree and watched Shahid spin in a desperate struggle to break free. All movement stopped as Colm fingered the flint wheel of his Zippo lighter, a diabolical gleam in his eye. Satisfied that he'd done enough to be able to extract as much or as little as the wretched lad knew, he fished out the stolen cell phone which he'd stripped and reassembled as the last wraiths of darkness had reluctantly given up on their bloodstained feast. There had been no bugs in the phone. Colm needed answers and he was going to get them. But first he had to check on more important matters. He walked into thicker trees and dialled a number.

'Thad? I need a sit rep on Orla. Please tell me you're still watching her.'

'Hey dude! Yeah man! We're all good here.
I'm right outside the only door into the labour ward and Orla has just gone into the last stages, I guess. Ridge went in an hour or so ago so all's fine here. You've escaped death again amigo? What the fuck, right?'

'The Yanks? Did any of them get out?'

'Negative. The asset? Is he with you?'

'Yep. I'm just going to have a serious chat with him. Try and work out where we stand.'

'Sure man. He's got to be the key to this. Hey! Let me tell you something Ridge told me earlier. He's pretty fucking mad at you, for killing the girl but I guess you had your reasons and we can talk it out later, but listen to this, man. This goes no further right? Ridge said that immediately prior to your kill shot, he heard the asset call Zakia by a pet name, *Boo*, that she had previously asserted would only ever be known by a man who'd shared her bed. So we got prior relationship there and not just a passing acquaintance either.'

Colm swung a long stick with frustration, bludgeoning the surrounding plant life as he did so.

'So just who is this guy? That's what I need to find out.'

'Sure but be careful dude. I gotta bad feeling about this and no-one here is talking. My unit, all of the ghost battalion, has split already. I'm here strictly on a personal leave basis but I'm kinda spooked, to be honest, so I took the liberty of tracking the whereabouts of the 'Dogs and it seems they been kickin' some ass over in North Africa. Would sure feel a hell of a lot safer knowin' those queer dudes were watchin' ma ass, you know what ah'm talkin' about.'

'No Thad, that's a good call. I was after thinking about getting you to mebbes check in with 'the man who can' and seeing if he could rustle us up a fast chopper for evac once Orla is safe. Tell your Dad it'd have to be under the radar, to be sure. Meet me at reference Lima Zulu as we discussed before, okay?'

'Copy that.'

Chapter 50

Colm knelt down so his voice was an inch from the terrified boy's sweat drenched face. He flicked the lighter on and off continually as he spoke.

'D'ye know just how slowly I could burn you to death?
Whilst keeping you awake throughout, of course.
Barbequed would be a fair description.'

Shahid wriggled desperately but it was obvious he wasn't going to be escaping any time soon. He'd just exhausted any last reserves of energy that hadn't already been leached from his aching body during the night and all he could think about was relieving the agony from what was now an excruciatingly painful leg. He'd lost all feeling from his arms and his eyes stung from the sweat and blood co-mingling down his face. He also knew that he'd soiled himself and his thick head of hair felt heavy and wet.

He sensed he was completely out of his depth with this guy and for the first time in his life he'd been unable to talk himself out of a problematic situation. Untouchable thus far, he'd finally grasped that universal truism about not being able to fool all the people all the time. But was he going to have to pay for this valuable lesson with his life? There was a lot of blood on his hands but he suspected that there were few players in this precariously balanced game who could claim otherwise. He was out of options for now and this mad man seemed to be so deadly serious that Shahid resolved to try a strategy completely unfamiliar to him. He would tell this man the truth.

Colm could not have been aware of the epiphany just experienced by his quivering hostage and so for expediency he'd plumped for the 'Phantom meets bad cop' persona but with bells on.

> An' was I after telling ye what I my job was back in the day, when I was in the Real IRA?
> I was in the 'nutting squad,' so I was. Not content with killing innocent by-standers, that was too bleedin' easy for us. What got us out of our stinkin' pit of a morning was the thought of catching one of our own; an informer, a nonce or a traitor!
> IS THAT WHAT YOU ARE THEN?
> I learned all the ways to inflict pain so I did.'

Colm spun his heavy stick effortlessly in a slow arc and whacked Shahid's already shattered knee and the forest echoed with the frenzied scream of a man at the brink of sanity.

Colm knew this and waited yet further. The timing had to be just perfect. He watched dispassionately as Shahid choked on the last contents of his stomach and whimpered like an injured dog.

'It was grand, so it was.

We'd set them up in an old out of the way place, a bit like this, where no-one could hear them scream. They'd be trussed up and helpless, just like yerself here. Of course we had to be cognisant of the old forensic an' that, so we'd have had you sitting on plastic sheeting, to catch all the blood and other body parts that might be fallin' off ye.

Once we'd finished, maybe a day or two later, yer own mammy would never had known we'd been there. Spotless it was. But sure, I don't need to worry about that over here so ye can spew up all ye want, so ye can!'

Colm turned and walked off leaving the boy hanging there. He'd picked up a couple of items a few hours earlier and he knew the boy would be imagining him returning with an assortment of medieval torture implements and he couldn't help smiling, despite the grim situation. He was a bad bastard, he knew that, but he had been trying so hard to be good.

Now it was time for the switch.

When he popped the lid from the bottle of mineral water and poured it over the boy's grimy face, Colm could see that Shahid couldn't work out if it was some fiendish trick or not. Once he'd ascertained there were no electrodes being assembled, his face relaxed and he allowed his mouth to receive some of the beautiful clean water.

'Right then lover boy! I'll get to Nasreen in a wee minute but first I want to know how long you've been fucking Zakia?'

Even a seasoned pro like Colm was taken aback by the boy's reaction. It was even better than if he *had* actually applied a current to his bollocks, Colm decided and he knew then that he'd have no problems with this one.

Shahid was crying like a baby and Colm saw that he was broken now perhaps beyond the point of repair. He started babbling and once the words started they became a torrent and it seemed to Colm that the boy was talking as much to himself as to him.

'It was an accident really! Just like the way that any other relationship might begin. We met…there was a spark and then we began seeing each other. For me it was more the physical side but I quickly realised that she was falling in love with me... it was a crazy time! When I wasn't with her, I was sitting up on-line

330

through the night… my beliefs were
changing so fast at that time… I suppose
I'd become completely brain-washed by
the jihadi cause. I'd already distanced
myself from most of my previous life but
somehow Zakia managed to infiltrate her
way into my new world...'

The boy started to drift off and so Colm
splashed his face with more of the mineral water
and that seemed to bring him back to life.

'I was being so heavily influenced by
others that when they discovered that
Zakia was a cop they encouraged me to
continue the relationship so as to keep
myself safe and perhaps to gain
important knowledge to further the cause.
I had no idea at that point that she would
have become as infatuated with the jihad
movement as she was with me but I
supposed that the whole thing seemed to
make sense even though I was feeling
uncomfortable at the intensity of our
relationship and I actually tried to break
it off a few times
My star was shining in the organisation
and I wanted to go overseas and fight
alongside my brothers and so Zakia made
me promise that we'd marry and she
would come and fight with me.
It was around that time when I began to
have nightmares about going abroad. I

331

thought I'd lost my zeal for the cause and was continually questioning my faith. Every day I'd want to run away and have a normal life, but then every night they'd groom me to hate the West even more. There was no-one to turn to, just to talk it all through...'

Colm poured some more water onto the boy and grunted.

'So you were after being scared? I don't think that's anything to be shy about.'

'Yes!
I think I was just plain scared at what I was about to do. That's when I made a schoolboy error and was picked up what I thought was the plain clothes police and I used my connection with Zakia shamelessly. But these guys were American and I found myself being bundled into a plane and taken to who knows where. They gave me the choice of working for the CIA or being arrested and spending the rest of my life in prison, probably never seeing the UK again. But they didn't like the fact that I was with Zakia as they found it too dangerous and they suspected her of being a mole for MI5. They were going to kill her, simple as that. I offered to break it off and they agreed to spare her but they told

me I also had to compromise her in such a way that no-one would ever take her testimony seriously if she ever did turn. So I went with Nasreen just to sour our relationship but my plan worked too well. She found us in bed together. I'd never been so terrified in my life at that point and I thought she was going to kill us both.

I promised to end it with Nasreen and told her I'd doubted her dedication to the cause. I said that she had to prove her love for me and for the cause by doing this one thing for me.'

'She killed the Brigadier?'

The stick hummed with a latent fury as it swung low and fast in a powerful parabola practised for a thousand years, trailing death in an arc of vengeance.

Chapter 51

The crack was strangely muffled this time. There was no echo as the wood broke against the boy's ribs and Colm knew from experience that it was the sound of breaking bones he had heard. He thrust out the jagged shard and howled like a wolf caught in a gin-trap, the veins in his neck bulging and red. He wanted to pierce the boy's flesh, to drive the stick deep into his chest and roar his anger to the forest as the hot red blood flowed over his shaking hands.

But he needed to find out the truth. His anger was directed more inwards than at the boy which was the only reason he spared his life, slowing the sweep of his attack so as to just cause a reasonable amount of pain. At least for now.

His anger which threatened to topple his trademark composure was not just because of his love for old Archie, whom he considered as a father. It was because he'd known in the pit of his stomach that she had been the one. That brief moment in the smoke-filled bunker, her diminutive shadow and those piercing eyes. They had exchanged a lifetime of emotions in that second and he'd instinctively known she was just like him. A stone dead killer. Strong and powerful to the point of being almost invincible apart from that same vulnerability, their Achilles' heel – those whom they loved. Venture down that dark road then they could be capable of any anything.

Shahid had momentarily passed out with the pain and now that he'd awoken he simply moaned the same word over and over again. 'No, no, no…' Meanwhile Colm circled him, never once taking his eyes off him, like a big cat stalking a defenceless prey, relentless and supremely in control.

But underneath the mask of 'The Phantom' he felt his guts roiling and he knew he didn't yet have the truth. He knew that she'd been the one who'd physically entered the building and poisoned the old Brig'. The tiny footprint had set off alarms straight away and Colm felt the bile rise as he thought of his old friend dying in such a way after all that he'd been through. But he also knew that people like Zakia, like himself, didn't often kill on a whim. They did what they'd been ordered to do, no matter what. He turned his venom on the boy, feeling the visceral hatred in his throat as he spat the words.

'So, was it your idea? Ye'd better tell me the truth, or I'll rip you to pieces, sure an' I will!'

'No! I mean, well not really. I'd been given a list of potential targets for attack. They were five names in Scotland and I told Zakia that she'd to kill one of them to prove herself but it was also to free me from the possibility of being betrayed.'

335

Colm twisted the sharp stick slowly into Shahid's chest, his black eyes screwed small as arrow tips. He suddenly knew the answer to his next question and he almost didn't ask it.

'Who gave you this 'list'? Where would yer Islamic chums get that kind of classified information and what the fuck did Archie ever do to them?'

'What? No. It was the Americans! They gave me the list and the Brigadier was at the top, number one. They told me he'd been involved in a massacre of some of my ancestors shortly after Partition and that he was a legitimate enemy of Islam.
I didn't really believe it but I also never thought that Zakia would do anything at all! I was more scared of the CIA than going to Pakistan so I just fled as quickly as possible. I finished it with Zakia and I disappeared without telling anyone where I was going. I never thought she'd kill anyone!'

'So you'd already left Scotland before the murder?'

'Yes! I'd forgotten all about it. It had been a tough baptism initially, but things were progressing really well with my unit in Pakistan and I was using every waking thought to make it a success. Until the two girls messed everything up. I never thought that Nasreen would come after me like a love-lost puppy and I certainly didn't think Zakia would have tracked down the Brigadier and then found me too!'

'So, she'd come to join you here?'

'Join me? No!
She'd come to kill me!'

Chapter 52

Colm was getting angrier by the minute.
He'd carried out enough interrogations to know
that you will always get to a point where the
hostage thinks they are going to die. At that
point they will confess to anything to save their
skins and then the real problem is sorting out the
truth from the wild imaginings of what they
thought you'd wanted to hear.

'Are you trying to tell me that Zakia
recruited my brother-in-law to find and
kill you and that the whole Nasreen
rescue was a clever smokescreen so she
could get to you?'

'Yes!
I couldn't believe it either!
She killed the Brigadier, not to prove her
love for me, as it must have appeared to
the Yanks, but to send me a message.
I was next.
Somehow she then made the connection
between him and Mr Walker. She set up
her family to be the unwitting conduit
and then you know the rest.'

'She couldn't have done all that on her
own. There's something you're still not
telling me, to be sure. My patience is
wearing very thin now and so if you want
to live, I strongly suggest that you just

cut the bullshit and give me everything
you know.
Was it the CIA that helped her to kill
Archie and then find you here?'

Shahid looked sideways in that classic
sign that he was going to lie and Colm looked at
his watch and realised he'd have to wind this up
soon, one way or the other. He picked up the
stick.

'It must have been. Yes!'

'What's with all this *must have been*?
Are you still in contact with the Yanks?
Did you have anything to do with the last
48 hours?'

'No! I've nothing to do with them
anymore and Archie's blood is not on my
hands I promise you!'

'So you're not involved with the CIA?
Do they know this?'

'Not exactly.
The honest truth is that I *was* working for
them but when they first recruited me in
Glasgow they made such an amateur job
of it. Not understanding the close knit
structure of Muslim society in Glasgow it
was known almost immediately that
they'd picked me up and so I'd been

given no choice but to work with them but then relay everything back to my jihad handlers.
They told me that if I didn't spy against the CIA then they'd kill my entire family. That's why I had to leave! It was just getting all too much for me.'

Colm could tell that Shahid had nervously read the scepticism that he so plainly felt and glancing at his watch, he also had a feeling that the boy wanted to tell him something else.

'So yer' after telling me that you're a *triple* agent now, is that it? D'ye seriously expect me to believe that?'

'I can prove it!
There was never any tribal leader coming into Islamabad!
There was no big meeting to take place and it was all a hoax set up to fox the Americans and lure them out into the open.
We had no prior knowledge of your bunker attack but the bombing of the High Commission would certainly have been ours and they would've wanted to sacrifice me before I could be interrogated. So you can see, if you spare my life there must be valuable information that I can give to you too.'

Colm's mind was racing. This level of duplicity was not unknown to him and he'd suffered at the hands of violence condoned by governments more than once before.

'Okay, so how do you explain the bombing of that government building we just scarpered from? There's no way your jihadi boys were after knowing where we were, not that quick anyways. Short of eviscerating you, which I've half a mind to do still, I can't see where you could be bugged. The Americans were only just aware of us and none of the Brits knew where we were.'

Shahid turned his bloody face towards Colm, wincing with the pain in his chest as he tried to lift his head so as to be able to look him better in the eye.

'It's obvious…'

'Jesus! The Yanks!
For sure! They must've realised you'd duped them and they had to save face. It was cleaner to get rid of both of us and blame the whole thing on your jihadi lot!'

'Hey! Where are you going?
You can't leave me here! I'm bleeding! I'll tell you more!

Please…! Help!'

As the cries became fainter, Colm stopped in his tracks. He was quite prepared to leave the boy to suffer a slow and painful death in the woods, although he doubted it would take too long for the local wildlife to descend upon such a tasty feast. But then his guts cramped painfully and he had a chilling thought. A thin smile cracked his granite complexion for only the second time in a day and he turned about and swiftly retraced his steps.

Chapter 53

Ridge couldn't stop smiling like an idiot and his face actually hurt with it. Through all of the madness, the dust and then plain old fatigue he'd never anticipated sitting like this in the sterile white of the hospital with a tiny new born baby in his arms. He could hardly believe it. They had their own perfect child, a beautiful little baby girl.

Orla was sleeping and Ridge watched her proudly, her breathing steady and strong. The poor girl was exhausted after a fairly tough natural labour in the end, the baby having chosen to fight her way into the world by the conventional route. There for the birth, Ridge was brimming with love and admiration for his wife. Thad had been in earlier and had joked about Orla having been too cosy with one of his 'brothers' due to the dark complexion of the wee girl and her thick head of jet black hair. Thankfully a nurse was on hand to explain to a relieved husband that the child was severely jaundiced and the natural colour should become apparent after a few days.

Orla had set upon 'Isla' for their little daughter's name, which Ridge was not too sure about but he was too deliriously happy to raise any concerns at this point. It was a play on the beautiful wee island close to Sorsay called Islay and was a popular name on the west coast of Scotland. But it was when Orla explained that she chose the name to always remind them of the somewhat unusual circumstances of the birth that he was confused.

> 'That's why you're never any use with the bleedin' crosswords my love!
> She's going to be called Isla after the place of her birth, eedjit that you are. Islamabad, of course!'

Ridge had gulped like a goldfish.

> 'Thank God we never landed in Karachi then, or you'd be calling her Kara I suppose?'

> 'Now! That's after being a lovely Irish name so it is and you know fine well that it's the name of one of my best friends. But the spelling's all wrong, so it is, it's spelt with a 'C' as in Carragh! But maybe for a middle name, or at least one of the-'

They both jumped as the double door crashed open and the harsh reality of the world flooded in on a tide of angry voices. It was Thad and he was back in black and moving fast. Even at this time, in his happy daze, Ridge wondered how Thad had managed to find a clean set of battle fatigues in his size around here. The hubbub of voices followed the tall soldier and then Ridge saw the cause of it all. Surrounded by a flurry of white coated hospital staff was a dishevelled and blood stained man pushing and

344

swearing like a sailor on shore-leave. Ridge felt the tears pour down his face as Orla screamed at the top of her lungs.

'Uncle Colm!
Would ye mind yer bleedin' language in front of the baby!'

Chapter 54

Ridge had never seen Colm so affected. He couldn't take his eyes of baby Isla even as he whispered orders to Thad and soaked up the play by play account of the birth from his excited sister who had begun a continuous barrage of words from the moment of his arrival. Ridge had handed his daughter back to her proud mother, Colm was forbidden to touch her due to his filthy state and so he just stared at her, eyes gleaming from a mud-splattered face.

But Thad had a far more serious demeanour and Ridge had that horrible feeling in the pit of his stomach that this perfect little cocoon was about to be ruptured. Despite the wonderful last few hours, he hadn't forgotten that one of these men had just killed a young girl that he'd considered a friend. A friend? Ridge felt sick and unclean as he looked upon the purity of his daughter and thought of his unfaithfulness.

Colm had asked about a second helicopter and Thad seemed to have everything organised for them to be transported somewhere safer or more comfortable. He wasn't too sure what was happening and he felt a sharp twinge deep under his old bullet wound as he looked at the sleeping baby and realised he now had a new mission in life, to protect this perfect little girl and keep her safe, at all costs. He shook himself and shouted over the white noise of his excited wife.

'What's going on Thad?
You're worrying me, pal. Aren't we going to stay here for a few days, to let mum and baby get stronger?'

Thad and Colm exchanged a quick glance and Colm nodded.

'It's all good, man, all good!
But we gotta get clear of this hospital, like now, man.
You know me, Ridge, always watchin' your back and now as we got ourselves a regular 'family situation' to protect, then old Uncle Thaddeus ain't shirking his responsibilities, no sir.'

Thad read the quizzical look on Ridge's face and he was about to speak when Colm interjected.

'Guys, it's still not safe for us around here and I asked Thad to organise a helicopter to take us out of Pakistan. Being the genius he is, he second-guessed me perfectly and we've got two jet helicopters outside, with the rotors running.
And Orla me girl! Do you think you could stretch this 'Uncle' thing to some more miscreants?

Yep! We've got all three of the Diamond Dogs hovering two feet off the ground out there but they're not going to be waiting too long. The locals are going ape-shit already and we've got a prisoner to transport just to complicate things further.'

Ridge felt his heart beating faster. If the Dogs were here then things must still be serious. He'd not seen the three ex-Marines since they'd all been plucked from a vicious fire-fight and almost certain death by another unit of elite US Special Forces led by none other than his beautiful and infinitely surprising wife Orla. He looked carefully at her flushed face and she answered his unspoken question with a forced smile.

'Sure I can move love, but just don't be asking me to be breaking any speed records, alright? Colm as long as you're positive we'll be safer out of here and you promise me I can get a nice bath at the other end, then Isla and I are good to go!'

It only took a few moments before Thad and his men had swept Orla out of the hospital, the soldiers deaf to the protestations of the medical staff. Ridge and Colm followed behind, one carrying and one gazing at their precious little passenger. Minutes later they were aboard the first helicopter, Colm having rigged up some tiny ear defenders for baby Isla before signalling to Ridge that he'd be on the second following machine. The noise was deafening and her mother and father huddled tightly around their day old daughter as the helicopter rose into the air, a violent silhouette against the late afternoon sky.

Despite the dramatic situation, both mother and baby drifted off within minutes and Ridge glanced nervously around the helicopter, searching for a familiar or even a friendly face amongst the black uniformed men. Even allowing for the huge helmets and dark visors he knew none of them could have been one of the 'Dogs.' Not a single one of them appeared to be wearing lipstick for starters. He smiled as looked across the darkening sky at the other helicopter and he realised just how much he was looking forward to catching up with the world's most lethal cross-dressers and showing off his baby girl. Ridge could just see big Patrick, biceps like pineapples, cradling little Isla and he laughed as he wondered what she would make of her rough tough 'Uncles' as she grew up.

Just then he saw the other chopper dart away from them and he felt his stomach heave as their own machine seemed to fall several feet through the air. Ridge saw the other men lurching to the edges of each door, brandishing large weapons and gesticulating angrily at each other and he instinctively put a protective arm around his little family. An electric shock of terror run up his spine as the men pointed to an orange streak unzipping the dark blue sky and then they all spilled across the cabin as their world tipped sideways. Ridge clung on to Orla but she just muttered and fell back into her well earned slumber, her baby safely ensconced within her arms. With his ear protection numbing his hearing, Ridge sensed alarms going off rather than heard them and he could see various flashing lights that he hadn't noticed before and that's when it hit him.

They must be under attack.

He felt his heart pound and his armpits throbbed painfully as he gripped Orla tight, feeling utterly vulnerable in this huge black metal bird.

A second missile streaked past them and this time there was a subsequent explosion of the like he would never forget to his last days. He knew from the looks of the other men what it meant. Even above the tremendous roar of the jet engines, he had heard the sound of rending steel as their sister aircraft had been blown to pieces. Ridge just buried his head into the mass of blankets covering his wife and child and waited for the worst. He knew he would never shake that feeling and he vowed silently that if they ever survived this day, he would never, ever, get into a helicopter again. They rose and fell like a fishing boat off the north head of Sorsay in a vicious autumn storm and he clung on to his new family and prayed that he had been mistaken.

He'd lied to his wife once about the fate of her brother in the last twenty four hours and now he couldn't bear the thought of having to repeat his perfidy once more.

Somehow he must have fallen asleep and the next thing he knew they were being half-carried off the helicopter and into a small private jet. Orla and the baby were still as sleepy as him and the three of them drifted off as the fast jet powered up into the clear black night leaving the heat and turbulence behind.

Chapter 55

It was the evening of the following day by the time they got together properly and Thad had already guessed it couldn't be anything but a subdued affair. He knew he was going to have to be strong for his newly adopted family and he wasn't sure how they would all have coped without his help.

They were safe at least. After a long and treacherous chopper ride they had met with one of his dad's private jets on an American base in Afghanistan and they were now in Germany, at the Ramstein air base, where his dad had built what was one of the most advanced drone headquarters in Europe. It was somewhere that Thad had lived for several years as a youth and a place riven with emotions for him. Had they not been worried sick about Colm and the 'Dogs' then he would have been entertaining or horrifying them all with countless tales of hormone-fuelled excesses and feats of daring. But that would wait, he figured.

Thad alone was still hopeful that Colm had survived the missile attack as he'd spoken to one of his men who had sworn he saw several dark shapes fall from the helicopter just before it turned into a fireball and plunged to the ground. However, the ex-marine had figured they were too low for a successful parachute landing but too high to have rappelled down and so the overall picture was still gloomy.

Thad had already been given confirmation that the pilots were both killed and that two other bodies had been recovered from the wreckage, one being their precious 'asset.' The simple fact that their four friends were not amongst the dead was good enough for Thad but Ridge had told him he'd grown weary of any further shadow play and so he'd sat silently by Ridge as he told a distraught Orla that she should not get any hopes up that he was still alive.

Orla, although exhausted, seemed to be coping reasonably well and had transferred all her attentions onto the little girl who needed her more than anyone. Thad was grateful for that small mercy but it was Ridge that he was worried about right now. He'd turned in on himself and resurrected his old hang-up about being the root cause for all their problems.

Way back, in wilder times, when they'd first been friends in San Francisco, Ridge had been on a collision course with destiny, mistakenly believing at that time that he was somehow culpable in the apparent death of his young wife, Orla.

Leaping headlong from that frying pan into the even more inflammable cauldron of a Central American drugs war he had contrived to involve Thad, Colm and Thad's three ex-Marine buddies in a fire-fight that none of them would ever forget. Despite the fact that they lost a valued friend, the 'mission' had proved incredibly successful, but Thad knew that Ridge had been haunted by the guilt of dragging them all into such danger in the first place.

It was only afterwards, as they all recovered in hospital, that his little Scots buddy had discovered the dark secrets that had underpinned his marriage. Keeping the intrigue as an in-house family affair, they were all then taken on a whistle-stop tour around the murky world of the international assassin as Colm lifted the curtain just a little on his past life as undercover-agent-gone-bad. It was partly these stories that strengthened Thad's belief that Colm must still be alive. After hearing tales of so many near misses in the past it was almost inconceivable that he should be taken in such a simple and unequivocal manner.

Ridge looked around, feeling hopeless and confused. They were camped out in a drab yet efficient Officer's Mess which seemed to be unused apart from them and reminded Ridge of a Mid-West US airport departures lounge. Orla nodded over to him and the unspoken message was that she was about to go off to feed their daughter and sleep. She hadn't said much since they arrived and Ridge felt his insides tighten as he saw her walk slowly away, holding Isla tightly to her chest.

He sought out his big pal who was regaling the suitably impressed catering guy about his various exploits around the globe. They grabbed a couple of German beers and found a quiet area in front of a plasma screen showing wall-to-wall US news footage. Ridge knew Thad hadn't given up on his friends and so he determined to find out what more Thad had discovered and if between them they could work out what the hell had happened and more importantly what to do next. He had spread out the phones which he'd charged up earlier and various scribbled notes from his time with Jake and he stared at them as if they could miraculously provide all the answers.

'So why did Colm kill Jake, I mean Zakia? I just don't get it.'

Thad could see the anguish in those grey, puffy features and he felt bad for his friend. Not for the first time, he'd been catapulted into a situation that he was ill-equipped to deal with. Thad was a successful model and an ex-Marine, not a spy or anything remotely like it. He was up-front when it came to everything whether it was his unashamedly insatiable appetite for raunchy encounters with either sex or his confrontational attitude towards anything that hinted of racism or oppression of minorities of any category. But he knew he was a whole level above Ridge in his understanding of the politics of international affairs and the duplicity inherent in that arena. His father had taught him well over the last year or so in the ways of the 'real' world. The world that few ever get the opportunity to see. Despite years of estrangement, the two had now formed a strong bond, something Thad had Ridge to thank for, and having an incredibly rich and powerful father certainly had some advantages.

'I hear you, buddy.
But I guess there's a whole heap of shit going on over there that we're just beginning to uncover. I know that the CIA got us out of that arms dump but I'm not so sure that the hand of friendship wasn't short-lived, you hear what I'm saying?'

'But she was just a wee lassie from Glasgow!
Okay, maybe not quite. She was a kick-ass cop who saved my life, for sure, right?'

'I think there was a hell of a lot more to that girl than you gave her credit for, amigo. Did you know she had been involved with that Shahid guy? That she used you as a cover to find him?'

Ridge thought back to that humid hotel room and he felt his face flush with recrimination.

'Yeah, maybe. But why did Colm shoot her? Who told him to do that? We'd never have found Nasreen without her. I mean it is one thing to …'

Ridge stopped talking as it had become obvious his friend wasn't listening to a word of it. Thad was staring at the TV screen and he leapt over the table to grab the remote control turning the volume up as he flung himself back down beside Ridge.

'What's going-?'

'It's CNN man. Shut the fuck up, that's your Logan guy, right?'

Ridge blinked hard and rubbed his crusted eyes, disbelievingly. It was Logan! There he was as large as life, on the international news and looking resplendent if not even more red-faced than normal in a coruscatingly white suit. His flaming hair stuck up untamed, Logan presumably having resisted the affections of the make-up department.

The footage turned to the first bombing in Islamabad where Ridge and Zakia had escaped and for the first time Ridge saw the true extent of the widespread damage and injury caused. Then followed brief images from Rawalpindi and the horrific scenes over on the border when they had flown across the Asian continent. They watched in horror as the ruins of the High Commission flashed up, the café where

Ridge had sought sanctuary now a mess of broken walls and strewn metal.

'That's us good buddy…' Thad muttered, as he felt Ridge clutch his shoulder and together they watched smoky plumes rising from the arms dump and then the sickening image of the crashed helicopter. Ridge turned away in horror but then returned his gaze as Thad thumped him hard.

'Woah! That's last night!
But *after* we left! Holy crap!'

Ridge didn't understand the significance of this last piece of the montage which showed the scene of an enormous explosion and significant fighting with several helicopters and other vehicles burning in the background and then thousands of rounds of ammunition and rocket grenades lined up alongside a dozen men sitting bowed and trussed. He was just about to ask Thad when Logan appeared again, this time with the audio being broadcast.

'I'd just like to thank the co-operation of the Pakistani authorities and the tremendous job done by the British Special Forces in the elimination of one of the Taliban's most powerful and influential warlords. Let this be a warning to Jamaat-al-Jasari and any further Taliban leaders who are

*considering switching their allegiances
to ISIL and Abu Bakr al-Baghdadi.
Today marks a significant step forwards
in the war on terror and my thoughts and
prayers go out to the families of those
who died in today's operation. Thank
you.'*

*'Mr Ross, you said this was co-ordinated
as a response to the bombing of the
British High Commission, but what
would you say to witness reports of
seeing incredibly tall female soldiers
wearing brightly coloured feather
scarves, make-up and nail varnish?'*

*'Are you mad?
That would be absurd. After all, we're
British, old bean!'*

Ridge and Thad stared at each other and
Ridge felt the emotion rising in his face. Thad
whooped and lifted him right out of his chair and
the barman must have thought they had lost their
senses. Ridge struggled to understand as Thad
spun him around his head screaming and
laughing.

'It's them, man! It's gotta be them!
Feather scarves, that's Barbarella for sure!
They're alive, Ridge, I know it!'

'But Colm…
Do you think?'

Thad put him down and regained his composure.

'I don't know bud. Let's see if we can find any more footage then I gotta call my dad and see if he's got any better intel.'

Ridge slumped into the comfortable plastic chairs again and stared up at the screen as Thad raced through the news channels. He heard a strange humming sound and looked down to the heavily scored plastic table. It was one of the phones! The one with the scratch across the screen! He snatched it up, hardly daring to believe it could be Colm. But there was no-one there.

'I thought that it…
Shit!'

He flung it down onto the table and as it resumed a muted reverberation, Thad gave him a brief hug before jumping over him and grabbing it again.

'It's a SMS message you dumb-ass!
Wait – here it comes now.
Make any sense to you?'

Ridge stared at the screen for half a
second then let out the loudest scream of his life.

The screen simply said;

Get drinking trousers
ASAP
We got bairn's head to wet right?
C x

Chapter 56

It was another bleak morning in Glasgow.
The lone piper had just begun his sad rendition
of what seemed to be the default refrain at police
or military funerals, The Piper's Lament. Being
a Highland boy, Ridge had always known the
tune as *The Flowers Of The Forest* and he
bowed his head in anger as the piercing sound
bounced unsympathetically off the cold wet
granite buildings surrounding the square.

He hadn't wanted to come here on this
bitter day. It was Orla, surprisingly, who'd
pushed him into attending. Both Masood and
Nasreen had beseeched her to use her powers of
persuasion after he'd politely but firmly declined
their invitation.

It was the hypocrisy that got to him, even
after everything he'd seen. It wasn't just the
traditional Highland airs that had been stolen and
repackaged.

It was also his memories.

Of course, Zakia was being given the
works - a full police ceremonial service. Ridge
looked around at the extent of the sickening
spectacle; the long lines of serving officers, their
arms held in a fixed salute, statuesque horses
groomed to perfection, banners and pennants
displaying proudly all the solemn pride and
pomp that accompanies a death in the field.

There would only be a handful of the
assembled throng who had actually known her
and an even smaller number who were party to

the ugly truth of her death. Nasreen, grateful to have been allowed a second chance, had been only too willing to shield her family from the reality of her miraculous rescue.

Ridge, once again, had emerged from his escapades as a hero, narrowly avoiding unwelcome publicity but having to accept the praises and financial rewards from the family. Only his wife was aware that he'd forwarded his second payment directly to a charity which dealt with the de-radicalisation of young Muslims in the city.

He gritted his teeth as the tiny coffin slowly passed him, swamped by the Saltire flag and an undemanding burden for the six strong policemen. This was not the girl he had known, albeit briefly. He closed his eyes, as the piper began the beautiful Skye Boat Song, and he pictured the effervescent girl laughing and taunting him once more.

Perhaps it was always like this, for people like himself and Orla. Had they not had bogus funerals conducted on their own behalf? Who would ever know why a promising and capable young girl should grow up vicious and twisted in an attempt to destroy all around her? Ridge likened her to the fierce but beautiful bramble bushes he was currently battling at their cottage across the sea. He squeezed Orla's hand and turned away from the dignitaries and uniforms to look up at a fleeting patch of sparkling blue sky. He made a mental note to graft a small piece of the thorny plant and grow it up against the south-facing wall of their new garden. He would harvest the delicious fruits next autumn and make them into red wine. Not that he ever drank much himself.

Next Time...

When Thad is arrested for a series of murders he didn't commit on the wrong side of the planet, Ridge Walker must find the real killer in order to prove his best friend's innocence. But as Ridge crosses swords with a merciless adversary and the savage ethos of centuries of warrior culture, the death toll speeds up and the seemingly random slayings take on a laser-sharp accuracy slicing ever closer to those he loves.

Two worlds collide in this race against time. As he sinks deeper into the macabre quagmire of a sick and vengeful mind Ridge begins to realise the full horror that awaits him.

They say 'the apple never falls far from the tree' and it's going to be a bitter harvest this season.

[Find out what happens in this third Ridge Walker novel in 2016]

That gives you plenty time to catch up with the first roller-coaster Ridge Walker thriller *He Who Pays The Piper*.